CATHERINE CAVENDISH

THE HAUNTING OF HENDERSON CLOSE

This is a **FLAME TREE PRESS** book

FLAME TREE PRESS
6 Melbray Mews, London, SW6 3NS, UK
flametreepress.com

Distribution and warehouse:
Baker & Taylor Publisher Services (BTPS)
30 Amberwood Parkway, Ashland, OH 44805
btpubservices.com

Thanks to the Flame Tree Press team, including:
Taylor Bentley, Frances Bodiam, Federica Ciaravella, Don D'Auria,
Chris Herbert, Matteo Middlemiss, Josie Mitchell, Mike Spender,
Cat Taylor, Maria Tissot, Nick Wells, Gillian Whitaker.

The cover is created by Flame Tree Studio with
thanks to Nik Keevil and Shutterstock.com.
The font families used are Avenir and Bembo.

Flame Tree Press is an imprint of Flame Tree Publishing Ltd
flametreepublishing.com

A copy of the CIP data for this book is available from the British Library
and the Library of Congress.

HB ISBN: 978-1-78758-103-6
PB ISBN: 978-1-78758-101-2
ebook ISBN: 978-1-78758-104-3
Also available in FLAME TREE AUDIO

Printed in the US at Bookmasters, Ashland, Ohio

CATHERINE CAVENDISH

THE HAUNTING OF HENDERSON CLOSE

FLAME TREE PRESS
London & New York

For Colin. We travel the Closes, roads
and winding lanes together...

PROLOGUE

November 1st, 1891

The tall woman lifted her skirt as she crossed the filthy, narrow street. Her nose wrinkled at the stench of human waste, rotting fruit and vegetables and all manner of foul remains that sloshed their way down the gutters of the open sewer that was Henderson Close, deep in the squalid heart of Edinburgh's Old Town.

Henderson Close. The very mention of the name sent shivers down the spines of most of the woman's acquaintances. They couldn't understand why she did this. Helping those too feckless, in their eyes, to help themselves.

A second-floor window rattled open. "Gardyloo!"

Along with everyone else in the vicinity, the woman scurried for safety, just in time before a torrent of stinking night waste splashed onto the street. The stench hit her with a renewed force that made her eyes water and her stomach heave.

Breathing through her mouth, the woman hurried on. The sooner she reached her destination, the sooner she could complete her mission and return to the safety of her cozy, lavender-scented flat in the more prosperous New Town.

As she quickened her step, she passed poorly dressed humanity of all ages. Children in little more than worn-out rags, on such a cold day as this too. She pitied them their filthy bare feet, pock-marked with chilblains, and scabs that wouldn't heal for want of a decent diet. She averted her eyes from the young girls, barely in their teens, who cradled their swollen bellies. The woman knew what went on. Some of these girls knew the fathers of their unborn babies all too well. They were closely related to them. Others wouldn't be able to pick the right one out of a police line-up.

She passed old women with no teeth and sparse grey hair. Yet most of them were probably barely past forty. Her age in fact. With her gloved hand, she adjusted the wire-rimmed spectacles a little higher on her nose, and arrived at number seventeen. A now-familiar clutch of apprehension tugged at her and she glanced around. No, everyone on the street was going about their normal business today.

She stared up at the dilapidated tenement, nine stories high, as she had done many times before. With land at such a premium in Edinburgh's teeming Old Town, they built upward, as high as the foundations would stand, and through lack of proper maintenance these old buildings sometimes collapsed, killing and maiming hundreds of inhabitants. Number seventeen was no better nor worse than any of its neighbors. Doors, and any remaining windows that weren't boarded up, had once been painted in a long-forgotten color, now chipped and flaking off, revealing the rotten wood beneath. It used to be that the richer you were, the higher up you lived. Those at the top of the building could see the sky and were furthest away from the stinking street below. But, for the past century or more, the well-to-do had moved away to the elegant streets of the Georgian New Town. No noxious odors for them.

The woman shook her head. Back to the purpose of her journey. The family she had come to see – the McDonalds – lived a wretched existence on the ground floor, barely able to afford the single room the mother, father and the youngest five bairns all shared. And the mother had another on the way. It had been like this all the years the woman had known them. Babies came. Babies died. More babies arrived. Mrs. McDonald must be in her late thirties or even older. Still they came. Her older ones were off her hands now. Her oldest....

Well, with any luck, at least what she had brought them would ensure food in the family's bellies for the rest of the week. That's why she came in the morning, when she knew the man wouldn't be there or, if he was, he'd be sleeping off the last of the previous night's ale. Not that Mr. McDonald was such a bad sort. At least, so far as she knew, he didn't beat his wife or the children and, when he was sober, he would do anyone a kindness, but she couldn't take a chance on the money getting into his hands. Too much temptation.

So lost in her own thoughts was she that she was unaware of the three youths who had formed a semi-circle behind her. As she raised her hand to knock on the worm-eaten door, they grabbed her. A fourth assailant – older, in his twenties – seized her. Shards of pain shot through her shoulders. She cried out as the four of them manhandled her round the corner into an alleyway.

The older one spat at her, threw her to the ground and kicked her. "Give us the money, woman!"

She tried in vain to curl into a fetal position as the four boys threw kicks and punches. Fists slammed into her face, knocking off her glasses. Blood poured from her nose. A sickening snapping noise and screaming pain tore through her jaw. She closed her eyes and prayed for them to stop. Pain burst through her chest as her ribs cracked. She pleaded for merciful death to release her.

A man's roar. The oldest thug stamped on her hand, breaking her fingers. He tore the purse from her broken arm and made off. Hobnail boots thundered as men pursued them.

Through the red mist of her agony, the woman recognized a familiar voice. Mr. McDonald was home, sober and here to help her. She felt him kneel beside her. He cradled her head. She tried to open her eyes but they were already swollen shut. Or the effort was simply too much. She tasted blood, felt it drip down her cheeks, mingling with the tears that cascaded down her face, and the muddy, stinking wetness of the ground beneath her face.

Mr. McDonald stroked her forehead. "Oh Miss Carmichael, what have they done to ye?"

Other voices joined his. Mrs. McDonald tried to wipe the blood off with the ragged hem of her rough wool skirt. "Lord preserve us. Who would do such a thing? Miss Carmichael too. All she ever does is out of the goodness of her heart."

The voices floated to the dying woman on echoing waves through the pathways of her mind, becoming fainter and fainter. Mr. and Mrs. McDonald leaned closer as Miss Carmichael struggled to speak. It was no more than a whisper, barely possible with her fractured jaw. "I am so sorry. They took it. Every penny."

A final tear tracked its way down Miss Carmichael's face as the darkness enveloped her for the last time.

*   *   *

In the shadows, a well-dressed young man moved, unnoticed by the crowd gathered over the dead woman.

A smile creased his lips as he walked away.

CHAPTER ONE

2018

"You have to remember, Hannah, people didn't live underground in Henderson Close. It was only built over after the last of them had left."

Hannah screwed up her nose as she stared around her. A dark street. Tenements on both sides, claustrophobically close, soared upward, only to be abruptly cut off by the foundations of the newer building above.

"They certainly lived close together in those days," Hannah said. "If they'd leaned out of their window, they could have shaken hands with the person living opposite."

Beneath her feet, the street was pockmarked with holes and littered with loose stones. At least it was dry though, which is more than it would have been back in the time when Henderson Close was a bustling, filthy hive of activity.

Ailsa, the general manager, went on, "Of course, in the old days, you would have needed to pick your way very carefully along here. As you can see, it's quite steep and you would have met all sorts of rubbish washing down the gutters."

"I can imagine." Hannah followed Ailsa up the silent street, clutching at the handrail for support.

"Sensible," Ailsa said. "I always advise my visitors to hang on. It's quite gloomy down here and so uneven. I've tripped a few times myself, and *I* know where the potholes are."

Hannah laughed. Above her, someone had hung Victorian-style shirts and a couple of sheets on a line stretching across the street. Ailsa kept up a running commentary while Hannah concentrated on trying to memorize her surroundings and the stories associated with each location. She would be given a script later and would need to perfect her role.

Each of the Henderson Close tour guides portrayed a character known to have lived there at some stage – some at the top of society and some very much on the bottom rung. Hannah would start next week dressed as Mary Stratton, English housekeeper to Sir William Henderson, an eighteenth-century banker and philanthropist, after whom the Close was named.

For Hannah, newly arrived in Edinburgh from her native Salisbury, this was her dream job – even if the pay wasn't up to much.

Ailsa stopped outside an open door. "Now this is a significant stop for you. Sir William Henderson lived here with his wife and two daughters."

Hannah peered inside a workshop, which contained all the trappings of a Victorian printer.

"Obviously, Sir William and his family would have lived higher up the building, so their quarters were destroyed when the redevelopment began in the late 1890s. The lower down the pecking order you were, the closer you lived to the stink of the street. Everything got poured down there. And I mean everything. Then you had chimneys belching out clouds of filthy, stinking smoke that coated the whole city with black soot. No wonder Edinburgh earned its old nickname of Auld Reekie."

"The effluent ended up in the Nor' Loch, didn't it?" Hannah had read about the disgusting foul lake.

"Yes, that's right. Along with all the so-called witches they dunked or drowned. They drained it in the early 1800s and constructed Princes Gardens. You wouldn't think what it had been when you look at all the lovely flowers, would you?"

Hannah smiled. "Maybe that's the reason the flowers *are* so lovely."

Ailsa gave a light laugh. "You're probably right."

They moved off. Ailsa pointed out places of interest along the way. "Once you've told them a couple of anecdotes about Sir William, and old Murdoch Maclean, whose printing shop you were looking at, move your guests off and around this corner." Ailsa turned to the right.

"Just around here, you'll see where Miss Carmichael was

viciously slain. You can make a fair meal of this." She stopped.
"Now, look down. What do you see?"

The light wasn't bright, but Hannah could make out a
dark stain.

Ailsa lowered her voice. "Miss Carmichael's blood."

Hannah stared. "Really?"

"Probably not, but it makes a good story. The guests love a
ghost story and Miss Carmichael is the perfect subject. Little is
known about her – what we do know is in the notes – but we're
fairly certain that this is the spot where she was beaten, robbed
and kicked to death by a gang of four ruffians. Three of them
were captured and hanged. The fourth escaped and was never
apprehended. It is said that, to this day, Miss Carmichael wanders
this street, looking for her murderer and demanding justice."

Hannah shivered. Ailsa laughed. "That's exactly the reaction
you want."

"Well, it *is* pretty gruesome," Hannah said. "Mind you, the
creepy environment helps. It's so quiet here. Eerie."

"Especially just here."

The two stood in silence for a few seconds. The stillness
lay between them in the gloom. Hannah swallowed, feeling an
almost uncontrollable urge to move on but not wanting her new
employer to think she was spooked. She forced herself to stand
motionless, as Ailsa was doing. Listening. When Ailsa finally
spoke, Hannah jumped.

"You can't hear any traffic from above," Ailsa said. "So
it's pretty creepy. I've often felt as if someone was behind
me, but when I've turned, there's been no one there." She
paused again. Was she looking for some reaction? Hannah
concentrated on breathing steadily. It always calmed her in
fraught situations. Maybe it was some sort of test. The place
was eerie and no doubt there were guests whose imaginations
began to run away with them. It wouldn't do for the tour
guide to be the nervy type.

Ailsa exhaled. "OK, come on, I want to show you Eliza's
room. She's another character you can get some mileage out of."

The manager led the way further down the dark, narrow

street. An unexpected ripple of cold air ruffled Hannah's hair and she shivered.

"You'll get used to that," Ailsa said. "All sorts of unexplained drafts and sudden chills. Sometimes even smells, and not always pleasant either. If you shut your eyes sometimes, you could almost believe you were there, back in the days when it would have been a seething mass of humanity."

Hannah smiled and wished she meant it. That chill had been strange. Almost as if someone had breathed cold air on her.

*　　*　　*

"You certainly look the part." Ailsa straightened Hannah's white cap and stood back. "Yes, every inch the eighteenth-century housekeeper, newly arrived from London, Mrs. Mary Stratton."

"Whatever happened to Mr. Stratton, I wonder?"

"He probably never existed. Mary would have been given the courtesy title of 'Mrs'. Same applied to the cooks. You didn't find too many married servants in the 1700s."

Hannah drew a sharp intake of breath.

"Nerves?" Ailsa asked.

Hannah nodded. "It feels like a flock of butterflies are dive-bombing my stomach."

Ailsa laid a hand on her arm. "You'll be fine. We've all been there. Just treat this dress rehearsal as if we were normal paying visitors. You know your part and you know the anecdotes and history of the Close. Just relax into your role and let Mary Stratton take over."

Hannah had an almost hysterical desire to laugh. "Sounds like a case of demonic possession."

Ailsa smiled. "You'll soon get the hang of it. Come up to the gift shop and we can get started. We open in just over an hour, so there'll be just enough time for the tour."

Hannah inhaled and picked up her long skirt as she followed Ailsa up the stairs.

A small group of ten people was waiting for her. Some were familiar, some not, but all were her new colleagues and they would assess her performance before she was let loose on the general public the following day. All the rehearsing, research and practice had been leading up to this.

Hannah said a silent prayer, moistened her lips, and began. "Good morning, ladies and gentlemen. I trust your journey here was a pleasant one."

Smiles and murmurings greeted this.

"My name is Mrs. Stratton. Mrs. Mary Stratton. And I have the honor to be housekeeper to Sir William Henderson, who owns a private bank and also prides himself on his good works. Something we all know bankers like to engage in."

A ripple of laughter killed at least three of Hannah's butterflies.

"But more of him a little later. For now, I want to take you down the stairs, underground to a secret world known as Henderson Close. Please follow me and do take care to hold the handrails. The Close is inclined to be uneven and we wouldn't want any accidents. Medicine was a little primitive in the eighteenth century and I am advised that we are clean out of leeches." More giggles.

Hannah led her group through a door at the back of the shop and down a flight of stone stairs.

At the bottom, she steered them past some shattered old wooden doors and into a room devoid of any furniture, whitewashed and illuminated only by a few flickering candle lamps hanging on the walls.

Hannah took up her position in the center of the room and began the story of Eliza McTavish.

"She and her family of eight children and a ne'er-do-well husband lived in this one room. They cooked here, babies were born here, ate here, slept here and even died here. Eliza birthed sixteen children, lying on a meager mattress that was stuffed with hay." On cue, a corner of the room lit up gloomily to reveal a lifelike waxwork of a sickly looking woman, her face frozen in an agony of childbirth. She wore a filthy greying shift streaked with 'blood' and lay on one side, on the straw mattress Hannah had just described. The light shut off.

One of Hannah's male colleagues piped up. "Where did they go to the bathroom?"

Hannah pointed to a bucket in another corner of the room.

"Eugh!" the man said, echoed by his fellow 'guests'.

"Yes indeed, sir, 'Eugh'. Although after a little while, they do say you get used to it."

More laughter greeted this. Hannah gave an inward cheer as twelve more of her butterflies fluttered to the ground. Outwardly she wrinkled her nose and shuddered and slowly moved back to the far wall.

"The year was 1645 and plague spread through the streets of the Old Town. As always, it hit the poorest first. Those who lived at street level, amid the vermin and the filth and...." She pressed a button behind her and the silhouettes of two enormous rats flashed up onto the wall her guests were facing. A couple of them gasped and laughter erupted.

"Yes, ladies and gentlemen," Hannah said, lowering her voice to add gravitas, "the rats came and brought the fleas with their deadly gift of bubonic plague. Poor Eliza McTavish caught it. Soon she was gripped by a violent fever, chills. She coughed up bloody phlegm and then, at the last, her body erupted in massive boils called buboes. Pretty soon, her children started showing similar symptoms. Right as she lay dying in her bed, they called in the plague doctor."

Another press of the button and the rats scurried away to be replaced by an eight-foot-high profile of a frightening-looking creature sporting a floor-length cloak, hood and an enormous curved beak, like some gargantuan crow.

Gasps and nervous laughter echoed around the whitewashed room and Hannah marveled at how authentically her colleagues performed their current roles.

"Fearsome-looking figure, isn't he? Yet he was a courageous – if somewhat foolhardy – man called Dr. Philip MacIver. He believed that by stuffing that beak with sweet-smelling herbs, he would keep the plague at bay. You see, it was thought that this plague and noxious fumes went hand in hand and, while there is a grain of truth in there somewhere, no one had actually thought to ask the rats about their involvement. Needless to say, poor Dr. MacIver perished of the plague soon after and, as you can imagine, there was no great rush of applicants for the position he had vacated."

The group was firmly on Hannah's side. She could almost believe they were real members of the public. All her stage fright had evaporated and she was enjoying herself and ready to deliver the reveal.

"So, what became of poor Eliza and her family, you may ask." Hannah paused, as she had rehearsed so many times. She counted to five. "Well, go on then. Ask."

The group laughed. Ailsa put up her hand. "What became of Eliza and her family?"

"I'm glad you asked that question, madam." Hannah made a gathering gesture with her hands and the group moved closer. She looked around her before lowering her voice to a conspiratorial stage-whisper.

"They do say that her neighbors were scared they too would succumb so, late one night, while everyone else was in bed, a group of them gathered out there, in the Close. They came armed with wood and sturdy nails and boarded up poor Eliza's room so none could escape. The cries of poor Eliza faded away after a couple of days, but it took nearly a month before the last child's cry was heard. Now what do you suppose that child lived on for all those weeks?"

"Ratatouille?"

Hannah jokingly rounded on the light-hearted male heckler with the ginger hair. "Ah, I see you are a man of discernment, well versed in the culinary arts, sir. Maybe you are right. Or maybe he feasted on something that tasted a little more like... pork."

Laughter, exclamations of mock disgust and a few nods showed Hannah she had delivered her lines well.

"Now, good people, we must hasten away to the house where I reside and I will tell you how Henderson Close came by its name. Please be careful. The ground is more uneven here."

Hannah led her group through a narrow doorway, down to the left, and they stopped outside a tenement, with a partially open door leading into Murdoch Maclean's print shop.

"Are we all here?" Hannah began a head count, but caught a glimpse of a woman disappearing around a corner further up the Close. Hannah called out to her. "No, madam. It's this way, if you please. We go there later."

She was aware of puzzled looks among the group. Ailsa spoke up. "It's OK, we're all here."

Hannah counted. Ten. "Well, I definitely saw someone go down there. I'd better check. Maybe a visitor managed to get in before opening time. Please, ladies and gentlemen, wait here for a moment." Hannah set off.

"I'll come with you," Ailsa said, "just in case. If there's someone down here that shouldn't be, I'll deal with them."

Within a few seconds, Hannah and Ailsa had rounded the corner. The short passageway contained closed doors – each of which they checked.

"Locked," Ailsa said. "Exactly as they should be."

In less than a minute they had reached the brick wall blocking up the rest of the passageway.

"This used to be an alley," Hannah said, recognition flashing into her mind.

"Not just any alley, either." Ailsa pointed to the perpetual dark stain on the ground.

Hannah shivered. "Miss Carmichael."

"Looks like you've had the perfect initiation." Ailsa smiled.

CHAPTER TWO

Four a.m. Hannah stared out of the living room window of her small flat above a coffee shop on the Royal Mile.

By day bustling with as many nationalities as a UN meeting, now all was quiet. A stiff breeze sent discarded sweet wrappers swirling and dancing along the street. Hannah cradled her coffee mug and turned away.

Two table lamps at either end of the room cast a warm, comforting glow. Hannah rarely switched on the main light, preferring to relax, bathed in a gentle, candle-like softness.

She thought over her strange experience during her dress rehearsal that morning. She *knew* what she had seen – however impossible that might appear. Perhaps it had been a trick they played on new staff. Maybe one of *them* had been behind one of those locked doors.

In a few hours, she would begin her first official day. What if she saw that…whatever it was…again? How would she react? Ignore it? Could she even do that? Instinct had ruled her reactions earlier, but if her mind was playing tricks on her, as Ailsa and at least some – if not all – her colleagues appeared to believe, she would be humiliated in front of the general public. Someone might complain. Great start to her dream job.

Think back calmly. What exactly did I see?

In the sole fleeting glimpse, she had taken in a tall, slim woman in a long brown skirt and matching jacket, wearing wire-rimmed glasses and a hat. Old-fashioned. Not unlike a photograph she had of her great-great grandmother, taken sometime in the 1880s.

In her mind, she replayed the reactions of some of her colleagues. Puzzlement, incomprehension, skepticism even, on one face after another. All except one.

Mairead.

Hannah searched for the young woman's surname. Ferguson. Mairead Ferguson. That was it. Her expression had been different than the rest. Surprise yes, but something else. She had nodded, almost imperceptibly, but it had been a nod nonetheless.

Exhaustion overwhelmed Hannah and this time she was fairly sure she would sleep, because now she knew what she was going to do.

*   *   *

Hannah arrived an hour before her first tour was due. She needed to see the one person who she was almost certain had seen what she had seen.

"Mairead!"

The girl smiled at her. She was already dressed for her role as Emily, a young kitchen maid.

Hannah lowered her voice. "Before anyone else gets here, could I have a word? It's about what happened yesterday."

"Yes, of course." Mairead wound her long blonde hair around her hand before tucking it firmly under her white servant's cap.

Might as well go straight for the jugular. "You've seen her too, haven't you?"

Mairead's eyes opened wider. "Seen who?"

"The woman...ghost...what I saw yesterday."

Mairead cast her eyes downward and nodded.

"Is it a wind-up?"

Mairead shook her head. "No. When I saw it, I was on my own."

"Who...what is it?"

"I've no idea. I used to be skeptical about ghosts, but not now."

"And you've only seen it once?"

Mairead nodded. Her face had paled. When she spoke, her voice wavered, as if she wasn't sure if she should tell Hannah. "About a month after I started. One of the visitors dropped a glove in the Close, so I went to get it for her. I saw a woman in Victorian dress, who turned down the alley where Miss Carmichael was murdered, and then vanished."

"Did you think she looked a bit...out of place?" Hannah stopped. Out of place? Of course she was out of place. She couldn't even be there! But Mairead caught on to her meaning.

"She certainly looked too well-dressed to be out and about in Henderson Close in the time period she was dressed for."

"I suppose the obvious suspect is Miss Carmichael herself, but has she been seen by anyone else. I mean, really? I know she's supposed to haunt the place, but isn't that simply one of those convenient ghost stories to please the punters?"

"Don't let Ailsa hear you call the visitors punters. She hates it. But to answer your question, I honestly don't know for sure. I have had visitors who have said they've seen something out of the corner of their eye. One man swore a raggedy little boy tugged at his arm. The poor man went white and he was shaking. I'd say, with the sort of murky history Henderson Close has witnessed, anything is possible, but, as for Miss Carmichael—"

The staff room door opened and Ailsa and a male colleague entered, dressed for their roles. They greeted Hannah and Mairead.

"Well, Hannah," Ailsa said, "first time solo today. How are the nerves?"

Hannah had been so preoccupied with thoughts of the spectral that her butterflies of yesterday hadn't materialized. Now, they came flying in with a vengeance. She made a rocking motion with her hand.

"You'll be fine. Let's hope your vanishing friend doesn't choose to make a repeat appearance."

$\star$ $\star$ $\star$

She didn't, and Hannah's confidence grew with each tour. She relaxed, joked with the tour groups, enjoyed friendly banter and all thoughts of Miss Carmichael faded away.

A week later, she felt as if she had been doing the job for months.

"I'm hearing good reports about you," Ailsa said. "You've really taken to this and I'm delighted. I have to admit I had my doubts. Your CV was a wee bit sparse, to say the least."

Hannah grimaced. "I had to make the best of what I'd got in the way of transferable skills. At least my teaching background helped. I know how to make presentations."

"I think it was your Amateur Dramatics credentials that probably swung it for you. Your improvisation test was excellent."

"Thank you."

"No more mysterious encounters?"

"None."

"You're getting used to the atmosphere down there. It can be really daunting at first. We had one young chap who lasted one tour. I heard screaming, not far from Miss Carmichael's corner. When I got down there, all hell had let loose. He was shaking, white as a corpse and pointing at something it seemed he could see but no one else could. He was babbling incoherently and his eyes.... Well, I've never seen anything like it. Needless to say the visitors were well and truly spooked. One lady fainted in my arms and had to be carried out. As for him, he took to his heels and we never saw him again."

"What had he seen? Or thought he'd seen?"

Ailsa shrugged. "No idea. He never told us. Wouldn't answer our phone calls and sent his elder brother to collect his P45."

"But no one else saw whatever it was?"

"No. They all said the same thing. They were enjoying the tour. He had been telling them the usual stories and they all thought he was very good. Then, suddenly, he stopped in mid-sentence, pointed straight ahead and started screaming."

A shiver passed through Hannah.

"Cold?" Ailsa asked. "It's a wee bit chilly today."

"No, I'm fine. Just thinking about that poor lad. He must have been terrified to behave like that."

"Yes, I suppose he must." Ailsa sighed. "Probably best he left when he did though. We can't have the visitors upset. Bad for business. Ah well, better get on. Keep up the good work."

She left and Hannah glanced up at the clock in the staff room. Ten fifteen. Forty-five minutes before her first tour. Enough time to fully investigate Murdoch Maclean's print shop. She had noticed a pile of old local newspapers in one corner and, with any luck, she might find a juicy story to add to her collection. It would be good to ring the changes a bit. Keep her presentation fresh.

She opened the entrance to Henderson Close and made her way down the stairs, torch in hand. Emergency lighting was on twenty-four hours a day, but it would be too dark to see in the printer's shop. The papers were yellowed with age and the print had faded to grey.

She was alone down there. The silence wrapped around her like an uncomfortable cloak. Goosebumps rose on her arms and her palms broke into a cold sweat. Contrary to what Ailsa had said, it hadn't been particularly chilly upstairs but down here…it felt as if someone had opened a fridge door. Probably because no one had been down here since yesterday, but….

Hannah shook her head. *My imagination's off again.* A blast of cold air slapped her in the face. Her ears pricked. Footsteps.

"Hello," Hannah called. "Anyone down here?"

Silence. Hannah exhaled and waited. Then, satisfied that her ears must have been playing tricks on her, she carried on, her torch bouncing shadows off the walls and floor.

She had one foot over the threshold of the shop when muffled sounds wafted toward her. Chattering, cries, horses and carts clattering on the street. Growing louder. Nearer. Hannah froze. She clapped her hands to her ears and squeezed her eyes tight shut. *This isn't happening.* Behind closed eyelids, she was aware that her surroundings were becoming lighter. Then there was the smell. Horse manure, human waste, rotting vegetables, cheap tobacco all mingling in a soup of impossible reality.

"Well, lassie, will ye be coming in, or going oot?"

The voice was male and accompanied by a strong smell of ink.

Hannah slowly lowered her hands and dared to open her eyes.

A man who looked almost old enough to be her father stood, composition roller in his hand, all ready to apply to the old-fashioned bed of type prior to printing. For a second, Hannah recalled seeing an old 'hot metal' printing press on a school trip to a newspaper. Yet, here it was, being used by…. "Murdoch Maclean?" she asked.

"Aye, the very same." The man sounded impatient.

Hannah could barely hear him for the clamor of noise from

the street. She nodded and gave him a half-smile before stepping back into the Close, leaving Murdoch Maclean to carry on with his printing. She retched at the stench from the gutters and the fresh manure in the middle of the street. Hannah swallowed hard repeatedly and forced herself to look upward. Tenements soared eight or nine stories – or even higher. Above them, sky, where grey clouds promised rain.

Hannah's bewildered gaze returned to street level and took in the poverty. Women in ragged shawls, some staring and pointing at her. Of course, she was dressed a century out of date.

Barefoot children, coated in grime, played chase. Men leaned on rusting iron railings puffing on old clay pipes.

A coal merchant's wagon clattered past, his massive piebald shire horse whinnying.

Hannah shut her eyes tight again, willing the scene to go away. Panic welled up inside her, rushing like a geyser. Somebody brushed up against her. Took her arm. The street noises vanished.

"Hannah! Are you all right?"

Hannah opened her eyes. Instant relief as she saw Mairead's concerned expression. "Oh thank God."

"You look terrible, Hannah. You were clutching your head. Do you have a headache or something?"

Hannah gave a light laugh, as she took in the familiar surroundings. "Or something, I think. I just had the weirdest experience ever. I mean, totally off the wall."

"I came down to tell you your eleven o'clock tour is comprised of one complete party of Americans and they've arrived half an hour early. Someone gave them the wrong time or they got confused or something. Anyway, Ailsa said if you want to get started now, that's fine with her. I switched all the lights on. What were you doing down here anyway, all by yourself?"

Hannah started back with Mairead. "I wanted to see if I could find some more stories to use, but if I told them what just happened to me, I'd have a harder time convincing them it was true than I'd have of persuading them that the stain is actually Miss Carmichael's blood."

Mairead blinked. "Tell me about it later. I want all the details.

But now we'd better get back. When Ailsa says 'jump', she expects a leap."

Hannah approached the Henderson house – and Murdoch Maclean's print shop – accompanied by a dry mouth and a wave of nausea. She ran her tongue over parched lips. Seeing the silent room with its Victorian printing press, type blocks and all the tools of a printer's trade, she offered up a silent prayer of thanks. The pile of yellowing newspapers lay stacked against the wall, but Hannah no longer had any desire to search through them. *Just let me get through this.* She took a deep breath.

"Now ladies and gentlemen, here we have the house once occupied by my employer – Sir William Henderson. He and his family lived at the top of the building before the rebuilding took place. They lived nine stories up so, you see, Edinburgh was truly the home of the first skyscrapers. Sir William was a generous benefactor, giving money to countless good causes and, because he was also a canny businessman, he made sure everyone knew how generous he was."

"Oh my God!"

A woman clapped her hand to her mouth. Her eyes wild. Terrified. The others in her party of Americans clustered around her.

Hannah grasped the woman's trembling free hand. "What happened? Do you need some air?"

The woman shook her head and lowered the hand from her mouth. Her cheeks were bloodless, her lips ashen. "I saw.... I don't know what I saw. But it was there."

"What was there, Lindy? Where?" A man – by the ring on his finger, her husband – put his arm around her as the crowd murmured among themselves.

Hannah's palms grew clammy. She gently released Lindy's hand and cast quick glances around the room. All seemed normal enough.

"Lindy?" she asked. "Was it a person you saw?"

The woman stared at her for a moment, then gave a vigorous shake of her head. Her husband spoke. "What was it then? An animal?"

He addressed Hannah. "She had one of these turns a couple of days ago in York."

The others nodded and muttered.

The man continued, "We were all in this pub – The Golden Crown. It's supposed to be haunted. We hadn't been there ten minutes before Lindy screamed. Swore she'd seen a shadow flash across the bar."

"This one wasn't a shadow." Lindy's color was returning to her cheeks. "It was a dark shape. A figure. But not like a real person. More like…a scarecrow. Yes, that's the best I can describe it. A scarecrow. Eight, nine feet tall. With arms and legs that were no more than…. They looked like tree branches. No. Poles. Wooden poles. And it was standing right behind you." She pointed at Hannah, who swung round. Nothing there.

Hannah looked back at the group. "Did anyone else see anything?"

Much head-shaking and a general chorus of, "No."

Lindy's face drained again and her lips quivered. "What's happening to me? This has never happened at home."

"We live in Kansas," her husband said, as if that explained everything.

Hannah nodded. "It *is* very atmospheric down here. And I'm sure the same can be said for the pub in York. I've had some strange experiences there I couldn't explain either."

This seemed to help Lindy. She visibly exhaled. "Have you seen anything down here?"

Hannah would dearly have loved to share her earlier experience with the group, who now seemed to be hanging on her every word, but she knew better. Her experience was so far-fetched it could well land her in trouble with the cynical Ailsa. Retelling well-documented ghost stories was one thing. Frightening the lives out of a group already affected by the behavior of one of their number was an entirely different matter. "Bad for business," she would say.

"Let's just say that if these walls could talk, I'm sure they would keep us all entertained for hours." The group laughed and the tension broke. Hannah turned her attention to Lindy. "Do you feel able to continue now?"

The woman attempted a smile. "Oh yes, I'm feeling much

better now. Probably…a trick of the light." Lindy held Hannah's gaze a few seconds too long, clearly willing her to agree with her. Hannah nodded.

★   ★   ★

Mairead choked on her mug of tea. "*Scarecrow?* What on earth would a scarecrow be doing in Henderson Close? There are no fields anywhere near."

"I know," Hannah said, and sipped her coffee. "She was having difficulty describing what she'd seen, but she was adamant it wasn't human."

"Well, that's a new one on me, and, on top of your…I don't know what to call it."

"Time slip? That's what it felt like."

"Whatever you choose to call it, the activity seems to be heating up down there since you arrived. You're not a psychic or a medium or whatever, are you?"

Hannah smiled. "Not that I'm aware of. I grew up in Salisbury surrounded by stone circles and pretty much the whole of English history scattered around the countryside, but never once did I experience anything out of the ordinary. Then I move up here and…bang!"

"Why did you come to Edinburgh anyway? It's such a long way from your home."

Hannah sighed. "Long story. The short version is my marriage ended, and my daughter graduated from London University and promptly decided to emigrate to Australia. Salisbury is a small city and it was hard to escape some bad memories, so I decided I needed a fresh start. I'd been to Edinburgh a couple of times before I was married and loved it. I came here for the festival when I was a drama student. When I saw this job advertised, I knew I had to go for it. I don't know quite what I would have done if they'd turned me down. I'd sort of committed myself to staying here as soon as I got the interview. Looking back now, I suppose I took one hell of a gamble. I'm only glad it worked out."

"Well, it may not be a West End role, but it *is* a lot of fun.

Most of the time anyway." Mairead rolled her eyes.

"Oh that. No, that's just one of those weird things that happens. It already doesn't seem real. As if I dreamed it."

"And is that what that woman did? Dream up a scarecrow?"

Hannah shrugged. "Haven't the faintest. Maybe she did it to get attention. Who knows?"

"I saw the group leave. They all seemed to have enjoyed it. They spent well in the gift shop so Ailsa was pleased."

Hannah grinned. "Maybe Lindy from Kansas did us a favor then."

"They all had their photos taken down there and purchased them."

"Probably hoping something ghostly would come out on the flash."

Hannah glanced up at the clock in the staff room. "Time to go. Let's see what this next tour brings."

★   ★   ★

But none of the remaining tours produced anything other than the usual gasps, chatter, some lively interaction with a small party of Australians and sore feet from all that standing and walking around on uneven terrain.

Hannah arrived home, longing to relax her aching feet and legs in a lovely hot, scented bath. She unlocked her front door and the aroma hit her. The unmistakable smell of lavender wafted under her nose, reminding her of her grandmother's house. Gran had used a lavender-scented beeswax for her special furniture.

But I don't.

Hannah put down her purse on the hall table and made her way into the small living room. The smell seemed to be at its strongest here, but she was at a loss to know where it had come from. Goosebumps rose on the back of her neck, prickling her.

In the kitchen there was no trace of the scent. Neither was there in the bedroom or bathroom. The windows were all tight shut.

Hannah returned to the living room and glanced outside. No

visible window boxes. Nothing to indicate the presence of any lavender blossom. Anyway, it was the wrong time of year.

She shook her head and retraced her steps to the bathroom. Five minutes later she sank into a bourbon vanilla-scented bath, which wrapped her in its luxurious, velvety embrace. Hannah leaned back and closed her eyes. All thoughts of Henderson Close and inexplicable scents faded into the background.

She let her mind drift back. Salisbury. The city of her childhood, with its peaceful cathedral close. All through the years she was growing up, she spent hours sitting on the grass, chatting to friends, watching the endless parades of tourists craning their necks up at the tallest spire in Europe. She had loved that place. Yet it had become impossible for her to stay there.

"*You're* the reason your marriage broke up and my Roger went off the rails with *that* woman."

Hannah could see her now. Violet Lockwood at full volume, like some overblown Brünnhilde, stabbing her finger into Hannah's shoulder, her eyes wild.

"*He* left *me*, remember?" Hannah had said, fighting to control her temper, forcing her voice to stay calm and quiet. She mustn't let this woman get to her. "Roger left *me* for *her*. It was as much of a shock to me as to you. More so in fact, since I was his wife."

"Oh you always were so superior."

Hannah hated the sneering tone. Her mother-in-law had never come to terms with her little boy leaving home. In her eyes, Hannah had snatched him away and turned him against her. All rubbish, of course, and Violet's own husband had left *her* because, according to Roger, she was so clingy and needy, he felt smothered. But Violet wasn't finished with Hannah yet.

"You drove your own daughter away to the other end of the world, and now you've made sure I never see Roger again. You're nothing but a selfish, heartless little bitch."

Despite her resolve, Hannah snapped. "Don't be so ridiculous. Jenna is doing very well for herself. She has a brilliant job and she's happy. As for Roger...he only lives in London. Not exactly the far side of the universe. You can go and see him whenever you like."

Violet shook her head. "If it wasn't for you, he would be a couple of miles away and I really *could* see him whenever I wanted. As it is, their flat's too small and I would have to stay at a hotel."

Well done, Roger. It had to be deliberate. In truth the flat was probably plenty big enough to accommodate his mother for a couple of nights, but his opinion of his mother pretty much mirrored his father's. All through their married life, there had been the last-minute, late-night phone calls. A lightbulb had blown. A drain was blocked with leaves. The gardener couldn't come for a week and the lawn needed mowing – that was her favorite for a sunny early Sunday morning. And when Roger was away, it had been Hannah who had turned out at all hours to do her mother-in-law's bidding. Not that Violet would ever acknowledge that, or even thank her.

Hannah sat up in her bath. Damn the woman. Even from four hundred miles away she managed to invade her thoughts and raise her blood pressure.

Her relaxing bath time ruined, Hannah reluctantly pulled out the plug.

★   ★   ★

The next day was Hannah's day off. Lucky, she thought as four a.m. saw her once again standing by her living room window, clutching a mug of tea and contemplating the street below. The smell of lavender had disappeared as inexplicably as it had arrived. Yet another mystery to add to the growing collection.

Autumn had well and truly settled in. The silent street glistened from an earlier shower of rain. Hannah shivered at the sight of it. It definitely felt colder tonight. She took a deep swig of her tea, started to turn away and stopped. She peered out into the semi-darkness illuminated imperfectly by streetlamps. No she hadn't imagined it. There it was again. Down below, a shadow moved.

Hannah held her breath. Something didn't feel right about that shadow. It lacked substance, even if that didn't make any sense. She waited. Her heart pounded.

The shadow moved again. Lightning quick. Caught for the briefest of instants in the glow of a lit shop window. But it was enough. Hannah barely noticed the crash of her mug as she dropped it. The figure stopped. As if it had heard. It raised its head, directly up at Hannah.

A woman in late Victorian dress. Not just any woman. In a split second, Hannah recognized her.

The ghost from Henderson Close.

Who vanished. Like a snuffed-out candle.

Hannah staggered backward and sank onto the couch.

CHAPTER THREE

Summer 1979

The young boy swung his legs on the low-hanging branch of the old sycamore. He squinted through the bright sunlight at the girl in the dirty white dress. "Who are you? Where did you come from?"

The girl said nothing. She clung to the ancient rag doll in her arms.

"My name's Dougie, but I hate it. One day I'm going to change it. Maybe I'll be called Rob Roy or William Wallace. I'm ten years old. What's your name?"

"Isobel."

His mother always said Dougie could hear a pin drop but he had to strain to hear this tiny voice. "How old are you and where do you live?"

The little girl looked over her shoulder and shook her head.

"Why are you in our garden? Do you live in one of the other flats? I've never seen you before and we've been here over a week now."

Still no reply. Dougie was getting a bit fed up with his uncommunicative new companion. He wasn't particularly interested in girls anyway, especially if they couldn't even be bothered to talk to him. Maybe she was a bit simple.

"I don't live here," she said eventually, again in that small voice.

"Are you visiting someone? We haven't had any visitors yet. My grandma lives in Glasgow and my cousins all live in Dunfermline. Where do your parents live?"

She shrugged her shoulders and once again....

"Why do you keep looking over your shoulder like that? Have you run away from home?"

"I have to go now."

"Oh, all right then. Will you come back?"

She shook her head again. "But I will see you again. One day."

Dougie pushed himself off the branch, overbalanced and tripped over. When he righted himself, the girl had gone.

That's the way it is with girls.

★   ★   ★

"And she disappeared? What, in a puff of smoke or something?" His new friend, Alec, chewed on a long grass stem while the two boys sat in the tree.

"Well, not exactly. I mean, I didn't see a puff of smoke or anything, but it *was* odd. She appeared out of nowhere when I wasn't looking and she left the same way."

"No one like that lives around here. We're the only kids in this house and then there are four more in the houses next to ours. There are a couple of girls further along the street but they're older than the one you saw. I reckon she'd run away from home and then decided to go back again."

"My dad said girls are always changing their minds."

"Mine too. He said it's their pre…prerog…something."

"When *we* say something, we stick to it."

"Yeah."

The boys sat in silence for a few moments. Then Alec spoke. "Have you met old McDonald yet?"

"The landlord? Once." Dougie shuddered at the memory of the tall, thin man with the piercing stare who looked as if he would like to carve him up into small pieces and eat him.

"He hates kids. Boys especially."

"Don't know why he lets his flats to families if he feels like that."

Alec jumped down from the tree. "Mum says he wouldn't get a person living on their own to pay the rent he charges, and old people are too feeble to climb the stairs. So he's stuck with us."

"He told me off on the day we moved in. He said I was too

noisy. He said if I didn't keep quiet he would call the police and have me taken away."

"He's always saying that. Don't worry. He can't do it."

"He said my parents wouldn't be able to stop him because it was his house."

"Did you tell your parents?"

Dougie shook his head. "He told me if I told anyone, he'd find out and definitely make it happen."

"You've just told me."

"You're not a grown up. You won't say anything."

"True."

A window rattled open. "Dougie? Come in for your tea now."

Dougie waved at her. "That's Mum. I'll have to go. See you tomorrow."

"Let's go out on our bikes."

Dougie grinned. "That'll be fun. Old McDonald can't complain if we make a noise then, can he?"

He looked up to see his mother closing the kitchen window on the first floor of the building where they lived. Alec followed him into the house.

In a shaded corner of the garden, behind a rhododendron, Isobel watched them go.

CHAPTER FOUR

Mairead trod carefully over the loose stones as the street dipped steeply downward. She clung to the handrail. It creaked, juddered and a whole section of it split off from its wall mounts. With a cry, she let go and watched it clatter to the ground.

She froze. Surely someone must have heard. The handrail rolled to rest by the wall on the opposite side of the deserted, abandoned street. Only the sound of her breathing and the rushing of blood in her veins disturbed the heavy silence.

A strand of hair slipped over her eyes and she pushed it back over her ear. Her cap had gone. Where had she left it? She couldn't remember.

"Kirsten…Kirsten…." The call was no more than a whisper, but her jaw clenched and she pulled her shawl tighter around her. Shawl? But she didn't wear one. So why…?

"Kirsten…Kirsten…." The voice was closer. Much closer. Behind her.

Mairead spun around, peered into the gloom. No one there.

"Kirsten…."

She could feel breath on her ear, tickling her hair.

Something brushed her shoulder. Slowly, she dared to look. A black, clawed hand gripped her. Its filthy broken fingernails dug into her skin, ripping, tearing. Rivulets of blood poured from the wounds and streamed down her arms. The taste of copper filled her mouth from her bitten lip.

Mairead unclenched her jaw and screamed.

★ ★ ★

It took a few seconds to realize where she was. Home. In bed. Safe. That nightmare. The same one she had dreamed for years. It always went the same way and left her feeling….

Mairead burst into tears, smothering her mouth with her shaking hands. Her lip hurt. She really *had* bitten it this time. She grabbed her pillow and stifled her sobs with it. Her widowed mother slept in the next room and Mairead mustn't wake her. The walls were so thin and she wasn't well.

Mairead took deep, gasping breaths, fighting to control herself. Slowly her sobs abated and her tears stopped flowing. She took a ragged breath and dried her eyes on a tissue. Her clock gleamed its green light. Five a.m. She had lain awake until at least two, and then that horrible nightmare.... From past experience, she knew she wouldn't sleep again tonight.

★   ★   ★

At work, Mairead splashed cold water on her face and stared at her reflection in the mirror of the ladies' washroom. Her eyes – red-rimmed and puffy from too little sleep and too many tears. Sometimes she felt she was slipping from reality. There were days when she wasn't even sure where she lived and worked. She always remembered in time, but the uncertainty was growing day by day and, with it, her anxiety that there might really be something wrong with her. And now, that dream was back....

Kirsten. Where had that name sprung from? She had always wondered that. She had never known anyone called Kirsten, not even at school. At least, not that she could remember.

Mairead dried her face and hands on a paper towel she then tossed into the waste bin. She forced herself to straighten her cap, paste a smile on her face and get ready for her first group.

Her new friend, Hannah, eyed her curiously as Mairead wandered into the gift shop.

"You OK?"

"Oh aye. Just had a bad night, that's all. Insomnia. I get it sometimes."

Hannah rolled her eyes. "Tell me about it. I've had it for the past few nights. I think I'm starting to hallucinate. A couple of nights ago, I would have sworn I saw our resident ghost in the street outside my flat."

"*Really?*"

"Only for a second and, as I say, I was tired. It was very late. You know the sort of thing."

No point in Hannah trying so hard to convince herself. Mairead didn't believe her either.

A few minutes later, Ailsa gathered them all together in the staff room. "As part of our ongoing expansion, there will be some workmen in today. We're looking at the viability of opening up part of Farquhars Close, which originally joined onto Henderson Close. At the same time, we can repair the damage to the section of Henderson Close that collapsed a while ago."

A few giggles erupted. Ailsa smiled. "Aye, I know. Everyone will call it 'Fucker's Close', but I can't help it. That was its name. James Farquhar—" The repeated correct pronunciation of the name as 'Farker' led to more giggles. "He was a wealthy merchant in the early 1800s. I've no doubt people had fun with his name then too. The workmen will do their stuff outside opening hours, so it shouldn't affect anyone too much."

"Apart from the dust." George Mackay, dressed as Sir William Henderson, raised his eyes heavenward.

"Hopefully not too bad. They'll put up boards and work behind them."

"When are they due to start?" Hannah asked.

"Six o'clock tonight, after the last tour."

"Wonder what they'll find?" Mairead asked.

"A whole lot of rubble, I would guess," Ailsa said.

George laughed. "As long as they don't let anything out, eh?"

"Thank you, George," Ailsa said. "I think we're all aware of the stories about Farquhars Close."

"Actually, I'm afraid I'm not," Hannah said.

"Don't worry," Mairead said, "I know them. I'll bring you up to speed."

"Thank you, Mairead," Ailsa said. "OK everyone, have a good day."

The staff dispersed to their stations. Hannah hung back to talk to Mairead. "More ghost stories?" she asked.

Mairead shuddered. "More ghoulish really. George was referring to the old legend that Farquhars Close was some sort of gateway to hell. It was one of the first Closes to go and was sealed very quickly. The story goes that a devil was walled up there and if he should ever be let loose, Edinburgh would burn."

Hannah grimaced. "Charming little night-time tale."

"I believe mothers did tell it to their bairns. Stopped them misbehaving. The mother would threaten a naughty child with being sent to the Farquhars devil."

"I think I'd be tempted to behave myself if I got a threat like that. Was there a physical description?"

"He was supposed to be eight feet tall, with arms and legs like tree trunks, and flaming red eyes."

"Sounds suitably demonic."

"There'll be a grain of truth in there somewhere. There usually is. He was probably a nasty, crooked man of above average height and strong sociopathic tendencies."

"Sounds about right. Funny, that woman from Kansas I told you about – Lindy – she described seeing a sort of scarecrow behind me. She said it was about that height, with wooden poles for arms."

"Maybe she had heard the old legend and her mind did the rest."

"Yes, maybe."

Mairead made for the door. "I'll go and collect my first group. See you later."

Hannah nodded and watched her go. There was something different about Mairead today. Something troubling, and Hannah couldn't help feeling that whatever it was wasn't going to go away anytime soon.

★　★　★

Hannah felt a chill on her face.

"Rachel…Rachel…."

Hannah stopped halfway down the steps to the Close. Behind her, the group jostled each other.

"Oh there you are. I thought I'd lost you." A middle-aged woman with fussy black hair grabbed the arm of a teenage girl who sported a bored expression and green hair.

"Sorry, folks," Hannah said, relieved. "I thought there was a problem."

The woman laughed. "Oh no, I'm always losing my daughter, she keeps wandering off."

Hannah addressed the girl. "Probably best if we all stick together."

The girl responded by rolling her eyes and mouthing, "Whatever." She pulled her mobile phone out of her pink bomber jacket and her face lit up in the bright light of the screen. Hannah didn't say anything. She knew what would happen. The girl tapped a few keys, frowned, scowled and returned the phone to her pocket. No signal. There never was down here.

The tour proceeded as normal. Hannah was a few minutes ahead of Mairead, so was the first to arrive at Murdoch Maclean's print shop. As they approached, Rachel's mother gave a little cry. "Can you hear that? It sounds like an old machine clanking. So realistic."

Hannah heard it all right. A clattering, clashing noise that shouldn't have been there.

One of the men cleared his throat. "Sounds like an antique printing press to me. I used to operate an old letterpress machine. Many years ago, of course."

"It's stopped now," Rachel's mother said. "That's awfully clever. I suppose you have a tape playing somewhere."

Hannah's mind froze. She must think. Now. They were all looking at her, waiting for the explanation, or punchline. *Come up with something. Anything, as long as it's now.*

"Ah yes, ladies and gentlemen, Murdoch Maclean, busy at his press as he always is. Day and night. Let's have a look at his shop."

Hannah stared at the sight in front of her. She swallowed hard to suppress her panic. Instead of a neat pile of newspapers, they were scattered all over the floor, as were his tools.

"Not very tidy, is he?" the retired printer said. "I'd have been shot for that."

"Yes, I agree." Hannah willed herself to come up with yet another plausible explanation. Finally, "Looks to me as if some of the local ruffians have been in and ransacked the place. It happened a lot in the Close, I'm afraid."

"Tough times," the printer said. Did he believe her? His calm expression gave nothing away.

"They certainly were, sir," Hannah said, remembering her role. "Now, let me take you a little further. I need to show you something quite remarkable."

Hannah went through the now familiar routine of describing Miss Carmichael's grisly murder, while her mind raced. Who could have done that to the print shop? The workmen hadn't started yet, so it couldn't be any of them. Worse still, Mairead would be in for a similar shock when her tour arrived there and Hannah had no way of warning her. Not without deserting her group. But Mairead was a trouper. She would cope. Just as Hannah had. Wouldn't she?

"Rachel! Rachel!"

Hannah pasted on what she hoped was a suitably helpful smile. "What's the matter, madam?"

"She was here a second ago and now I can't see her anywhere." The woman's panic was beginning to infect the others. Hannah had to take control.

"Now, don't worry, I'm sure she simply got distracted. If you'll all wait here, I'll pop back and find her." And with any luck she might be able to warn Mairead before she made it to the print shop.

She left her group muttering among themselves and trying to calm the agitated mother.

Hannah searched up and down Henderson Close but found no sign of Rachel. Where was the girl? She heard voices approaching and stood on the threshold of the printer's shop. Mairead appeared, closely followed by her group. Hannah cleared her throat.

"Good day to you, Emily," she said, trying to ignore Mairead's questioning expression. "I see you have brought some friends to Mr. Maclean's shop. Sadly he is closed for business today. As you can see, some of the local hooligans have ransacked the place and he has gone in search of a policeman."

Mairead picked up the thread. "I see he has left you in charge, Mary." She turned to her group. "Poor Mr. Maclean. This is the third time this year he has had need of the local constabulary.

Kids today, eh?" The group giggled and there were some nods of agreement from some of the older members. "Still, with Mary in charge, they won't dare return, will they?"

"Indeed not, Emily."

"Very handy with a broom handle is Mary."

"Indeed I am." Hannah made a gesture resembling a golfer teeing off. "Now, Emily. You don't happen to have seen a young lady with green hair pass this way, do you?"

Mairead's eyes opened wide and she shook her head. "Green hair, you say? No, indeed. I think I should have remembered that. I think we all would, wouldn't we?" The conservatively dressed group were clearly enjoying the exchange and probably thought it was all part of the usual tour.

The sound of running feet brought one of Hannah's party dashing up the Close. "She's back," he said, panting a little. "But I think you'd better come and see."

"Thank you, I shall come at once, and bid you all a pleasant visit and a good day," Hannah said, determined to stay in her role. No point in two groups being upset by the antics of one silly girl.

She followed the guest back and spoke softly to him. "What's happened? Where was she?"

He shook his head. "That's the point. She doesn't know. Swears she never left her mother's side."

Rachel's mother was beside herself, wringing her hands and acting as if she were in a Victorian melodrama. Rachel meanwhile was red-faced and angry, protesting her innocence.

"I'm telling you. I was here all the time. It's you lot that went off somewhere. And then it all went funny."

"What sort of 'funny'?" Hannah asked.

"I could see up to the sky, and there was this awful smell. Like manure. Then there were these horses. One nearly knocked me over. And these people came from nowhere and started pointing at me and laughing. Then you all came back and it stopped."

The expressions of disbelief on the majority of people in front of her spelled potential trouble ahead if Hannah didn't immediately take hold of the situation. Rachel's mother was sobbing in the arms of a sympathetic female of a similar age, but far greater self-control.

"Now, ladies and gentlemen, I'm sure there is a simple explanation for all this, but, for now, let's finish the tour and return to the gift shop and your own time. This lady and her daughter will be well looked after, I can assure you."

The group had fallen silent now. Only the odd whisper and an atmosphere you could have sliced through. The only sound was the occasional sob from Rachel's mother.

Back upstairs, Hannah took the mother and daughter aside. "I'd like us to go into the office for a cup of tea and ask you exactly what you saw, Rachel, but first I need to tell my manager what's happened and also make sure there is someone to cover my next tour." She addressed the older woman. "I'm sorry, I don't know your name?"

"Jackie." Her voice trembled.

"Thanks, Jackie. Will you both be all right for a couple of minutes?"

They nodded. Rachel had stopped looking angry now. More confused if anything.

In Ailsa's office, with strong cups of tea, Hannah prompted Rachel to repeat to her manager what she had seen earlier. Her account was identical. When she had finished, Hannah wished she could bottle the startled expression on Ailsa's face.

"You say you could see the sky?" Hannah asked.

Rachel nodded.

"So the tenements were their full height. Not covered?"

Again she nodded, but said nothing.

"Did you feel as if you had, somehow, gone back in time?"

"Yes. That's exactly how it felt. Seriously weird, or what? Freaked me out." She shuddered.

Still Ailsa said nothing.

Hannah turned to Jackie. "How exactly did she reappear?"

"It was strange. One minute she wasn't there and the next, she tapped me on the shoulder and asked me where I'd been…where we'd all been and why had we left her on her own."

"That's right," Rachel said.

"This is all most peculiar," Ailsa said. "I don't think anyone has reported this sort of thing before."

"No, but I've experienced some strange stuff and I'm not the only member of staff to…." Hannah wished she could cut off her tongue. Rachel and her mother were clearly keen to know more and Ailsa looked as if she would like to strangle her.

Ailsa glared at her. "I think that's enough for now." She addressed Jackie. "All I can do is apologize for the fright you've had."

To Hannah's surprise, Rachel's face broke into a grin. "The most excitement I've had since we got here. Wicked. Wait till I get home and tell me mates. They'll never believe it."

"Rachel!"

The two left, with the mother still scolding her daughter. Hannah made to leave too. She knew it wouldn't be that easy though.

"Just a second. A word please."

Ailsa shut the door. "I assume the incident you were referring to happened on your dress rehearsal?"

"That and…. I'm sorry, Ailsa, I shouldn't have said anything."

"Correct, not in front of our visitors. You mentioned someone else had experienced something similar. No one has brought this to my attention. Who was it?"

"I really can't say without getting their permission first, but I can describe what they told me."

"No, I don't want hearsay. Get their permission and come back to me at closing time today. Both of you."

⋆   ⋆   ⋆

"Bloody hell!" Mairead's eyes blazed with barely restrained fury. "How could you do that, Hannah? I told you in confidence. Ailsa'll think I'm a lunatic now." Mairead's teaspoon clattered into the sink of the staff room.

"I'm sorry. It slipped out. If it hadn't been for that girl—"

"She had nothing to do with it."

"Oh excuse me, she had everything to do with it. I have my experience and then a couple of days later, she has an almost identical one. I think it's worth comparing the two, don't you? Maybe something is going on here and we need to work out whether it's harmless or potentially dangerous. We have hundreds of members of the public in and out of here every week." Hannah felt her own righteous anger boiling up inside her with each word she uttered.

Mairead wasn't having any of it. "Ailsa is cynical about anything she can't see, feel or touch. She only lets us go so far in our storytelling because she doesn't want us exposed as charlatans or to be in trouble for frightening some poor old dear into an early heart attack. Now you've blurted that out in front of visitors and landed me in it with you."

Hannah stared at her, biting her tongue, so as not to lash out. The door opened. Ailsa strode in.

"I heard most of that. Thank you. Please come to my office."

         ★   ★   ★

Ailsa sat on her side of the desk and Hannah and Mairead sat side by side opposite her.

"Right, Mairead. You first. What do you allege you saw?"

Mairead repeated her experiences in a voice that barely registered above a whisper. When she had finished, Ailsa moved on to Hannah.

"You saw something similar on your dress rehearsal."

"Yes, Ailsa."

"And that's all you've seen?"

Hannah caught Mairead's eye. "Something else happened." She explained her strange encounter. Ailsa listened, occasionally tapping the desk with her pen.

"It does seem remarkably similar to the girl today. The question is, what caused the hallucination?"

Hannah spoke before thinking. "Why does it have to be a hallucination? Can't it actually have happened?" Why did she have to open her mouth at that precise moment? What was the matter with her today?

Ailsa's lips narrowed. "It can't have happened because things like that don't happen. A trick of the light. Hallucination. Too little sleep. Have you been sleeping well, Hannah?"

"Well, no, actually—"

Ailsa slammed her hand on the desk. "There you have it.

Hannah was suffering from lack of sleep and that girl? At her age anything could be responsible. Wishful thinking. Being impressionable. Drugs."

Hannah clenched her hands in her lap. Was she being serious? *Drugs?*

The silence in the room grew deafening until, at last, Ailsa seemed to make up her mind.

"Right, here is what we're going to do. I don't want to hear any more about this from either of you, do you understand?"

They both nodded.

"Good. Provided that is the case, I suggest we forget today's incident. Put it down to mass hysteria or something, I don't care. But if I find out you've been passing this story around, either among the rest of the staff or, God forbid, to the visitors, I shall have no hesitation in dismissing whoever is responsible on the grounds of gross misconduct. Am I understood?"

"Yes, Ailsa."

"Good. Now I suggest you both go home and, Hannah, you make sure you get a proper night's sleep."

Hannah nodded and followed Mairead out of the room.

Once out of earshot, Mairead spoke. "I'm sorry, Hannah. I overreacted. I shouldn't have lashed out at you the way I did. I've been so tired recently and the nightmares...."

"Let's put it behind us. Personally I don't understand why Ailsa reacted like that. This place thrives on ghost stories. Half our visitors come hoping they'll have a close encounter with something they can't explain."

Mairead shrugged. "I think it's a wee bit odd too, but she's always been like this. Maybe she doesn't want Henderson Close to lose credibility or something. I've never understood it either." She passed her hand over her forehead. "I could do with a drink right now."

"Good idea."

Mairead rummaged in the side pocket of her dress. "Damn. I've left my keys down there."

"I thought you were supposed to carry them with you?"

"You are, but I found they clanged and jingled so much, it

distracted my visitors. Every time I moved, it was like Marley's ghost, so I discovered a wee hiding place I tuck them into at the foot of the stairs, near the entrance. I'll get changed and pop down for them. Won't take a sec."

"OK."

★　★　★

The workmen had arrived and there were sounds of shouting, laughing and the thumping of tools and equipment when Mairead opened the door to Henderson Close. With so much coming and going, they had left the entrance unlocked. She stepped inside and the door swung shut behind her, as always. With the main lights off, the place was gloomy and Mairead had forgotten to bring her torch.

She grabbed hold of the handrail and felt around the nearside wall, touching the familiar cold stone.

A breeze lifted her hair. The workmen had put on a fan perhaps. She found the little crevice and her fingers touched cold metal. She retrieved her keys.

"Kirsten...Kirsten...."

"Oh please, no," she breathed. "I didn't hear that."

Something brushed her shoulder, caressed her hair, stroked her ear. An insect. God forbid, a spider. She put up her hand to brush it away and touched nothing but herself.

Whatever it was had moved. It was on her shoulder. She couldn't breathe. It didn't feel like an insect anymore. More like....

No, please, no.

She saw it out of the corner of her eye. The hand in her nightmare. Black, scaly, clawed. Filthy. Crawling down her arm.

Mairead screamed.

CHAPTER FIVE

"Mairead? *Mairead*." Hannah felt her way down the stairs, the atmosphere gloomy with only the emergency lighting to light the way. Her voice echoed along the Close, seeming to resound back at her from every nook and cranny. She listened hard for Mairead's answer but there was no reply. Where could she have got to? Uneasiness swelled inside her as she stepped on the uneven surface.

"Mairead!" Still nothing. Hannah peered through the few open doors, entered the printing shop, stopped. Listened for the tiniest sound. Maybe Mairead had tripped and fallen. Hit her head. Knocked herself unconscious.

But she only came to get her keys. And they were at the foot of the stairs. Why would she go any further than that?

Hannah pressed on, pausing at Miss Carmichael's corner. She glanced down at the 'blood'. Nothing unusual there. The stain was visible, as always. Dry. Old.

"Kirsten...Kirsten..."

Hannah caught her breath. The voice was male, but it sounded faraway, almost a whisper.

A sudden sound. A sort of pattering, as if someone with small feet...a child...running down the Close. Hannah shivered.

A man's cough. Hannah stifled a scream.

"You all right, lassie?"

She could have kissed him. One of the workmen.

"You look like you've seen a ghost."

Hannah forced a light laugh. He might not be far off the truth there. "I'm looking for one of my colleagues. She came down here about ten or fifteen minutes ago. Have you seen her?"

He shook his head. "No. You're the only one I've seen. I thought everyone else had gone home. Then I heard a noise and thought I'd better investigate."

"I must have missed her somehow then. She's definitely not here."

"She's probably waiting for you in the shop."

"Yes, you're probably right."

Hannah left the workman, who continued on his way to start his night's work.

Upstairs, the shop was dark, empty. No sign of Mairead. Hannah couldn't even call her because she didn't have her mobile number. Maybe she had gone straight to the pub, thinking Hannah had gone there already.

Hannah had intended suggesting the nearest one and hoped Mairead would have had similar ideas. She made her way over to the busy bar, and squeezed through happy, laughing tourists and office workers newly released from a day's work.

She searched the main and small bars and even tried the Ladies'. No sign.

She bought herself half a pint of cider and found a seat near the door. If Mairead came in now she definitely wouldn't miss her.

Half an hour later, she drained her glass and gave up. She would see her friend at work tomorrow and find out what had happened then. No harm could have come to her. After all, she had only gone to grab her keys. There would be a simple explanation.

★   ★   ★

But Mairead wasn't at work the next day. Nor the day after that. No one had seen or heard from her. It was as if she had simply vanished. Hannah now had Mairead's number. She rang it repeatedly but there was no answer.

Hannah racked her brains to think of any explanation for the sudden disappearance, but failed every time. None of the other staff could understand it either. Hannah had been the last one to see her as far as anyone knew and Mairead wasn't the type to not turn up for work.

★   ★   ★

Hannah knocked on Ailsa's office door.

"Come in. Hello, Hannah. What can I do for you?"

"It's about Mairead. I wondered if there was any news? She's been off nearly a week now and I can't get her to pick up on her phone."

Ailsa's brow creased. "I know. We're all very concerned. As I told you before, someone left a message on the voicemail, saying she was sick with flu and wouldn't be coming in. That was on her first day of absence and since then...nothing. She'll need a note from her doctor from tomorrow. Have you called round to her house at all? She lives with her mother, doesn't she?"

"Yes, but I don't know her address."

"I do. I can't give it to you, I'm afraid. Confidentiality. But I think I'll go round this afternoon. I've been calling the landline but it seems to be disconnected."

"That's a bit odd, isn't it?"

Ailsa sighed. "Maybe. But I think a lot of people are relying on their mobile phones these days. Telephone rental is so expensive."

"I just thought. With her mother living there as well.... I think I would always want my mother to have a landline. In case of emergencies."

"Me too." Ailsa stood up. "Right that settles it. I'm going round there now. I'll let you know what happens tomorrow. Lock up for me, will you? The builders aren't in tonight."

"No problem." Hannah closed the door of Ailsa's office. Mairead might be sick, but why wasn't she at least answering her phone? Sending a text? Responding to voicemails? Anything other than this awful silence. It wasn't as if her mobile phone was switched off either. Before long, if she wasn't recharging the battery, it would die. Not only was it worrying, but she was also risking her job. Ailsa seemed OK about it now, but if it went on more than a day longer, it could be a very different story. If she didn't produce a doctor's note – certifying her absence – after seven days off work, she could lose her job.

"Come on, Mairead. Pick up." The phone continued to ring. At the seventh ring, the voicemail kicked in as usual. After the tone, Hannah spoke. "Hi, Mairead. Look, we're all really worried about you. Ailsa is on her way round to see you. Please call me as soon as you get this message."

She clicked off her phone and opened the door to the deserted gift shop. George had changed into his own clothes and was about to leave. "Oh there you are." He smiled at her. "I'll leave you to it then. Didn't want to go until I knew you were here to lock up after me. Still no news of Mairead, I hear?"

Hannah shook her head.

George frowned. "It's not like her. I mean, first off, she's never sick. I don't think she's had one day off, apart from holidays, since she started here a couple of years ago. And she's always so conscientious. She's the last person I would have thought would fail to keep in touch. We all know to ring in every day unless the doctor has signed us off. I can't understand it. Hope she's all right."

"Me too," Hannah said, and wished the heavy weight pressing on her chest would go away. "No doubt Ailsa will update us tomorrow."

"If Mairead still has a job tomorrow."

"That thought had crossed my mind too," Hannah said.

"See you, lass."

"See you, George."

She locked the door securely behind him and switched off the shop lights, leaving only the emergency ones casting their dim glow across the store.

Alone in the building, she pushed away the increasing sense of unease and walked quickly to the entrance to Henderson Close, grabbing a torch as she did so. She would now have to go all round, making sure no one had managed to separate themselves either deliberately or accidentally from their party. Her heart beat faster with each step she descended. Down here, all the lights remained on, but they would go off automatically at any moment.

Her footsteps echoed off the walls. Hannah forced herself to maintain a steady, unhurried pace as she moved around the meandering narrow passageways. She peered through the windows and checked the doors were locked. As she passed the Henderson House, she noted the tidiness of the print shop. Someone had cleared it up on the day it had been 'ransacked', though how that had happened in the first place remained a mystery. Hannah's gaze took in the dirt floor, tools and printing machine and a memory flashed into her mind.

Murdoch Maclean setting his type blocks. Asking if she wanted anything. It seemed more real when she stood here. She gave a little shiver and moved away, turned into the alley and—

Whispering, like the echo of some far-off conversation. "Who's there?" she called, her voice echoing all around her. Silence. It came again. Closer now. Indistinct. Chatter.

"Who *is* that? Who's down here?"

Silence.

Giggling.

More angry than scared, Hannah's anger rose from the pit of her stomach. "This isn't funny. No one is supposed to be down here. Show yourself. This instant."

"I don't think you'd like that."

Hannah gasped. A male voice. Stronger than the last time. Different. Where had it come from? Unlike last time, she'd heard it – not with her ears. In her brain.

She breathed heavily. "You can stop playing your silly games now because I'm not having it. You shouldn't be down here. Come out before I call the police and have you arrested for trespass."

"I don't think so."

Laughter. Behind her. Hannah spun around.

A shadow flashed across the wall and vanished.

Hannah stared, her mouth desert dry.

She stumbled back, past Miss Carmichael's corner and the printer's shop, back up Henderson Close. She staggered up the steps, her clammy palms clinging to the handrail.

She was almost at the top when the main lights went out, thrusting the Close into the gloom of the emergency lighting. *Six-thirty. The lights always go out at six-thirty this time of year.*

She reached the door and slammed it shut behind her, locking it. She leaned against it, breathing hard. *Dear God, let me have imagined that*. Now it was *her* inner voice speaking to her. Last time? A stranger.

★   ★   ★

Ailsa handed Hannah a cup of coffee and sat behind her desk. She was frowning. Hannah waited while she collected her thoughts.

"I'll tell you, Hannah, I don't know what to make of it all. It keeps getting more and more crazy. I rang the doorbell, knocked at the door. Nothing. There's a gate that takes you down a path to the side door, so I went down there. The garden is all overgrown with weeds and briars, so it looked as if no one had been down it in weeks. Months probably, because all that growth must have happened last summer at the latest. Anyway, I knocked hard at that door and that's when a neighbor came out. Bit of a stern old wifey. Asked me what my business was. I told her I was Mairead's boss and she looked surprised. Apparently she hasn't seen Mairead in a couple of *years* or more. Thought she'd moved out when…now get this, when her mother *died*."

"*Died?*"

Ailsa nodded. "That's what I said. Anyway, the woman could see I was shocked and asked me in for a cup of tea. Turns out she's got a kind heart underneath the gruff exterior. She told me Mrs. Ferguson had been ill for a long time. Multiple sclerosis. She developed it in her thirties when Mairead was only a child. I never knew any of this but Mairead grew up as her mother's caregiver."

"I had no idea."

"The neighbor – Mrs. Lauderdale – wasn't wholly surprised at that. She said the two of them lived in their own world mostly. Mairead went to school and then on to university to study English and Drama, but she always lived at home and Mrs. Lauderdale doesn't ever remember her bringing friends home. No school friends or boyfriends. Probably didn't want to disturb her mother. *She* gradually deteriorated and it was clear Mairead was having trouble coping toward the end. Her mother couldn't walk, and some days, she could barely use her hands, or speak. One day, Mairead went out shopping and when she came home, she found her mother slumped over in her chair. She'd been saving up her painkillers. Morphine. Took a massive overdose. She left a note. Must have taken ages for her to write even though it was quite short. She said she didn't want to be a burden any longer and that Mairead should have a life. Heartbreaking stuff. Must have been devastating for her daughter."

"And this was all a couple of years ago?"

"Yes. Must have been around the time she started work here."

"And she never mentioned it?"

"She never really talked much at all about her private life. Just that she lived with her mother. No details. Certainly not to me."

"Nor me, now I think about it. But some people like to keep themselves private, don't they? Even with their friends. They tell people what they want them to know."

Ailsa gave her a knowing smile. "Yes, they do, don't they?"

Hannah quickly returned to their original subject. "You said this neighbor hadn't seen Mairead for a couple of years?"

Ailsa nodded. "According to Mrs. Lauderdale, Mairead left quite abruptly a few weeks after her mother's funeral. The house belongs to the council and, for some reason, it still hasn't been re-let yet, even after all this time, but you know what councils are like. Never do today what you can put off for a few years."

"Did she say where she was going?"

"Not to Mrs. Lauderdale. She wouldn't have known when she'd gone, but she happened to be dusting her windowsills and saw Mairead piling bags into a taxi. Mrs. Lauderdale waved at her, but Mairead totally ignored her, as if she hadn't seen her, but Mrs. Lauderdale was sure she had. A few weeks after she left, Mrs. Lauderdale could see mail piling up behind the door. It's glazed so a dead giveaway to any potential burglar that no one was at home. She rang the council and they had no idea she had gone, beyond the fact that they weren't receiving any rent. It was paid by direct debit out of Mairead's mother's account and when that was closed after her death, no more payments were made. They hadn't been able to contact anyone and were about to issue an eviction notice."

"I don't know what to make of it," Hannah said.

"Join the club. I can't understand it. I mean, where has she been living and why did she give that old address? I can kind-of understand the moonlight flit – although it was in broad daylight apparently – I mean, if the girl was in financial difficulties and couldn't afford the rent…. But where has she been these past two years? Sleeping on a friend's couch? Living rough?"

"Hardly," Hannah said. "She's always so smartly dressed. Always clean…no, she couldn't have been living rough."

"Did she ever speak of any other friends?"

Hannah thought back over their brief acquaintanceship and shook her head. "Not that I remember and I think I would. Oh, this is ridiculous. She can't vanish into thin air. Where on earth is she?"

"People do though, don't they? Vanish. Years ago, that politician. John Stonehouse. Disappeared for years and then turned up again. Then there was Lord Lucan. They never found him, did they?"

"But he was supposed to have murdered the nanny and, as far as we know, Mairead's done nothing illegal. Apart from running out on the council rent that is. But she hasn't murdered anyone, committed fraud, robbery."

"Not that we know of, but as we've now discovered, there's so much about Mairead that we hadn't a clue about until now. How much more is there to uncover?"

"Shouldn't we report her as missing or something?"

"I've already done that. I called in at the police station on the way back and told them everything I know. I need to drop her staff photo in later."

"Let's hope they can find her. And that she's safe and unharmed."

"They want the voicemail message that person left, so they can try and analyze it. I heard it back again and you can't even tell if it's male or female. Do you want to listen?"

"Please."

The voice was indistinct, muffled, as if the caller were holding something over the receiver to disguise his or her voice. The accent was distinctly Scottish but Hannah couldn't place it any closer than that, not that she was any expert on Scottish regional dialects. The tone sounded gruff and Ailsa was right. Impossible to tell whether it was male or female – or even Mairead herself. The girl was a good enough actress to pull that one off, for sure.

"Mairead Ferguson won't be in to her work today. She has the flu." The phone cut off.

Ailsa switched off the voicemail. "See what I mean? Male or female?"

Hannah shrugged. "No idea."

"Good thing the police have these sophisticated machines these days. They can analyze wave patterns, tones, pitches, all sorts. They should even be able to tell us where that accent comes from."

"Assuming whoever it was wasn't putting it on."

"That thought crossed my mind too. But why do this?"

Hannah left soon after, not sure whether she should be confused or scared for her friend – and feeling both.

★   ★   ★

Rain pattered onto her living room window. Hannah reached up to draw the curtains and glanced down at the glistening street below. In the evening darkness, the puddles of water shimmered in the silvery glow of the streetlights. The normally bustling street was deserted. It looked cold, unwelcoming on a typical Scottish October evening. Anyone without a roof over their head would suffer tonight.

Mairead. Where was she? Hannah paused, her hands on the curtains.

A sudden movement below her window grabbed her attention. Hannah stared. A female, dressed in a long dark coat and old-fashioned hat, stared back up at her through her wire-rimmed glasses. Hannah's mouth ran dry. Her lips pulled taut over her teeth. A pulse in her temple throbbed.

"It can't be you," she said. "You can't be here. Not now."

Almost imperceptibly, the woman inclined her head in a nod, turned and vanished into the shadows.

CHAPTER SIX

George sipped his pint of Guinness thoughtfully as he and Hannah sat facing each other across a small table in the Greyfriars Bobby pub. In the week since Mairead's departure, Hannah had welcomed the company of this slightly balding, ginger-haired man of similar age to herself. His down-to-earth common sense was what she needed with all the craziness going on around her. Nothing seemed to faze George. He took everything in his stride and almost convinced her that nothing was amiss and that Mairead was off somewhere enjoying herself. The laughter lines around his blue eyes creased as he stood and indicated her almost empty cider glass.

"My shout," he said.

"Thanks. Just a half please."

Minutes later he was back, brimming glasses in hand.

"I had a cousin who disappeared," he said, before taking a massive swig of Guinness. The foam gave him a creamy mustache that he proceeded to lick off.

"Did he ever turn up? Or she, that is?"

"No, definitely he. Yes, six months later, he sent a postcard from Canberra. He'd been a busy lad. Fallen in love with an Aussie barmaid at his local. Decided to leave everything and fly back with her. They were getting married and she was three months pregnant."

"Wow! Is he still out there?"

"Och, no. He was back in Dunfermline a few months later. Left her behind. Everything had been going fine until her boyfriend was released from prison."

"Huh?"

George laughed. "Massive chap. Did a lot of boxing. Turns out the girl had been living with him until he got nicked for armed robbery. He did his time and expected to pick up where he left off. My cousin decided discretion was the better part of valor and scarpered. That was five years ago. When the divorce came through, he married a nice, quiet, mousy girl from Inverness and they run a sweet shop together. Two wee bairns, a spaniel called Benny and a Siamese cat with three paws, called Cleopatra."

Hannah laughed. She could never quite be sure whether George's stories were fact or fiction.

He winked at her. "I know you're worried. But there'll be a simple explanation and probably a misunderstanding. Someone has got their wires crossed and my money is on that nosy neighbor. Some of these wifeys love nothing more than a good gossip – never let the truth get in the way though."

"But it's not just Mairead's disappearance, is it? It's all the other stuff that's been going on. The printer's shop...."

"Kids."

"But how could they have got in? They're not allowed on the tours."

"Builders probably left a door open somewhere, or, if they were over fourteen, they could have hung back. Got back in or something. Happened at my last place. Put the wind up one of the older tour guides. Like you, she became convinced ghosts were at it. Until they caught the little buggers."

"OK, well what about the other stuff I told you? Both Mairead and I have seen the same woman. A woman who couldn't be there. Then I have that experience of going back in time. And the voices...."

"You told me you haven't been sleeping. It's a very atmospheric place and we all get a little carried away sometimes. Even me. I think I see things out of the corner of my eye on occasions." He stopped and shook his head. "Henderson Close has that effect on you, and on some of our more susceptible guests. Like your Rachel the other day."

He could be right. It certainly made more sense than what Hannah feared. So why couldn't she make herself believe it?

★   ★   ★

At home later, Hannah switched off the television and sipped a mug of strong tea, lost in her thoughts. Inevitably her mind drifted back over the past weeks and months.

Leaving Salisbury had been a momentous decision for her, made easier by her increasingly erratic ex-mother-in-law, who had taken to calling her up at all hours merely to bombard her with insults.

She's lonely. No matter how many times she reminded herself that, it made precious little difference. Yes, the woman was lonely. Hell, so was Hannah on occasions, but the difference between the two of them was that Hannah had determined to do something about it. The redundancy provided the spark she needed to ignite her decision.

Two choices presented themselves. Either stay in Salisbury and try and get another job there, or, move away, start afresh. Free, single. Definitely single. After Roger, she had no desire whatsoever to start another relationship, however many times well-meaning friends had tried to hook her up with allegedly eligible candidates. No, for the foreseeable future at least, that ship had well and truly left port.

As the days progressed, and Violet's phone calls made her seriously consider taking out an injunction against her for harassment, the thought of a complete break with her past grew more and more attractive. So, what would she do? Carry on teaching? Or something quite, quite different.

Her divorce settlement and redundancy would keep her from destitution. She didn't have to earn the sort of salary she had been used to, so....

With a pen and paper, to list possibilities, she booted up her laptop and started a search for different jobs using her preferred job criteria. The results were interesting, if mostly predictable. Aside from teaching and allied professions came acting. *Oh yes, very practical....* But then something struck a chord.

In London she had visited the Dungeon and thought how great it would be to have a character guide's job. To play the part of a person from a different era, steering groups of excited visitors around a haunted attraction, telling them ghostly, macabre tales.

Her excitement mounting, Hannah began her search for themed venues and any associated job opportunities. It turned out there was an increasing number to be found. Evidently, in this crazy world, people loved nothing more than a good, old-fashioned scare. Like the ghost trains of previous generations.

City after city. Manchester, York, Chester, Liverpool, Birmingham …and then she found it.

Edinburgh.

"Can you bring history to life?"

Yes.

Her application was off the same day. A week later, her interview was confirmed, and two days after that, she set off for a week in Edinburgh.

And the moment she stepped over the threshold of the tourist attraction that was Henderson Close, she felt a strange sense of belonging. Though for the life of her, she hadn't a clue why.

★   ★   ★

Mairead's disappearance continued to concern Hannah but, apart from that, a few mercifully uneventful days followed in Henderson Close, but it was an uneasy lull. Hannah had a hunch the calm would not last.

One morning, she opened the entrance door and her group filtered through. A gasp came from one of the women. "I can't go any further. I can't go down there."

The woman's voice trembled. Panic etched into every syllable. Hannah stood with ten of the group at the bottom of the stairs. The others started muttering among themselves. Someone giggled nervously.

"Are you all right, madam?" Hannah asked, careful to stay in character.

"She'll be all right in a moment." A man of similar age to the woman took hold of her arm and tried to drag her down the stairs. Meanwhile, the rest of the group had descended, and all eyes were on the terrified woman.

"Come on, Beth, you're making a spectacle of yourself."

"Sir, I'm sure if your wife doesn't want to come down here, she doesn't have to. She can always wait for you upstairs."

"No," he retorted, "I paid good money for these tickets."

"Don't worry about that, sir. I can make sure the lady's ticket is refunded."

He relaxed his hold on the woman, who was now shaking.

"Is it claustrophobia?" Hannah asked, more in hope than expectation. She guessed what was coming.

The woman shook her head. "Can't you feel it? Can't you see it?" She wrinkled her nose. "Smell it?"

Hannah sniffed, as did other members of the group. All looked as baffled as she felt.

"I'm sorry, madam, I don't quite follow—"

The woman held on to the handrail and began to back away up the steps. Her husband stood halfway down, casting quick, uncomprehending glances at Hannah.

The woman's voice was a hiss. "There's *evil* down there. It's growing. I've…I've got to get out of here."

She turned and stumbled up the rest of the stairs and out through the door. It banged shut behind her.

The group was hushed. Shocked into silence. Hannah cleared her throat.

"Well, ladies and gentlemen, as you can see, Henderson Close has a profound effect on some people but I can assure you, we haven't lost a visitor yet." *As for the staff, that's a different matter.* "Shall we proceed? I have some interesting stories to tell and time's a-pressing."

As always these days, Hannah's heart beat a little faster as she came upon Maclean's shop. A wave of relief washed over her when she saw it, neat, tidy. Everything in its proper place.

The group had settled. Even the man whose wife had been so agitated. They laughed at her jokes, said "Ooooh" and "Ahhhh" when the lights went out and the 'rats' dashed across the wall. They were suitably impressed with the plague doctor and his crow-like mask, and intrigued by the legend of Miss Carmichael's murder.

They had just rounded the last corner when a sudden, stiff breeze hit them.

Hannah thought quickly. "Some work is being carried out on Farquhars Close, which runs across the bottom of the street. I expect it's coming from there," she said.

A woman who had made it her business to stick like glue to Hannah throughout the tour suddenly spoke. "What a great idea to have the workmen dressed in Victorian workmen's clothes."

Hannah looked at her. "No, madam, there are no builders here today. They work in the evening and through the night."

The woman's look of surprise made Hannah wonder if she was right after all.

"But…but I just saw…a man in corduroy trousers, a cloth cap, old-fashioned clay pipe, bandanna round his neck. He had a hod of bricks over his shoulder."

Hannah's heart started to pound again. "Where did you see him, madam?"

The woman pointed a shaking finger off to the right. "Oh God, I've just realized," she said. "He went straight through that wall."

The group erupted in excited chatter and a few shocked gasps.

Hannah fought to come up with a plausible explanation but couldn't think of one. There was nothing else for it. "Ladies and gentlemen, it seems you have had an added bonus on your trip today. The ghosts of Henderson Close have decided to pay you a visit. Well, a couple of you anyway."

Polite, slightly edgy, laughter.

"Right, if you will all follow me, we'll return to the twenty-first century. I trust you have had an enjoyable tour today."

Murmured thanks, nods and an excited American woman of indeterminate age and the fixed expression of a Botox-devotee pressed Hannah's hand. "That was the best ghost tour ever. You guys do a wonderful job here. Thank you."

Hannah smiled. "Glad you enjoyed it, madam. Please tell your friends."

"I sure will."

As she was the last to leave, Hannah followed her up the stairs. At the top, the woman paused and turned back to her. "That waxwork man in the shop. You know, the printer? He's so lifelike. I swear I saw him move. I don't know how you did that. Awesome."

Hannah forced a smile on her face and said nothing.

There was no waxwork man in the print shop.

CHAPTER SEVEN

George, dressed as his character, Sir William Henderson, eased himself into a comfortable armchair opposite Hannah in the staff room.

"Ailsa's in a foul mood," he said, raising his coffee mug to his lips.

Hannah nodded. "One minute she's angry, the next she seems in a world of her own. I think she's really worried about Mairead. It's been ten days now and the police have found no trace of her."

"What about the voicemail?"

"Inconclusive apparently. Their money is on it being Mairead herself. They say it sounds as if she had put a scarf or something over the mouthpiece and faked an accent."

"So they're sure it's a woman's voice?"

"Not entirely. Their attitude now seems to be that if she wanted to disappear, that's her prerogative. She's an adult. No known history of mental illness. As to where she's been living this past two years...the only address anyone, including her bank, has for her is the one Ailsa visited a few days ago."

"I suppose in this day and age when everyone does everything online, an out of date street address is no biggy."

"I suppose...." Hannah sighed. "It's so peculiar. I know we had a brief falling-out when I let Ailsa know we'd experienced something weird in the Close, but I'm sure we cleared that up."

"You had a weird experience?"

She hadn't meant to mention that to anyone. Her promise to Ailsa....

"Oh, it was nothing really. One of the visitors played a trick on us. Had me going for a minute, that's all."

Hannah hoped her casual tone would throw George off

the scent. He frowned, seemed about to say something, then thought again and moved on.

"I hope we hear something soon," he said. "About Mairead. If Ailsa bawls me out once more, I swear I'm jacking it in here."

"Hang on in there, George. Sooner or later, Mairead will have to draw some money out of her account and then they'll be able to trace her. Goodness alone knows what she's been living on this past week or so anyway."

"Maybe she has a savings account no one knows about?"

"Or maybe—" Hannah stopped short of voicing her ultimate fear. That if, and when, Mairead turned up, she wouldn't be alive and kicking.

George glanced at his watch and stood. "Better get going before Ailsa gets on the warpath again. You coming?"

Hannah smoothed her dress down. "Let battle commence," she said, smiling.

The afternoon's tours went smoothly. One woman swore she could smell garlic around Miss Carmichael's corner.

"She wasn't a vampire, was she?"

Hannah restrained herself. "Not that we are aware of, madam."

Others in her group tittered and giggled. The woman blushed and hung back when Hannah ushered the group on to the next point of interest.

At the end of that tour – the last of the day – Hannah said her goodbyes and accepted the thanks from another set of satisfied customers. The woman who had asked about the smell of garlic was the last. Her awkward expression reflected the embarrassment she must be feeling.

"I'm sorry to be such an idiot," she said.

"That's no problem at all. People have all sorts of strange experiences down there."

"The thing is, I really *did* smell garlic. I didn't mention the other smells. Like our herb garden…and the nasty stink of manure as well. The different smells kept wafting over me, but I could see I was the only one, so I shut up. The rest of the group already thought I was a nutter."

"It's a very atmospheric place."

"No, it's more than that…I felt something down there. Something so dark and rotten…as if someone had opened an old coffin. It smelled of…death."

Hannah stared.

The woman shook her head. "I'm sorry. I must go. I'm not making any sense. Thank you. Please be careful."

She had gone before Hannah could respond.

"Lock up for me, Hannah. *Hannah.*"

Hannah had been completely unaware of Ailsa approaching her. "Sorry?"

"I said, lock up for me, would you? I've got a stinking migraine and I need to get home while I can still see properly to drive."

"Yes. Of course. No problem. Hope you feel better very soon."

"I just need my bed."

Hannah locked the shop door behind her boss and drew an unsteady breath. The last tour had finished early and the builders hadn't yet arrived, so she was on her own. She opened the door to the Close and started her descent.

The lights were still on. Hannah reached the stony street and began her check of the doors and accessible buildings. Above her, the occasional car horn, the rumble of a particularly large vehicle, a distant police siren, fading as she moved further underground and away from the road above.

As always these days, she approached Murdoch Maclean's shop with trepidation, then exhaled in relief as she saw everything in order and not a figure in sight. She was moving off when something caught her eye.

She stepped over the threshold and smelled the familiar odor of printing ink and musty paper. But something didn't feel right. The pile of newspapers against the wall. They looked different somehow. Reordered. She went up to them and picked up the one on the top. The paper was fragile, brown with age. The front page was a mass of advertisements. Carefully, she turned the page. She gasped. A familiar face looked out at her from page two. Quickly, she read the caption underneath.

"An early photograph of Miss Carmichael, who was murdered yesterday on Henderson Close."

But that's impossible. It can't be her.

Hannah closed the paper, folded it once and tucked it under her arm. She half ran round the rest of the site, tested doors, peering in every nook and cranny, finding nothing untoward.

Noisy male chatter came closer. The builders. A smell of cigarette smoke. "You shouldn't be smoking down here," she said, loud enough for them to hear. Nobody responded and the smell grew stronger.

She faced the floor-to-ceiling boards that now formed the barrier with Farquhars Close. Here the chatter and smell was at its strongest. "Did you hear me through there?" she called. "I said no one is allowed to smoke down here."

Still no response. The chatter grew louder. Women's voices mixed with the men's. A horse neighed.

Don't let this be happening.

In front of her, the boards seemed to pulsate, fade in and out. She caught glimpses of another street. Like Henderson Close but open to the sky. In a shop doorway, a shadow moved. It raised its right hand and beckoned to her. Instinctively she stepped back as it emerged from its shadowy doorway.

It was male, tall and thin. Impossibly thin. Skeletal even. But with sagging, dirty skin hanging off its sunken jowls. A filthy, black claw-like hand with yellowing talons beckoned to her. The creature's eyes blazed. It opened its thin-lipped mouth and exposed long, tobacco-stained teeth. It laughed. Raucous. Its straggly, greasy hair hung limp below its shoulders. It spoke, but its voice was in her head.

"You have no business here."

Hannah cried out, hitched up her skirt and ran back to the stairs, still clutching the newspaper. She didn't look back. Maybe it was following her. Maybe not. No time to lose. She had to get out of there.

Back in the shop, panting and trembling, she dropped the keys twice before she could lock the door. She leaned against it, trying to catch her breath. Through the door she swore she heard that laugh.

The scrape of a key sent her reeling across the shop. The door opened and a figure appeared. He saw her. "You all right, lassie?"

Hannah wanted to hug him. It was one of the builders.

"I'm fine." Her voice said otherwise.

"Didn't mean to startle ye. Just checking if anyone was still here."

"I'm OK, really. I wasn't expecting anyone and it's a bit spooky here when you're on your own. I'll go and get changed and then I'll be off."

"I'll lock this door now." He moved to go back down to the Close.

"Just one thing," Hannah said. The builder turned back to her. "Did you see anyone else, or smell cigarette smoke down there?"

The builder looked confused. "No. Only my mates of course. We all arrived together."

"And no one's had a crafty cig down there?"

"No chance. Not on my watch. I don't want to go up like a bonfire. There've been too many of those in Edinburgh as it is." He smiled at her. "But you're right. It *is* spooky down there. I thought I heard a horse whinnying once. My mate Pete swore he heard someone yelling. We reckoned it was just noise filtering down from the street above."

"Yes, probably."

★   ★   ★

The staff almost filled the small office as Ailsa stood in front of them.

"We've had a request from a group of paranormal investigators based in Leith. They want to do an all-night vigil."

Groans echoed around the room. Ailsa raised her hand.

"All right, I know. It'll be five or six hours of utter boredom and the need to keep a tight lid on your desire to giggle, but it brings in good money and gets us publicity we don't have to pay for."

Every nerve in Hannah's body was twitching. "Are you sure this is a good idea, Ailsa?"

Her boss blinked and looked at her as if she had made an

improper suggestion. "Why wouldn't it be? Without these events, we wouldn't have the money to keep developing the site. Those builders don't work for free, you know."

Hannah looked around at her fellow tour guides. They said nothing, but watched the exchange intently.

She couldn't help it. She had to speak up. "I know, but some peculiar things have been happening down there lately. And then, Mairead's disappearance—"

Ailsa seemed to grit her teeth. "I am well aware of the impact of Mairead's disappearance, Hannah. I'm as worried about her as you are. More perhaps, because I've known her longer, but in light of the little we know now, I wonder if any of us ever knew her at all."

Her voice sounded sharp and her words harsh. Hannah reached for her bag and pulled out the carefully folded newspaper she had retrieved from Maclean's shop the previous day. She unfolded it and, as Ailsa and her colleagues watched, puzzled looks on their faces, Hannah laid the paper out on her boss's desk. The team crowded around and peered at the faded print.

George spoke first. "My God, it's the spitting image of her."

"What do you mean 'spitting image of her'?" Hannah demanded. "It *is* her."

Ailsa huffed. "Don't be ridiculous. This newspaper is dated November 2nd, 1891. It *can't* be her. Besides, look at the caption. It's a photo of Miss Carmichael, taken a few years before she was murdered, by the looks of it."

Hannah and the others stared at the impossible photograph. The clear eyes of Mairead Ferguson stared back.

The others muttered among themselves. Hannah got the distinct impression they were as skeptical as Ailsa. All except George. He tapped the picture. "Ailsa, don't you think it's remotely possible that there is something in all this? I know there have been all sorts of reports of sightings, people being touched and so on over the years, but the activity does seem to have escalated in recent weeks."

Ailsa nodded and stared hard at Hannah. "I have noticed that there has been an increase since Hannah arrived and I wondered if she has an explanation for it."

Now it was Hannah's turn to stare. Anger brought an edge to her words. "If you're implying I have had something to do with any of this, you're wrong. I've *experienced* some unexplained events, not *caused* them."

"Nevertheless, it is quite a coincidence, you have to admit," Ailsa said.

"Mairead had experienced much the same kind of activity as I did. And that was *before* I came here."

"If she did, she never reported it."

"She probably knew this was the reaction she would get. She wouldn't be believed and would be accused of making it all up."

"I'm not accusing you of anything, Hannah."

"Not much!"

The silence echoed around the room.

George coughed. "May I make a suggestion?"

Ailsa nodded, her lips in a tight white line.

"Let this paranormal group come and do their overnight vigil. Maybe they'll tap into something. We need a couple of us to be with them. I'll volunteer. How about you, Hannah?"

Hannah shot him a glance. An overnight séance down in Henderson Close was the furthest thing from what she wanted to do but she was aware all eyes were on her. She couldn't back out now. Her mind screamed at her to say, "No."

"OK," she heard herself say. "I'm up for it."

A slight smile twitched the corners of Ailsa's lips. "Excellent. They'll be arriving on Saturday night at around eleven thirty. I expect they'll be well bladdered from an evening in the pub, but I understand they're a pretty good-natured bunch. They'll be bringing hand-held video cameras and the usual paranormal paraphernalia. I don't think anyone else need volunteer. I'm sure Hannah and George are more than capable of handling them." She treated the assembled staff to a broad smile that stopped short of Hannah.

From nowhere, a chill crept up Hannah's spine. Why had she agreed? Every instinct told her it was the last thing she should have done, but she couldn't back out now. All she could hope was that she didn't live to regret it.

★   ★   ★

Freezing rain and a biting wind on Saturday had sent the temperature plummeting toward zero by nighttime. Glad that she had chosen to wear a warm, fleece-lined jacket, chunky scarf and thick woolen gloves, Hannah exhaled. Her breath billowed ghost-white. She switched on the shop lights and closed the door behind her. Footsteps approaching made her turn. George smiled at her from the shop doorway.

"Beat me to it, I see," he said. "You're keen."

Hannah grimaced. "Not quite the word I would have chosen. Railroaded more like. I can't help feeling this is a mistake. If we unleash something we can't control...."

"Let's wait and see, OK? Now, how about a coffee before the hordes arrive?"

"Thanks, George. I had one before I came out but I think it's worn off." Hannah followed him into the staff room. Five minutes later, steaming mugs in hand, they returned to the shop to wait for the group.

"What time is it?" George asked.

Hannah peered at her watch. "Twenty past. They'll be here anytime now."

"Hope they're not too wasted. We don't want any of them falling down those bloody stairs."

Hannah smiled. In the pit of her stomach, a snake of fear uncoiled itself and shifted. She fidgeted on her stool behind one of the two tills. Sitting a few feet away on the other one, George noticed.

"You really don't want to do this, do you?"

"How did you guess?"

"You'll be OK, honestly. I've done a couple of these before. They're just a bit of good-natured fun. People scare themselves and each other. They usually manage to convince themselves they've heard something, or that something has touched them. They all have a jolly good time and then at six a.m., they go home completely knackered and ready for their beds. As we will be."

"I hope you're right."

"You'll see. I will be."

So why did George look so apprehensive? Hannah shivered. "It's certainly cold tonight." She patted her hands together in their snug gloves. "I can hardly feel my feet." The trainers she had selected were more for the practicalities of the uneven surfaces. Even with an extra thick pair of socks, her feet yearned for a long, hot soak. Her toes already throbbed painfully.

Excited chatter wafted in and then faces appeared at the window. Smiling, laughing, some slightly anxious and apprehensive. George opened the door, while Hannah stood to greet their guests.

"Hello, we're the Phantoms." A tall, well-built, twenty-something male with black hair and a sunny smile introduced himself. "I'm Rory. This is my girlfriend, Kate." A shy, slightly younger girl stepped forward. "Then we have Andrea, Dave and Scott." Each member of the group smiled and waved as they were introduced. A slight but identifiable aroma of beer danced around the group.

"I'm Hannah and this is George," Hannah said. "We'll take you down and let you get set up."

George unlocked the entrance door to the Close. "Now if you all follow Hannah, I'll lock up the shop and turn off the lights again. Hope you've all brought warm blankets. It's freezing just now."

From what Hannah could see, they all seemed well-prepared. Each group member had a rucksack, apparently filled to bursting with everything they needed. Rory carried a camera tripod and Dave had a small collapsible card table under his arm. "For the séance," he explained to Hannah.

"I guessed," she said, smiling outwardly while the snake of fear reared its head, ready to strike.

"I think Murdoch Maclean's printer's shop would be a good place to start," George said, as they approached it. "There's room enough for you to set up that table and we can all squeeze in there. It's also been the site of some reported anomalies, hasn't it, Hannah?"

Hannah threw him a look, but retained her composure. "It certainly has," she said.

"Such as?" Rory asked.

"I'd rather not go into detail yet," Hannah said. "Let's wait and see if anything happens tonight."

"Have any of you been on the tour here?" George asked.

Four hands went up. Kate piped up. "Something stroked my arm," she said, her voice trembling slightly.

George smiled. "Probably a spider. It's a wee bit dusty down here."

"Oh no. It wasn't a spider. Definitely not. I felt the fingers. On my bare arm."

"Creepy," Andrea said.

Rory put his free arm around his girlfriend. "That's why we're here really," he said. "I was with Kate when it happened. She nearly fainted."

I don't doubt that, Hannah thought, then chided herself for being uncharitable.

The group all seemed to know their roles in setting things up. Hannah and George waited on the sidelines and watched them, setting up the table, mounting the camera on its tripod.

Rory spoke up. "I usually get some shots of the place, using night vision, but when it comes to the séance itself, I'll walk around with the camera and try and capture any table turning or whatever may occur. If we're lucky we may capture some orbs, or even a mist."

"I think it's quite likely you'll see a bit of mist tonight," George said.

"*Really?* How do you know?"

George exhaled deeply. A cloud of breath drifted away from him.

"Oh. I see. Of course. Obviously. Good one, George. You had me going there for a second."

George grinned. "All part of my job."

"Right, everyone," Andrea said, "if you'd like to gather round. To begin with, George – if you wouldn't mind joining us – you, Kate, Dave and myself will sit at the table. Rory's on camera as usual. Scott, you take notes and Hannah? Could you observe please? Remember—"

A general chorus. "No one moves the planchette."

She smiled. "That's right. If nothing happens, nothing happens. We need to be sure what we experience is the real deal."

Hannah stood behind Andrea as the four seated at the table placed their right forefingers lightly on the planchette in the center of the Ouija board.

Rory moved slowly and quietly around, his camera running. When Andrea began to speak, he stopped and focused on the board.

"If there are any spirits here tonight, we welcome you. We come in peace and wish you no harm. Is there anyone there who would like to talk to us?"

Silence. The planchette didn't move.

Andrea tried again. "We'll introduce ourselves. My name's Andrea."

"I'm George."

"My name's Dave."

"I'm Kate. Oh." She gave a slight start. "Did you feel that? It moved. I swear it moved."

"I felt a sort of trembling," George said.

"So did I," Andrea said.

"Me too." Dave.

"It didn't register here," Rory said. "Maybe when we look at the film later, we'll see a little movement."

Andrea took a deep, audible breath. "Is there anyone there who wishes to talk to one of us?"

Nothing happened. Seconds ticked away. Only the sounds of nervous breathing punctuated the stillness.

Until Kate screamed.

"Something touched me. It did. I swear. It touched my arm."

"OK, Kate, calm down," Rory said. "I didn't get anything on camera."

"I *felt* it. Only for a second but...oh my *God*." She pointed behind Hannah. Everyone turned.

"I've got it," Rory said. "Bloody hell, I've really got something."

At the entrance to the shop, a mist swirled and weaved

around itself, as if it were trying to form into something solid. A shape. Human, maybe.

"What are you seeing with the camera?" Dave asked. "Are you getting any more detail?"

Rory peered hard, looked away, blinked and peered again. "It's a child. A young girl. There's something…not right. Oh fuck." He lowered the camera.

"Don't do that," Kate yelled. "You'll lose the footage. This is the first time—"

"She has no face, Kate."

"What?"

"The little girl in the mist. She has no face."

The mist dissolved instantly as if it had never been there.

No one spoke. Each of those seated around the table still had one finger on the planchette.

It quivered. A general gasp echoed around the room.

"It's trying to move," Kate whispered.

Apprehension tightened Hannah's throat. The planchette began to move uncertainly, dragging across the board randomly as if trying to orient itself with the letters and characters. It stopped. Hannah held her breath.

Kate coughed. Rory spoke. "Do you wish to speak to someone in this room?"

The planchette started to move again, slowly, uncertainly at first but gaining momentum, until it shot across the board to 'Yes'.

"OK," Andrea exhaled. "We've made contact. Please could you tell us who you wish to speak to? Is it me, Andrea?"

The planchette immediately shot across to the opposite side of the board. 'No'.

"Is it Dave?" Again, 'No'.

"George?"

The planchette shot across the board, almost tearing itself out of Andrea's reach. Twice more it landed on 'No'.

"So it's someone in the room but not at the table."

The planchette didn't wait to be asked. It shot across to 'Yes', and immediately began to spell out a word.

"Scott, are you getting this down?"

The blond-haired man with a shorthand notepad was scribbling down letters. "Yes. H, then A. N. N. A. H." The planchette came to rest.

"OK, Hannah, would you join us at the table, please? Kate, please would you step out and observe?"

Kate nodded and bolted out of her chair, clearly relieved to be out of the action.

Hannah's fear clenched her muscles, tightened her jaw and drained her saliva. She took Kate's seat and placed her gloved finger lightly on the glass.

"Right," Andrea said. "Introduce yourself, Hannah, and we'll see what the spirit wants to talk to you about."

Hannah tried to moisten her dry lips. Her words didn't sound like her. Her voice wavered and she cleared her throat. "My name is…I'm Hannah. You have something to…to…say to me?"

The planchette circled around the board, until it came to rest on 'Yes'.

Andrea nodded at Hannah, urging her on.

"What do you want to say?"

The planchette threw itself off the board. It sailed past Hannah's left shoulder and suddenly she was somewhere else.

The noise and clamor were almost deafening. Horses, carts, costermongers shouting out their wares. Drunken men singing outside a crowded pub. Inside, someone was attempting to play an out-of-tune piano. Badly.

Hannah looked around. She was standing outside Murdoch Maclean's printing shop and, as she glanced down at her twenty-first-century clothes, she understood why she was drawing some unwanted, curious attention.

Behind her, Murdoch Maclean spoke. "Ye'd better come in, lassie. That's if ye dinnae want tae get yersel' mugged."

Hannah caught the eye of a man of indeterminate age, face blackened with grime, leaning against a railing across the street. His trousers were tied at the waist with a piece of filthy twine and were more rags than whole. He leered at her, showing blackened teeth. Hannah hastily retreated into the shop and banged the door shut.

"Dinnae do that. Ye'll have me hinges off."

"Sorry."

"Now what can I dae for ye?"

How could she answer that? Ask him to point her in the direction of the twenty-first century?

"I seem to be a bit lost."

Murdoch Maclean tossed back his hair and laughed. He wiped his ink-stained hands on his apron. "Ye can say that agin, lassie. In those clothes, ye certainly dinnae belong here. Where are ye frae?"

Might as well tell a little white lie. Being a Scot he probably hated the English anyway. "I'm from Wiltshire. England."

"Aye. English. I guessed as much. The accent. So what's a Sassenach lassie doing in the erse-end of Auld Reekie?"

"Erse-end?"

The printer tapped his backside.

"Would you believe me if I said I haven't the faintest idea?"

Murdoch Maclean carried on wiping his hands and his eyes never left hers. Finally, he reached for a clay pipe and tobacco pouch. "Aye, lass, I would. I dinnae ken where ye come frae, but I do ken ye were in my shop not two weeks back. Dressed like ma auld granny." He looked Hannah up and down. "Now I dinnae *what* to make of ye."

"You *remember* me being here? I almost believed I'd dreamed it."

"No, lass, ye were here awreet. Now, where was it ye wanted to go? Maybe I can tell ye how to get there."

Hannah wished she could tell him. She wanted to be where she was, but apparently more than a hundred years into the future.

"I'm sorry...I...." The room darkened, as if a total eclipse had blocked out the sun. The cacophony of street noise grew muffled and faded as rapidly as the daylight.

"Hannah. *Hannah.*"

She realized her eyes were tightly closed and opened them. A sea of concerned faces studied her closely.

"Where were you?" Rory asked.

"You mean I wasn't here?"

"You were physically here, but as for where your mind was...." He shook his head.

"Why? What happened? What did I do?"

George touched her hand. "You were talking to someone. You seemed to be answering questions. Something about being lost, not having the faintest idea about something and believing you'd dreamed it – whatever *it* is."

"But I was here all the time?"

"Of course," Dave said. "We've all been sitting or standing around this table for the past twenty minutes. It's been fascinating listening to you. Best trance I've ever seen."

"Trance?"

"Something like it," Andrea said. She indicated the planchette, which had been replaced to its central position on the board. "Now let's try again. Hannah, ask it what it wants to say to you."

Hannah pushed her chair away and stood. "No, I'm sorry. I really can't. I'll stay and watch, but I'm not going to participate anymore tonight. Not after...."

Andrea frowned. She looked as if she was about to reprimand Hannah but thought better of it. "OK. Let's see if anyone else wants to talk to us tonight. Kate, come and sit back down." She did so, hesitantly, and the four who were now seated placed their forefingers on the planchette. Andrea called out.

"We welcome any spirits who are with us here tonight. Is there anyone who wants to talk to one of us?"

Slowly the planchette began to move. Scott had his pen ready and started to write as it quickly made its way around the board, stopping at letter after letter, until it finally came to rest.

Andrea cleared her throat. "What have we got, Scott?"

"Just deciphering it now. Got it. It says, 'Tell Hannah to come and find me.'"

"Find who?" Hannah said. "*Mairead?*"

The planchette stirred and moved again. More rapidly this time. Scott seemed to struggle to keep up. Once again, it stopped.

"Did you get that?" Andrea asked.

"Think so. OK, it says, 'In the graveyard. By my plaque. Come tonight.'"

"What?" Hannah's heart was racing.

"Do you know who this is, Hannah?" Rory asked.

"I think she does," George said. "I think we both do. It isn't Mairead, is it, Hannah?"

Hannah shook her head. "I don't know."

"OK, you probably don't know. Maybe some of you do. Anyone here familiar with Greyfriars Kirkyard?"

A few murmurs and nods.

"Well, you'll all be aware of the ghost of old George Mackenzie, who persecuted the Covenanters when he was alive and takes great delight in frightening unsuspecting tourists now he's dead?"

A little nervous laughter this time.

"What you probably don't know is that not too far from the prison where he incarcerated all those people is a plaque on a wall. All it says is 'Miss Carmichael'. No dates. No first name and no one knows who commissioned it, or what their connection might have been to the lady of that name."

"Is that the same Miss Carmichael who was murdered here?" Rory asked.

"It's generally assumed so, although no one can actually say for certain."

"And you think Miss Carmichael has been in touch with us tonight," Hannah said. "And that she wants me to go to her plaque tonight?"

The group exchanged glances with each other, as George nodded.

"You're not going on your own though," he said. "I'm coming with you."

The planchette shot out from under their fingers and landed on 'No'. Then it moved again.

"Alone," Scott said. "It wants you to come alone."

"No chance!" Hannah stared at the now-still planchette. "I never believed in those things before. I always thought people used magnets or something to make them fly across the table."

Andrea's voice was harsh. Indignant. "I can assure you no one interfered with that planchette. I don't ever remember it doing that before."

The others murmured their agreement.

"And what about that mist?" Andrea was in full flow now. "And the child with no face Rory caught on camera?"

"I'm the resident skeptic in this group," Dave said. "If that was a special effect, hats off to you guys. It's the best I've ever seen. Most convincing."

"I can assure you that was nothing to do with us," George said. "We don't do that kind of special effect."

"It was real," Kate said. "Why do you find it so hard to accept, Dave?"

"After tonight, I doubt that I shall. It's the first time I can honestly say I've been scared, and I've lost count of how many vigils I've been on."

"I'm sorry, Andrea, I shouldn't have said what I said," Hannah said. "I'm still trying to rationalize what's going on here."

George stood up. "I think we should stop this. Now. This has moved on from being a harmless bit of fun into something none of us understands. I'm sorry but as the most senior member of staff here, I'm taking the decision to end this séance right now. Maybe another night and without Hannah present."

"Then nothing will happen," Dave said. "It doesn't usually. This is the best manifestation I can ever remember. That mist. The child with no face...."

"I'm not risking Hannah's welfare."

"And what about the graveyard?" Rory asked. "Are you going there tonight?"

Was she? A part of Hannah desperately wanted to go – but alone? Surely that was asking for trouble. She knew none of these people, except George, and she didn't know him particularly well. What if someone here had an ulterior motive for getting her alone in a deserted graveyard in the dead of night? No, it was far too risky.

She shook her head. "Not tonight. And certainly not alone."

"Wise decision," George said. "Now folks, if you don't mind, I think we'd better call it a night. We'll refund your money. I'll talk to Ailsa tomorrow."

The group muttered and took their time packing up their equipment.

★   ★   ★

George walked Hannah home through the deserted streets. A chill wind whipped up Hannah's hair and her cheeks and nose tingled. Occasional icy raindrops splattered onto her coat and face.

"Dreich tonight, isn't it?" George said.

"Dreich? Oh yes. Very wet and cold. I hate this time of the year. Everything is so grey and dead."

Their footsteps echoed on the silent street.

"Do you want to go to the graveyard?" George asked.

Hannah thought again before speaking. "On a fine night maybe. Daytime would be better though." She stopped. A strand of hair blew into her mouth and she brushed it away. "Has anything like this ever happened to you before, George?"

He faced her and laughed. "Not as such. But since I've been working at Henderson Close, I've become used to odd things happening. People tell me strange tales. One visitor swore he was possessed by the spirit of Miss Carmichael for about thirty seconds. He said she showed him who her murderer was. The one they never caught. I asked him who it was and he said she had left his body before revealing his identity. I could have simply dismissed the man's story, but he was white-faced, shaking, and swore he wasn't making it up. His wife assured us all that he wasn't given to flights of fancy. Rather the reverse. He was a total skeptic about ghosts and such things. That was a couple of years ago and I'm still not sure whether he was telling the truth, having a hallucination or it really did happen to him. These days I keep an open mind. I find it's the best way. But if you want to go, and you're going at night, promise me you'll let me know. You've got my number, text me or give me a call."

"Thanks, George. I will." They carried on a few more yards. "This is me."

He nodded at the café. "Handy if you want a coffee."

"I could murder one. But they're closed. I'll have to make do with instant, at home."

"I'd invite myself in to join you, but it's late. Not as late as it would have been if that séance hadn't imploded, but I'm away to my bed now."

"Thanks for shutting it down tonight. It was getting a bit too intense. I'm still not sure what really happened."

"Beyond going back in time to visit the real Murdoch Maclean." Hannah smiled. "Who knows?"

"'Night, Hannah."

"'Night, George."

Hannah unlocked her door, ran up the stairs to her apartment and felt grateful for the warmth of the central heating that greeted her at her door. No smell of lavender tonight and she found she missed it in an odd sort of way.

She undressed and put on pajamas and a warm fleecy dressing gown before making herself a comforting mug of hot chocolate. She would be warm and snug on the sofa. She curled up on it, her feet cozy in her sheepskin-lined slippers.

Picking up the remote, she turned on the TV, and rapidly became increasingly irritated by the trashy shopping channels and endless re-runs of ancient programs best forgotten. Late night viewers and chronic insomniacs had little to cheer them from the hundreds of channels available.

She switched off, closed her eyes and sipped her delicious chocolate. Her tension released and her mind wandered back a few years. Like a series of snapshots, she remembered her wedding day. So young and pretty in her long white dress and veil.

Their reception. Her father had always been a traditionalist. He slipped her hand into Roger's at the altar, a tear in his eye. Her mother had wept copious tears 'of joy' she insisted, while drenching a pretty, but useless, lace handkerchief. Roger's best man gave a funny speech. In her mind's eye, Hannah could see him now, standing, smart in his grey suit, telling outrageous stories of his and Roger's exploits when they were teenagers backpacking in Europe. Hannah couldn't remember his name. Strange how daft things like that simply wiped themselves from your memory when they were no longer needed.

The years flashed by in her memory. Jenna's birth. The smell of her as she lay, all pink and chubby-cheeked in a soft blanket. Tiny fists pumped the air, commanding the attention of anyone within sight or sound of her. Her legs kicked and bucked like an excited kitten.

Her baptism. The poor young vicar almost dropped her in the font when she suddenly let out a plaintive wail he hadn't expected at that moment. Maybe she had already decided her stance on religion even at that early age. She certainly hadn't shown any inclination to attend since.

Jenna growing up. Her early love of reading put her well ahead of the rest of her class when she began school. Between games and books, Jenna had not been a difficult child to please. Only if the weather turned nasty in the summer holidays and she had run out of reading material. Then she would be under everyone's feet until a trip to the local library was forthcoming or the sun came out.

Hannah sipped her hot chocolate and allowed her mind to drift further. She and Roger had done better than many and enjoyed fifteen or more years of a mostly happy marriage before things started to go wrong. She never saw it coming although she probably should have done. But she had been too wrapped up in her own career and Jenna.

Roger seemed self-sufficient. Absorbed in his own career, which started to go from strength to strength right at the time Jenna was studying for GCSEs. He was promoted and began to work later at night. Sometimes his job would take him to London and he would stop over there for a night or two. Jenna achieved eight good GCSEs, followed by a clutch of A Levels and a degree in English. Then followed training as a teacher, and her unexpected decision to emigrate to Australia.

"I've landed this amazing job in a school in Brisbane, Mum. You'll be able to come and visit and I can come back over here for holidays. Please be happy for me. It's the sort of opportunity I'd probably never get in this country."

Hannah refused to be one of those clingy, whining mothers – she had seen enough of that already – so didn't question why her daughter could only apparently get a decent teaching post thousands of miles away from home. Instead, she stiffened her backbone and plastered a beaming smile across her face. Jenna went off happy, excited at her new life. Hannah dried her tears. At least she still had Roger. And her career. She too had achieved promotion and the pressures of teaching and an increasingly heavy workload of administration kept her occupied day and night.

Looking back now, she couldn't understand how she could have missed all the obvious signals. With Jenna gone, enjoying her new life, she and Roger had nothing left in common. They were two individuals sharing a house. Sharing a bed they never even cuddled in anymore. Going through the motions of a marriage that, in truth, had been dead for years.

Then it changed. At first, she enjoyed the flowers, the unexpected bottles of champagne. In all their years of marriage, he had never been one to shower her with gifts. Always something nice at birthdays and Christmas and he never forgot an anniversary, but spontaneous bunches of flowers? Never. Now, whenever he came back from a trip away for more than a day or two, he would arrive back home and shower her with gifts. Hannah would be amazed and thank him. She told colleagues at work. She saw them exchange glances and she knew what they were thinking. But she knew better. Not her Roger. He would never betray her.

"I want to show my appreciation for everything you do for me," he would say, always managing to just avoid her eyes. "You've always supported me. Financially in the early days."

That was true. He had been a struggling accounts assistant, studying for his full accountancy qualifications while working at a low-paid, monotonous job. She, on the other hand, had taught Drama in a large Comprehensive School. His career had blossomed, as had hers.

Then she achieved a further promotion. She became Head of Drama. No sooner had they celebrated that, than Roger decided the time was right to give her some news of his own. But instead of telling her, he left her a note. She read it and re-read it countless times and could still remember every word even though she had long consigned it to the flames of the wood-burning stove in her former home.

Dear Hannah, I know this will come as a shock to you, but it really is the best way. I'm sure you know things haven't been right between us for a long time now. Ten years or more maybe. I stayed because of Jenna. I didn't want anything to disrupt her education. But now she is off our hands and happy in her new career – and you have your exciting new role to occupy you – the time has come for me to admit what has been in my heart for so long. I met Liz at the London office about eight years ago. She's an accountant too and we hit it off immediately. We've been together ever since and now we feel is the right time to put things on a proper course. I've picked up my things today while you were at work and I'm moving in with her in London. My solicitor will be in touch about all the legal stuff. Sorry about the letter, but I thought it was best this way. It must be a huge shock for you and this way we can avoid a scene and maintain our dignity. Thank you for everything. I wish you all the very best for the future. Roger.

And that was it. All she got for twenty-five years of marriage. Oh, and the house if she wanted to buy him out. She didn't. The house was duly sold and she moved into a rented flat. When the school had to make cuts, the Drama department was the first to go – officially merged with English. 'Efficiencies' they called the savage reductions in both staff and resources. According to the last Ofsted report, those so-called 'efficiencies' had left the school under-resourced and understaffed to the point where it was now in 'special measures'. Hannah gave a light laugh at the irony.

She put down her empty mug and wandered over to the window. Drawing back the curtains, she peered out over the glistening street. The rain twinkled in the streetlights. A steady, heavy drizzle. Down below, a lone figure stopped to look up at her.

Hannah gasped. The figure beckoned to her.

In one sweep, she closed the curtains and turned her back on the window. It couldn't be her. Miss Carmichael. But as the light had caught her and illuminated her face, Mairead Ferguson's eyes had met Hannah's. Mairead…but not Mairead. A dead woman who looked the image of her.

Hannah knew what she had to do. Tomorrow night she would go to the graveyard.

CHAPTER EIGHT

Greyfriars Kirkyard at night. Chill. Dark. The church ghostly in the silver moonlight. Trees denuded of leaves, their branches reaching out their skeletal fingers to the heavens. It didn't take much imagination to see ghosts walking among the gravestones of the generations of the Edinburgh dead, slumbering – or lying unquietly – beneath their granite blankets. Hannah shivered and stamped her almost-numb feet and her breath misted in the night air as she spoke. "I'm so grateful you came with me tonight, George."

"Not at all. If it wasn't so damn cold, it would be quite a pleasant night."

Hannah stared up at the twinkling stars in the clear sky. "There'll be a frost later."

"It's started already. Come on, let's find this plaque. Have you got your torch?"

Hannah waved it at him.

"Good, let's switch on, and off we go."

Hannah didn't know or care whether George was faking his light-hearted attitude. She was glad of it.

The promised frost was already in evidence as their feet crunched the ground beneath them. In the dimly lit grounds, blades of grass twinkled with ice crystals. Hannah led the way. She hadn't a clue where she was going, but something seemed to direct her, moving her forward, then to the right, until they reached the back wall.

Look up.

Hannah obeyed the voice in her head, shining her torch on the wall.

"There!" Hannah said. The grey stone plaque could not have been more than two feet by one foot and the only two words carved into it almost filled its surface. 'Miss Carmichael'.

"What happens now?" George asked, his voice no more than a whisper.

"I don't know. I suppose we just wait and see."

"Is it my imagination or is it even colder right here? It's bloody freezing."

"I know. We won't stay long. Then we'll go over to the pub for a shot of Scotch."

"That's the best idea you've come up with so far, lass."

Hannah switched off her torch. "No point wasting the batteries."

George nodded and switched his off too. His breath misted in front of him, mingling with Hannah's. Her fingers started to throb. Not even the thermal gloves she wore could keep out the bitter, penetrating cold. She couldn't feel her feet.

Hannah turned to face the opposite direction, away from the plaque. Ahead of her stretched the path they had come up. To the right of it, grandiose monuments to some of Edinburgh's finest citizens. To the left of her lay more graves, some elaborate granite structures with carved angels and Grecian pillars, silhouetted against the night sky.

A light breeze skittered around them, blowing a few remaining leaves off the ground and sending them dancing. Ancient trees creaked like old bones. Hannah gave a start at the ghostly shape of an owl as it unexpectedly took off from a nearby tree. It soared off into the sky, its plumage phantom pale. She realized she had grabbed George's arm and gently dropped her hand.

George craned his neck. He whispered to her and pointed. "There's something there. Moving in the bushes. I can't make it out but it's coming toward us. Switch your torch on. Let's get a look at it."

Hannah moved the torch so that an arc of light swept around the graveyard in front of them. For one second she thought she saw something. A tall figure, in shadow, darting out of the bushes, but gone before she fully registered it.

Her heart raced. "Did you get a proper look at it?"

"No. Not really. For a second, it seemed familiar.... No. I'm being stupid."

"Familiar?"

"Ignore me. My imagination's going haywire. Maybe it was the ghost of old Mackenzie." His laugh was forced.

Hannah swept her torch around. "There's nothing there now," she said.

"I told you. Old Mackenzie on his nightly rounds."

Hannah decided to play along with him. "Nasty piece of work by all accounts."

"It's a familiar story," George said. "People persecuted for religion. Mackenzie was a cruel and merciless character. It provides a lot of entertainment for the tourists and revenue for the graveyard tours now though."

"Well, whatever it was, it's gone now." Hannah shivered. "If I stay here much longer, I'll turn into one of those statues." She nodded over at an angel with folded wings silhouetted against the night sky. In this poor light, she half imagined it unfurling those wings and taking off, like the owl a few minutes earlier.

George snapped his torch off, pocketed it and slapped his hands together. "I don't think there's any point in staying here any longer. I'll get the first round in."

"OK."

"Hannah."

"Yes?"

George looked startled. "What?"

"You called my name."

"No, I said I'd get the drinks in."

"But I heard...."

George looked at her intently.

"Nothing. We're both seeing things and I'm starting to hear things. Let's get that drink." Hannah made to move forward. Something strong pulled her back. It clawed at her neck, dragged her back by her hair, tugging so hard, her scalp burned.

"I am not finished with you."

She had heard that male voice before. "George. Help me!" She struggled to free herself from the invisible grasp.

"Hannah? What's the matter?" George put his hand out to steady her, gave a cry and dropped it to his side. "For fuck's sake. What's going on?"

The invisible arms that held her tightened their grip. Hannah wriggled one way, then the other, but couldn't free herself. The more she struggled, the tighter the vise-like grip became. Invisible fingers dug into her upper arms, dragging them behind her back, almost lifting her off the ground. "It won't let me go. I can't get free. George, *please.*"

He seemed rooted to the spot.

The voice in her head grew louder, more urgent. *"You are here where you belong, Kirsten. Here where you'll stay."*

It tugged her back harder and she slipped on the frosty ground, struggling to regain her balance. Was the voice even in her head? Couldn't George hear it?

"Please. Let me go!"

Her cries snapped George into action. He tried to grab her arm and instantly recoiled. "It's like an electric shock every time I come near you. Like you've got a force-field around you. I can't get through it." He tried again. Again he shot back.

Whatever held Hannah tightened its grasp once more. It dragged her back further.

"You belong here, Kirsten. With the dead."

The voice was raw, grating. Loud enough to rattle her eardrums. She cried out, "Let me go!"

The creature strengthened its hold. It shifted position and leaped onto her shoulders, weighing her down so that she was bent almost double. She could see nothing. But George could. His mouth gaped.

"What is it? What have I got on my back?"

"I.... It's...a gargoyle. It's like a gargoyle!"

Hannah squirmed, trying to throw the thing off. The harder she twisted, the more it clung on. Hideous breath invaded her nostrils. Still she could see nothing. Then, between her legs, fingers. Claws, tearing at her trousers, trying to stroke.... A filthy laugh....

"No." Strength she didn't know she possessed rescued her. She wrenched herself hard left.

Without warning, the iron grip broke and she fell forward. Free. George caught her.

Hannah struggled to breathe. "What the hell was that thing?"

George shook his head. His hands trembled. "I only saw it for an instant. It looked like one of those stone carvings you get in old churches. It had this awful grin on its face. Gargoyle is the best I can manage."

"It spoke to me. Did you hear it?"

George shook his head. "Not a word. What did it say?"

"It told me I belonged here. With the dead. It called me Kirsten."

George put his arms around her, comforting her.

If only she could slow her heart down. It felt ready to burst from her chest. She remembered what that thing had tried to do when it had her in its grip and the nausea made her gag. "I must have been the only one meant to hear it. But why? What does it want from me? And why did it call me Kirsten?"

"I don't know, Hannah. I wish I did."

Hannah gently extricated herself from George's arms. "I really need that drink now. This was a crazy idea, coming here on a night like this. Let's go." She set off. George hesitated for a second, then followed her.

In the pub, Hannah's hands shook so badly she struggled to hold her glass. The neat Scotch burned her throat and made her cough, but it warmed and soothed her.

"I think we need some professional help," George said after a lengthy silence.

"So do I, but who? There are so many fakes around."

"I'll ask a friend of mine. She did a dissertation on mediums and that sort of thing at university. I remember at the time she said that she had come across some fascinating people in the course of her research. Some obvious fakes, some less obvious and some she couldn't begin to explain. Maybe one of them can help us."

"So, she reckoned some of them were the real deal?"

George nodded. "And you'd never have met a more skeptical person than Megan before she started on that. After she'd finished, she had to admit there could be something in it."

"I can't help thinking this is all linked to Mairead's disappearance."

"And Mairead generally. Where had she been living all that time she was supposed to be caring for her mother?"

Hannah shook her head. "And why is it that I keep seeing a woman dressed in Victorian clothes with Mairead's face? And the photograph in that newspaper I found in Murdoch Maclean's shop?"

George sipped his drink. "I'll speak to Megan. I'll call her tomorrow. Bit late now."

"Thanks, George. Anything to stop all this. And find Mairead."

★   ★   ★

At home, Hannah undressed. She remembered the creature's hold on her – its talons clawing her. *Kirsten.* She couldn't get that name out of her mind. It meant something to her but, try as she might, she couldn't remember ever knowing a Kirsten.

She peeled off her trousers. She must wash them before she could bring herself to wear them again. As she made to roll them up to put in the laundry, her fingers found perforations. And a rip. Holding them to the light, she stared. There...in the gusset. No way had they been there before.

She dashed into the kitchen, flipped open the kitchen waste bin and dumped the trousers in, her heart thumping. Then she turned on the hot water and scrubbed her hands until they were red and sore. Anything to get the filth of that creature off her.

CHAPTER NINE

Cerys Lloyd was a woman in her mid-forties with long, thick, scarlet hair, a flamboyant green velvet cape and a lilting Welsh accent. She smiled easily and seemed perfectly at home with her unusual calling. "There are so many legends associated with this place, I'm not surprised you've been having problems. Some highly unsavory characters have roamed these Closes. You know, there are times I have to run through the Old Town, so many voices all clamoring for my attention and none of them with the living."

"That must make life very…difficult," Hannah said, still not sure whether they were dealing with a charlatan or the real deal.

"Oh it is, but it is my legacy, I'm afraid. My mother was the same, you see. Had the gift. Curse more like." She rolled her eyes and then winked. "We had better get going. I never eat before I work and I'm starving, so the sooner we make a start, the sooner I can stop the hunger pangs. If you hear any growling sounds, it's probably me." She patted her flat stomach.

Hannah smiled. George opened the door.

The two of them followed Cerys as she descended the steps leading down to Henderson Close.

She had barely gone three steps before she stopped and leaned against the wall, her hand on her chest. "Oh, yes. I feel it already. Not it. Them. So much pain, so much…." She pushed herself away from the wall and took a few more steps until she reached the bottom.

She was breathing heavily and didn't seem anything like as composed as she had been a few minutes earlier. "There are so many lost souls down here. So many…. There is one who searches and one who does not wish to be found. A woman and a man. The man is young, in his early twenties, but his soul is much older. I feel it." She put her hands to her forehead as if a sudden headache had overpowered her.

Hannah and George stood in front of her, waiting for her to continue, but she said nothing. After a few seconds, she lowered her hands and, without a word, moved on, stumbling a little. They rounded the corner leading to the printer's shop and Miss Carmichael's corner. Cerys stopped dead. "He's here. Can't you feel him?" She spun around. "He's all around us."

"Who, Cerys?" Hannah asked. "Who's all around us?"

Cerys stared at her, wide-eyed. "He's here for you," she said.

Her words chilled Hannah's blood. She tried to speak but her mouth wouldn't form the words.

George seemed to sense her problem. "Who, Cerys?"

Cerys turned her eyes on him. "You've met him. Recently. Both of you. His spirit is ancient. Evil." She shook her head violently. "No. I won't do it again. I won't put myself at such risk." She backed away. "I'm sorry.... I thought it would be all right this time but.... I'm sorry...I can't do this...I have to leave." She pushed them aside to let herself pass.

George grabbed her arm. "Hang on, Cerys."

She shrugged him off. "I must go. I can't...."

She raced up the steps. Hannah and George followed close behind. Upstairs, Hannah threw the switch and light flooded the empty shop, closed after a busy Saturday. Cerys clutched the counter for support, her hands trembling.

Hannah touched her hand. "What happened to you down there?"

Cerys's bright blue eyes bore into Hannah's. "Something's been released. I told you. It's ancient, pure evil, and I've met something like it once before. It nearly killed me."

"You mean some sort of demon?" George said.

"If you want to call it that, I suppose demon is as good a name as any. I don't know its actual name. Others might have a name for it. But I recognize its power. It can travel and it can mutate. Someone has released it from its place of captivity."

"But you said you'd met something like it before," Hannah said. "And you said it can travel."

"I have and it can. But this evil isn't just one. It's many. A colony if you like. Yet it's all one entity. The part that's here was sealed up, but now it's free."

"Farquhars Close," Hannah said. "The building work...."

Cerys gasped. "Oh no. Tell me they didn't knock walls down."

Hannah and George nodded.

Cerys slammed her fist into her upturned palm. "Stupid, stupid idiots." Her face contorted in a sudden spasm of pain. "I've got to get out of here. I can feel it getting closer. If it finds me it will destroy me. It knows I can see and feel it. It can't let me live this time. Last time was too close."

"What happened...last time?" Hannah asked, afraid of the answer.

Cerys seemed about to tell her, then changed her mind and shook her head. "No. It's best you don't know. It can't do any good." She made for the locked door.

George stopped her. "But what are we supposed to do? Get the wall put back?"

"Oh, it's far too late for that. It's out now. Nothing can stop it. I certainly can't. I haven't the strength remaining in me." She put out her hand to turn the key in the door.

Hannah barred her way. "But it was captured once, surely it can be captured again?"

"Good luck with that."

"Cerys, you can't just leave us like this," George said.

"Watch me. Now please, Hannah, let me out of here. I can't help you."

Hannah stayed where she was. "Then what are we going to do?"

Cerys sighed. "Try praying. To any and all deities in the universe." She shoved Hannah out of the way, opened the door and slammed it behind her.

George watched her race down the street. "So what do we do now?"

Hannah shrugged. "I'd take her advice and try praying, but I pretty much gave up on that years ago."

"I'd like to say she was a fake but Megan insisted she was

the most genuine she had ever met. Uncannily so, it seems. She doesn't make a penny out of her mediumship and has been accurate so many times, telling total strangers things she couldn't possibly know. She's also cleansed a lot of houses and Megan never came across anyone who wasn't full of praise for her. We won't find better."

"Well, I wasn't particularly impressed," Hannah said. "So she needn't think she can add me to her fan club. I thought her attitude was appalling. I thought mediums and such like had some code of conduct. They're not supposed to go around frightening people. As if we didn't have enough of that already."

"Look, I'll speak to Megan again. Tell her what happened this evening and see if she has any other suggestions. Meanwhile, I don't think any of us should go down there alone. No point in frightening the others, so let's keep it between ourselves, but if it looks like any member of staff is going down there, one of us had better make some excuse and go with them."

"Agreed." She stared at the entrance to the Close and shivered. "When I first got this job, I was so happy. I never thought I'd say this, but unless we can stop this happening – unless Cerys is wrong – I don't think I can stay here."

"Me neither."

"But before I came here, you didn't experience anything like this, did you?"

"Not to this extent, admittedly, but this is a strange place. It does have a checkered history and inexplicable things have always happened. Objects moving, shadows I can't explain—"

"But nothing like this. Nothing like last night or what happened at the séance?"

George avoided her eyes and shook his head.

"So you think it's all down to me too?"

"I didn't say that."

"You didn't have to."

"Hannah. It's probably coincidence. Maybe this was meant to happen at this time. They would have knocked down the wall to Farquhars Close anyway, whether you had joined us or not. I think it's far more to do with that than anything you might have done or any influence you may have been. And what about Mairead's disappearance? You're not responsible for that and it's all linked up. It has to be."

"Where is Mairead?" Hannah said it half to herself. George didn't reply.

★   ★   ★

Back in her flat, Hannah sat on her sofa in the soft lamplight, a glass of smooth red wine within easy reach. Again and again she replayed the events at the kirkyard, the séance and then Cerys's extraordinary outburst. From nowhere, an old memory stirred. Probably nothing. Unrelated. But.... The nagging thought wouldn't go away. She glanced at her watch. Eleven fifteen. It would be quarter past nine in the morning in Brisbane. Sunday morning, so Jenna could be home. It was spring over there. She might be out and about with that new boyfriend of hers. Or enjoying a lie in.

Oh, what the hell. It was worth a try, wasn't it?

Hannah booted up her laptop, preferring the larger screen to her mobile phone. She went onto Skype and called Jenna.

Her daughter seemed slightly breathless as if she had scurried to answer the call. Her sleep-head hair was mussed and her face makeup free. She looked golden skinned, healthy and happy. Hannah almost changed her mind about what she was calling about.

"Mum, what a lovely surprise! I thought we weren't Skyping till next week."

Hannah forced a smile and hoped Jenna was fooled. "Oh well, you know me. I like to be spontaneous." Who was she kidding? She could never fool her daughter.

"OK, Mum now you are officially worrying me. What is it? Are you ill? You look exhausted. Is the job going all right? Has something happened?"

"Nothing to worry about, Jenna. I'm fine. The job's fine. I'm working hard but I'm perfectly well. Honestly." Stop insisting, she told herself. She definitely won't buy that.

"Then…what? Come on, Mum, don't keep anything from me. You know you can't."

"It's something and nothing really. I was sitting here, having a few quiet minutes chilling by myself and I got to thinking about when you were little and you had that friend. You remember. What was her name? Her mother was supposedly psychic or something."

Jenna frowned as she thought. "Oh, you mean Jacquetta? Jacquetta Hidalgo Lister. Yes, her mother was a real oddball. She developed some sort of fixation with you. Weird."

"That's right. Can you remember the details?"

"Oh God, that was years ago."

Hannah caught a movement behind her daughter. "How's Sean?"

"He's well. Come and say 'hi' to Mum, Sean."

A deeply tanned, dark-haired man with a friendly smile and expensive-looking teeth leaned over Jenna's shoulder. "G'day, Mrs. Lockwood."

"Hello, Sean. Nice to see you again." Hannah meant it. Sean seemed a decent man, who worked hard as a doctor and obviously cared deeply for her daughter. Jenna could do a lot worse for herself.

Jenna squeezed Sean's hand. "I'm going to chat to Mum for a little while. Catch you on the patio later?"

"You got it."

He moved out of shot and Jenna watched him go. She turned back to the screen.

"Looks like it's going well for you too," Hannah said.

Jenna smiled. "It is. He's moved in with me, Mum."

"I'm happy for you."

"I was going to tell you next week. It only happened a few days ago."

"As long as you're happy, I'm happy."

"We are. And before you ask, no, I'm not pregnant. We're not ready for all that yet."

"All in good time. No rush. You're both young."

"Where were we? Oh, Jacquetta and that strange mother

of hers. She was supposed to be Romany I think. I remember Jacquetta and I were playing at our house one day and her mother came to collect her. It was the first time she met you and she went…well…peculiar. Started swaying and putting her head in her hands. I remember she pointed at you and—"

As if someone had opened a gate, the memory flooded back. Hannah exclaimed, "That's right. Only she didn't point at me, she pointed behind me."

"That's it. She said she saw someone standing at your shoulder. She described it like an ugly hunched creature with red eyes, scales, claws, a hideous mouth and teeth. Like a…a—"

"Gargoyle."

"Yes." Jenna's initial expression of triumph quickly faded. "Mum, what aren't you telling me? Why rake this up after all these years?"

"Oh, it's nothing really. You know I work in this spooky place. It's great fun. People come to us with all sorts of stories. Strange encounters and experiences they've had and it was something someone said. For some reason it put me in mind of Jacquetta's mother and I was racking my brains. I knew you'd remember."

"I should do. I don't think I saw too much of Jacquetta after that. Well, it was a bit embarrassing, especially in front of my other friends, when this woman broke into hysterics every time she saw you. And she started calling you another name. Christine, I think."

In a shockwave, Hannah remembered. "Kirsten. She called me Kirsten."

"That's right."

"And she said she wanted to conduct a séance and contact the creature. I refused but she kept on asking."

"I seem to remember you steering me away from her and suggesting I spend more time with my other friends."

"Sorry, but…."

"Oh, that's OK. We didn't have that much in common anyway. Something tells me Jacquetta was destined to follow in her mother's footsteps."

"Do you know what happened to her in the end?"

"They moved away. I think they went to somewhere in Spain. They had relatives there and after Jacquetta's father's business folded, there were financial problems. I haven't heard anything of her for…oh, must be ten years or more."

It had only been a half-thought anyway. With Cerys's departure, contacting Jacquetta's mother might have been a possibility but even if she had done so, Hannah couldn't see herself being able to tolerate more than a few minutes in the infuriating woman's company. Jenna's memories had brought back images of awkward encounters. Rosanna was an overly emotional sort who could be guaranteed to wring the most drama out of any situation and made a great song and dance about her heritage. No, it wouldn't have been a good idea to contact her and rake up the past all over again. It had all seemed too far-fetched back then anyway. Even now. The gargoyle thing. Coincidence surely. Kirsten….

"Mum, are you sure that's all there is to it? You look worried."

"Worried? No, don't be daft. I'm fine. Now you go and get some of that spring sunshine and enjoy your weekend."

"If you're sure…."

"I'm certain. Thanks for filling in the gaps. You know how it is when you get something on your mind and you can't sort it out? You've done that for me so I can put it to bed now."

Jenna smiled. "Glad I could help. Love you, Mum, chat next week. I'll call you this time."

"Love you too, Jenna. Chat soon."

Jenna's face flashed off the screen as the call terminated. Hannah switched off her computer and sat back down on the sofa. Rosanna Hidalgo Lister. She stored the name away in her mind.

★   ★   ★

George listened as he sipped his pint of Guinness the following day after work. He set his glass down. "What you described is pretty much how I would have described it. The creature, I mean. And we do need professional help. It's a bit of a coincidence about the Kirsten thing as well. Especially from so many years ago."

Hannah frowned. "She is an absolute pain, unless she's had a personality transplant. And she probably still lives in Spain."

"You said Jenna thought her daughter was probably destined to follow in her mother's footsteps?"

Hannah nodded. "That's what Jenna said, yes. But as far as we know she still lives in Spain too."

"Facebook. You've got an account, haven't you?"

"Yes. I suppose I could at least search for her. It depends whether she's changed her name or not."

"I did some Spanish at school. Can't remember any of it now but I do know that Spanish surnames tend to be double-barreled. So her mother's patronym was Hidalgo and her husband's name is Lister?"

Hannah nodded. "Technically Jacquetta should have been Lister Hidalgo – father's surname first, followed by mother's maiden name – but they decided that was too complicated for living in the UK so they all kept their surnames the same. Jacquetta may have changed it back when they moved to Spain. And, of course she may be married now, so her surname will probably have changed again. Complicated or what?" She put her head in her hands.

"Try looking for Rosanna first. Then, if you really can't bear the thought of communicating with her, see if her daughter is among her friends."

"George, you're a genius."

He winked at her. "It has been said."

*　　*　　*

"Gotcha!" There was only one Rosanna Hidalgo Lister on Facebook and a half-remembered face beamed out at her. "Either you've had work or that's an old photo," Hannah muttered to herself. She clicked onto Rosanna's list of friends. Infuriatingly, her list of friends would only be available to her if Hannah sent her a friend request.

"Dammit."

Hannah searched for various permutations of Jacquetta's name but came up with no one who even marginally matched Jenna's former friend. She went back to Rosanna's page, hesitated, then clicked on the friend request button. After all, it wasn't as if she'd actually have to meet up with her again, was it?

★   ★   ★

Ailsa tapped her fingers on her desk. The staff sat in a semicircle in front of her. "The builders have quit."

Hannah spoke, "Just like that?"

"Just like that. A couple of them had a nasty experience, or so they said. They reported being attacked by some black shadow with claws. I mean, honestly." She laughed. A couple of the others snickered. George and Hannah remained stony-faced.

"The upshot of it is that, until we can appoint another contractor, work on Farquhars Close has been temporarily suspended."

"Will it be bricked up again?" George asked.

"Not unless you want to do the job yourself, George," Ailsa said. "It will remain as it is. The boards and the sheeting will stay in place and you need to make sure that your groups don't go wandering into hard-hat areas."

Hannah said nothing. Her mind swam with thoughts of the evil entity Cerys had warned them of. It remained down there, free and unfettered and if it could indeed travel, how far could it go?

George cornered Hannah in the staff room. "I've spoken to Megan. The first thing she did was ask what on earth we'd done to Cerys. Apparently the woman rang her in floods of tears, mumbled something about never going back there and made Megan promise she would never call on her professional advice ever again."

"I knew she was upset when she left here."

"Upset doesn't begin to cover it anymore. The result is that Megan is refusing to suggest anyone else. She said she has few enough friends as it is without losing any more. Then she told me to find another job and leave Henderson Close well alone."

"That might be a good idea if only that thing wasn't on the loose. Do you think that's what grabbed me in the graveyard?"

George poured a coffee and handed it to Hannah before

pouring his own. "I think it's highly likely and it's probably what frightened the builders."

"We'll see if Rosanna responds to my friend request, but meanwhile, there has to be something we can do. Is there any information on Farquhars Close around? I mean, someone in the latter half of the nineteenth century managed to wall that thing up, so surely we can do the same now?"

"You know what Cerys said. She clearly didn't think that was going to happen anytime soon." George drained his coffee mug.

"Yes, well, she didn't see fit to hang around, did she? She obviously doesn't have *all* the answers."

"We don't have *any*."

Hannah sighed. Did George seriously plan to do nothing? That was the one thing they couldn't afford. "We'd better find some. And fast. I'm going to have a word with Ailsa."

George did a double-take. "You don't mean you're going to tell her about Cerys?"

"How crazy do you think I am? Of course not. I'm going to ask her if she has any information on the history of Farquhars Close. Especially at the time it was decided to wall it up. I'll just tell her I want to add a bit of spice to my presentation."

"Fair enough. Good idea."

★   ★   ★

Hannah stood in front of Ailsa. She took in the dark circles under her boss's eyes, the way her mouth drooped at the corners. If she had known her better, she would have asked her what was wrong, but Ailsa was difficult to get close to. Instead, Hannah told her what she planned, and Ailsa managed a genuine smile. "Excellent idea, Hannah. I've got an old book here somewhere." She stood and reached up to the top shelf of her bookcase. "If you'd like to put something together and let me have it, we can share it around the other members of the team. Might as well get their appetites going for another visit when I can find a new building contractor."

"It's a big job. You'd think they'd be lining up." Hannah

watched as Ailsa located what she was looking for. An old leather-bound volume. Ailsa blew on the spine and a small cloud of dust scattered itself.

"Yes, you would indeed, but I'm sure we'll find someone before long. Here you are. McKinley's *Tales of the Edinburgh Closes.*"

Hannah took the dusty book, opened it, and the familiar fusty smell of old paper wafted up.

"It was my grandmother's," Ailsa said. "Long out of print now of course, but it used to fascinate me when I was growing up. It's probably why I do my job now, if I'm honest."

"I'll take great care of it."

"I know you will. I should have told you this sooner, but I'm glad you came to join us, Hannah. I know we had a bit of a rocky start but you've fitted right in and your enthusiasm for your work is infectious. I'm not surprised we get such excellent feedback from your tours."

Hannah hadn't been expecting such fulsome praise. "Thank you, Ailsa. I really appreciate that." She was tempted to tell the manager the real reason she wanted to borrow the book. She got as far as opening her mouth, but then shut it again. Best to quit while she was winning.

That evening, she opened the old book. Its hand-cut, thick pages were interspersed with tissue-covered pictures of the Old Town at the turn of the nineteenth and twentieth centuries. The front page of the volume showed the date of publication as 1910 and the slightly florid, yet chatty style of the author – George McKinley – made his subject easy to absorb. Each chapter was headed by the name of the Close concerned and Hannah skipped past Mary King's Close, Anchor Close and a host of others until she came across Farquhars Close.

She started to read the description of its location and the dates it was evacuated, walled up and covered. By the time she finished, she had a plan.

CHAPTER TEN

George and Hannah stood alone at the back of the shop half an hour before the first tour was due to begin.

George ran his hands through his hair. "I thought we agreed that no one should go down there alone anymore. It's too dangerous, Hannah."

"I know and believe me, if there was another way, I'd gladly take it, but we've got to deal with this…whatever it is. Rosanna hasn't got back to me and we can't afford to wait any longer. We know this…thing…demon…whatever it is can already leave the Close. I'm convinced that was what grabbed me in the graveyard and it was the voice I heard in my head. It all matches with the stories in Ailsa's book."

"What exactly did McKinley say?" George asked.

"He wrote about legends of the Auld De'il of Farquhars Close. Some say it was a ten-foot-tall creature with long, black claws and an ability to transport itself instantly from one place to another. It also possessed the ability to transmogrify. Gargoyles are mentioned more than once and there's a picture of one that's remarkably similar to what you and Rosanna described. You could be talking to someone you knew and then realize they weren't behaving as they usually did. When challenged, the creature turned back into its natural form. There were loads of reported sightings, dating way back to when the Close was called Deamhan Close – demon spelt the Gaelic way – so we're looking as far back as at least the sixteenth century, but probably earlier. Then there's another legend. Apparently, in the early 1890s, there was a series of grisly Jack the Ripper-type murders covering an area not far from Henderson Close. The killer was never caught, but many people said it was the work of the Auld De'il. That kind of fits with what Cerys told us, only she wouldn't give the demon a name. You remember she said that some people had a name for it."

"McKinley being one who identifies it as the Auld De'il. You think Mairead may have been targeted by this creature?"

"Possibly. I don't know. The builders had only just started when she disappeared, but one of the first things they did was knock the dividing wall down, and you remember how Cerys reacted when we told her about that."

"And that's when it got free."

"I think so. If it exists at all, of course. We still have to remember that there could be a perfectly logical explanation for everything." She was clutching at a vain hope and she knew it but, deep within her, was a tiny grain that craved the simple and tangible, however unlikely that now seemed.

George shot the little grain into smithereens. "Hannah, after all you've experienced and what I saw, how could you be in any doubt anymore? I know I'm not."

"I keep hoping we're wrong. I have no experience of anything like this and with no one prepared to help us professionally, we're just having to muddle through as best we can."

George laid a hand on hers. "We're friends, Hannah, we'll muddle through together. That's why I don't like the thought of you going down there alone. I'm going to come with you and I won't hear any more arguments."

Hannah smiled. "OK. It would be great to have company. Human company."

"Ailsa's away for a few days, so let's go down there after everyone else has gone. Pity we don't have any hard hats. Do you think we should take anything else with us?"

"You mean holy water, incense, a smoking sage brush? If what McKinley says is true, they would do us precious little good. A few years before they sealed up Farquhars Close, they allegedly summoned a ghost, who appeared and battled with the Auld De'il and sent it back to hell. Everything went quiet for months and they thought they were safe, but then things started happening. People were driven mad, children were scarred for life by being scratched and mauled by something they rarely saw, but felt. Then came the reports of the tall creature with scaly, skeletal claws. All horribly familiar."

"So they walled it up? But surely it escaped before they had chance to? It would have known it was in danger."

"They walled it up after the ghost had once again fought against it. It seems that when it returns, it must come back to the place where it did battle with its old adversary. By the time it returned, it was well and truly bricked up. It would have stayed that way too, if the builders hadn't demolished the wall."

"But it can move through walls. How else would it have got to the graveyard?"

"It can move through walls, George, but it can't escape from a devil's trap. You know what a pentagram looks like?"

"A five-pointed star."

"McKinley says that at the very spot where the ghost defeated the demon, the residents painted a special pentagram. When the entity returned, it would have been imprisoned there, unable to escape until someone, or something, damaged the devil's trap. My guess is that when we go down to Farquhars Close tonight, we'll find a pentagram with something missing. The builders probably paid it no mind and dragged some materials over it. It wouldn't take much damage to give the demon a chance to get out."

"And give those same builders a damn good scare into the bargain."

Hannah nodded. "I suggest we take some paint and a brush."

"Just one other question. Both times, a ghost was summoned. Do we know who this ghost is?"

Hannah shook her head. "McKinley didn't know, but his guess was that they just summoned a spirit and the one with the closest ties to the Close came through. I don't even know if it was a physical manifestation. It might just have been an invisible force."

"And we don't need a Ouija board?"

"Apparently not. McKinley doesn't mention one and it seems a group of residents simply stood together and called out for a spirit to help them. That's what we need to do."

"You're remarkably calm for someone who's contemplating battling a devil."

Hannah raised her eyes heavenward. "Am I? If you must know, I'm quaking in my boots here. I'd much rather leave this whole thing for someone else to sort out, but I can't. I'm obviously being targeted, and, like you, I can't shift the feeling that Mairead's disappearance – maybe even the mystery about where she lived – is all tied up with this. I owe it to her, as well as myself, to do whatever I can to get rid of this evil."

The staff room door opened, admitting the rest of the team, chattering among themselves.

"Hey, you two," Phil said. "You've missed all the fun. Someone must have got in last night and daubed graffiti on the boards between Farquhars Close and Henderson Close."

"What?" Hannah exclaimed.

"Sheelagh and Morag are down there now, trying their best to get it off. We're going to have to postpone the first tour, so I'm off to entertain the folks. Fortunately, it was only about half full, so we'll shift the folks onto the twelve o'clock. Whoever it was has a macabre sense of humor. Some very rude words." He laughed, then stopped. "Seriously though, Ailsa is going to do her nut. How could anyone have broken in? There's no sign of a forced entry, so we're all going to come under suspicion. And Mairead of course. Just because no one's seen her doesn't mean she couldn't still have a set of keys."

Hannah felt her blood heating. "Why on earth would Mairead want to do something like that? She loves this place. She wouldn't do anything to harm it."

Phil looked at her steadily, almost smugly. "Well, I know I didn't do it. I don't think you would do it, or George, or anyone else here present so that leaves...." He let his words trail.

That was too much for Hannah. "For fuck's sake, Phil, she's such an easy target, not being here to defend herself." Hannah pushed past him.

George called out to her. "Where are you going?"

"To see for myself."

"I'm right behind you."

The rest of the team said nothing, as Hannah and George hurried out of the staff room, through the shop and down the steps.

Voices drifted toward them and, as they approached, the sounds of harsh scrubbing. Hannah and George turned the corner that led to Farquhars Close. Hannah glanced down. The dark red stain was still there at Miss Carmichael's corner. Hearing them approach, Morag and Sheelagh paused in their labors.

George sucked in his breath. "Fucking hell!"

Hannah stared at the red-spattered boards and walls. "I can't even read what some of this says." She moved closer and peered at the strange, archaic symbols interspersed with words of distinctly Anglo-Saxon origin describing various intimate behaviors and body parts.

Morag resumed her scrubbing. "Grab a brush, if you like. It would be a help. This stuff is the devil to get off. Don't forget to put rubber gloves on. The cleaning agent is organic and supposed to be harmless but I wouldn't take any chances with your skin. I brought extra pairs just in case."

"It looks like gloss paint." Hannah donned a pair of yellow gloves and picked up a scrubbing brush. She soaked it in the hot water and solvent solution and scrubbed hard for a few minutes. Nothing was shifting. She peered closely at a name repeated half a dozen times among the swear words. 'Kirsten'. Her heart pounded.

"No idea who that is," Morag said. "Maybe the name of the person who did this. Perhaps she likes to sign her 'art'. Damn it to hell. It won't budge."

"It's what I said when we discovered it," Sheelagh said. "We're going to have to tell Ailsa and get the specialist cleaners in. This stuff is useless." Hannah and the others stopped.

"What about the tours?" Hannah said. "We can't have them seeing this."

Morag snapped her fingers. "I've got an idea. Maybe the builders left some more boards. We could rig them up so the graffiti can't be seen."

"There's a way in round there," George said, pointing to the corner.

The four of them trooped along to where one of the boards had a door. Morag pushed it open and they all filed in.

"Eugh, what's that smell?" Hannah covered her nose. Everyone else followed suit.

"It stinks like compost that's been left to rot for months," George said.

"It's more than that," Hannah said. "There's another smell. Like some dead animal. When I was a child, there was a terrible stench in my father's garden shed. Turned out to be a dead rat." She shivered at the memory of the maggot-ridden corpse.

"Yes, I know that smell," George said. "You're right. Only this is like a whole nest of them."

Morag shivered. "It's worse than creepy in here. Let's find what we need and get out."

Sheelagh was peering at the ground.

"Have you found something?" Hannah asked.

"Come and have a look. I can't properly make it out. Not enough light."

"I've got my phone," George said, fishing it out of his pocket. "It's got a flashlight on it." He switched it on and shone it where Sheelagh was pointing.

Hannah bent down and traced the drawing with her finger. The figure was damaged but there was no mistaking its shape and what it should have been.

"It's part of a pentagram," she said, standing. "Some of it has been scratched away." She looked at George. "Recently I would imagine. Looks like something heavy was dragged across it."

George nodded. "The builders. As we suspected."

"What an extraordinary thing," Morag said. "Och, well, it'll make a good story for the folk. That stench. I swear it's getting worse. Especially by this drawing."

From a few feet away, Sheelagh called, "Found some!"

Morag rushed to join her. George and Hannah lingered a moment longer by the pentagram. Hannah lowered her voice to a whisper. "At least we know where to come tonight. Might as well work with what's already here."

"Good idea," George said.

Hannah felt the butterflies that had been her constant companions for days now. They swooped and twirled, fluttered and dive-bombed her stomach until she felt physically sick. She swallowed down bile and joined Sheelagh and Morag, who were struggling with a large board.

George stepped in and took the bulk of the weight while the women steadied and balanced the rest of the board between them. They shuffled back to the graffiti-stained passageway and leaned it against the tenement. A few minutes later, another one joined it. In twenty minutes or so, they had the makeshift screen in place, secured by ropes and weights.

"Whatever you do, don't lean against it," George said, "and it should hold for a day or two until we can get the professionals in."

"Who's going to tell Ailsa?" Morag asked.

George sighed. "I'm technically in charge when she's away, so I guess that would be me."

Morag laid her hand on his arm. In mock dramatic style she said, "We're right behind you, George."

"Yes," Sheelagh said, laughing. "Well behind you."

"She can't seriously believe one of us would do this?" Hannah said. "No, someone else is responsible, and I don't mean Mairead either."

"Come on guys," George said. "Time's pressing. It's ten to twelve. Phil will be running out of anecdotes. He's probably telling rude jokes by now."

"Anything but that," Morag said. "We must save them!"

It felt good to laugh, after all the tension of recent days. Back in the crowded shop, Phil held center stage and the group – now swelled to the maximum number of twenty – were clearly enjoying themselves.

"Ah, here they are. My errant colleagues who left me, a poor legal clerk, to keep you amused while they did…whatever Sir William required of them. I trust your work is completed, Sir William?"

"It is indeed, Rudge. Carry on." With a flourish, and laughter from the group, George swanned away in true Georgian style.

Hannah watched him go. He might be putting on a brave face but she guessed at the consternation he must be feeling. His call to Ailsa would be far from easy.

Two hours later, one look at George's ashen face and Hannah knew Ailsa had given him a hard time.

"She was talking about disciplinary proceedings. I mean, how the hell could I have prevented it? I've heard and seen her in a temper before but she was screaming down the phone at me. She told me she wanted whoever was responsible for the mess caught and appropriately dealt with. I think in her mind that would involve removal of some of his or her more delicate body parts."

"She'll calm down when she's had chance to digest it all. Deep down, she knows none of us would do this."

"You didn't hear her. As far as she's concerned, this is a result of my incompetence. If it's not a member of staff, it must be a visitor who stayed behind after the last tour, and that means it's my fault for not checking properly. But I did, Hannah. I checked thoroughly. There was no one down there after closing time last night."

"No one human anyway."

"Exactly, and you know Ailsa. The minute I mention the supernatural, she'll be preparing my P45 and I'll be off down the Jobcentre before you can say 'Auld De'il'."

"Come on, I'll buy you a drink."

George stood. "Thanks. I need one."

In the nearest pub, they downed two Scotches and returned to the shop. It was dark and shuttered, exactly as they had left it.

As they passed through the entrance, the atmosphere of Henderson Close closed around them, dank and heavy.

Hannah wrinkled her nose. "It's worse than ever down here. It smells like rotten eggs."

"Sulfur," George said. "In my misspent youth we used to let off stink bombs to annoy Mrs. Laing, our teacher."

Despite her apprehension, Hannah couldn't help but smile. "I bet you were a horrible little boy."

"Indeed I was. Vile. But my best friend, Alec, was worse. At least I didn't drop worms down little girls' dresses."

"I'd have clocked you one with my duffel bag."

"I believe you would too. Come on."

They arrived at Miss Carmichael's corner. Hannah felt sick

from the stench, which was so much stronger there, but she spotted something else. She bent to peer more closely at the stain.

"Is it my imagination, or does that look wet to you?"

George touched the surface with one finger. "That's because it is." He turned his hand. The finger was red. Cautiously, he sniffed it.

"Blood."

"But that's not possible, is it?"

A rush of foul-smelling wind. George cried out. Hannah watched in horror as he levitated three feet off the ground. An ear-splitting roar, and a shimmering light enfolded him and extended at least eight feet into the air.

"George!"

The terrified man squirmed uselessly. His expression turned through shock, fear, to pain.

The shimmering became a glow. Pulsating. Strong. For the first time, Hannah saw what George must have seen in the kirkyard. A hideous dwarf-like creature with burning red eyes, scales, a hunched and crooked back. It looked made of stone yet it moved with surprising agility. George cried out as it leaped onto his shoulders. Long, black skeletal talons gripped his flesh. "Get it off me! For God's sake, Hannah, get it off me!"

Hannah pulled at his legs but the thing increased its hold.

George gave an agonized cry. "Stop! Stop! It's killing me!"

She wasn't strong enough to fight this creature – all she could see were its talons, gripping George so tightly rivulets of blood trickled down his arms.

With no weapons, Hannah knew she didn't stand a chance. She did the only thing she could think of.

"Miss Carmichael, if you are here, if you can hear my voice, please help us."

"You do not belong here. The grave is your place now, Kirsten. Faithless Kirsten."

Hannah clapped her hands to her ears. But the voice was inside her head. It didn't come from the creature. Someone else. Or some other part of it. Its raucous laughter rang in her brain, echoed through every fiber of her body, chilling her soul.

A roar bounced off the walls. George crashed to the floor with a scream. He covered his head with his hands.

Hannah rushed to help him. "George! Speak to me. *George!*"

George raised his blood-drained face to hers. He trembled, his eyes wide and terrified. "Did Miss Carmichael come?"

"I don't know. Maybe. I didn't see her but that…thing…left in a hurry so…."

George stood. Hannah steadied him as he winced. "I think I've sprained my ankle."

"Do you want to go back?"

"No, we've come this far, let's do this."

Leaning on Hannah, he limped with her to the site of the damaged pentagram. Using a coin, Hannah opened the pot of paint and dipped in the brush. She took out a folded piece of paper from her pocket and examined the diagram on it. While George leaned against the wall for support, she knelt on the uneven ground and drew the five-pointed star, then copied the ancient symbols carefully. All around them, the atmosphere grew heavier until it made breathing difficult. Hannah had to steel herself to keep a steady hand when every instinct told her to get out of there as fast as she could.

The smell of sulfur had faded, or maybe they had become accustomed to it, when Hannah completed her drawing, resealed the paint pot and stood.

"It's done," she said. "Now all we have to do is bring that…entity…back here and summon the spirit to trap it in the pentagram."

"If only we knew who to call out for."

"I have a theory. Remember the blood at Miss Carmichael's murder site? Why would that be fresh today? I think there's a good reason for that."

"You think it's her? That she's the one who battles the demon?"

Hannah shook her head. "I don't know, but why else would that blood be fresh tonight when we really need help to trap this thing?"

"Do you know what you're going to do?"

"No. Do you?"

George shrugged and shifted his weight. That ankle must be really aching by now, she thought. "Haven't a clue," he said.

"OK, I'll call out and see what happens. Wish me luck."

"You got it."

Hannah moistened her lips. "If you are there, Miss Carmichael, or if there is anyone there who wishes to help us, we respectfully call on you, beseech you, to come now."

Silence.

Hannah tried again. "If you are there, please help us. Help us to trap the evil once and for all that it may never escape again."

A deep sigh echoed around the walls. A chill froze Hannah's cheek. Still nothing. She opened her mouth to begin again. Then stopped.

A familiar, but unexpected voice called out from some distance away. "Hannah? Hannah? George? Is it you?"

Hannah and George stared at one another. Hannah spoke first. "What the…? Mairead?"

"It can't be," George said.

"Keep talking, you two, so I can find you." Definitely Mairead.

"We're near Miss Carmichael's corner," George said.

As if she had been there minutes earlier, Mairead's smiling face greeted them.

Hannah rushed toward her and hugged her tightly, so tightly, Mairead struggled to free herself. "Hey, what's this? Anyone would think you hadn't seen me for ages."

"We haven't," Hannah said. "Not for a fortnight or more. Where have you been? Everyone's been so worried."

Mairead frowned. "You've lost me. I was here earlier today."

"Er – I don't think so," George said. "What date do you think it is?

"October twenty-seventh, of course. Why?"

George removed his phone from his pocket and switched it on. "Have a look at that."

Mairead looked disbelievingly at him for a moment before lowering her eyes and reading the date on the screen. "But that's impossible. It can't be the twelfth of November. You're having a joke here, aren't you?"

Hannah and George both shook their heads. "I wish we were, Mairead," Hannah said. "You left here one day and the next, someone called in sick on your behalf. A week later, Ailsa went round to your house but a neighbor said you hadn't lived there for two years."

"That's not possible."

George persisted. "Ailsa said the place looked deserted and virtually derelict. The neighbor told her she had been in touch with the council a few weeks after you moved out and they had been planning to start eviction proceedings for non-payment of rent."

Mairead continued to stare at them. "I haven't a clue what you're talking about. I've lived there forever. I still live there. twenty-two Bishop Crescent. I stay there with my mother."

"You mean you've lived there since you moved here from Dundee?" George asked. "You told me you came from there originally."

"Yes. Of course that's what I meant."

Hannah caught the snap in her voice, wondered briefly at it, and then ignored it. She searched her mind for an explanation and came up blank. Around them, the temperature dropped.

"Do you feel that?" George hugged himself.

Hannah blinked as a shadow passed behind Mairead. "I think someone, or something, just joined us."

Mairead continued to stare at her companions, apparently oblivious to Hannah's words. Behind her, a shape – indistinct at first – began to materialize.

The figure was Mairead's height, could have been Mairead's twin, dressed in sensible Victorian costume. A brown floor-length tweed skirt and matching jacket, with complimentary unfussy hat and wire-rimmed spectacles, completed the picture.

Hannah wondered why she didn't feel scared. It was as if she had grown to know this person. She had seen her on a number of occasions in different locations. Maybe that was it. Perhaps it was the benevolent expression on the ghost's face.

"Mairead," Hannah said softly, "don't be scared, but please. Turn around."

George's mouth was slightly open. He must have been able to see what Hannah saw.

Like an automaton, Mairead slowly turned around. She gasped, her hand flew to her mouth. The spectral figure continued to stand where she was, no change to her benign expression.

Hannah knew it was time. She let her instinct guide her. "Miss Carmichael. Please help us. We've drawn the pentagram. Show us what we need to do to get the demon trapped in it."

The ghostly woman stared at her, unblinking, then seemed to grow before their eyes. Hannah stood rooted to the spot, horrified at the transformation going on in front of her. The calm features contorted, twisted, elongated, collapsed until what was left no longer contained any recognizable form.

In one swift move, the phantom threw itself at Mairead.

"No!" Hannah screamed. Mairead struggled to get free, but the ghostly grip proved too tight. Tendril limbs became black talons, scraping along Mairead's arms as the girl screamed and Hannah tried to prize her free of the vise-like hold.

George lurched forward and grabbed Mairead's other arm. "It's dragging her into the pentagram."

The creature formed a mouth. It opened, revealing razor-sharp teeth. The stench of sulfur choked them. It grew a serpentine neck and drew its head back. Any second now and it would bite Mairead.

Hannah yelled, "Let her go, you *bastard*!"

The creature completed its transformation. A monster covered in scales, its long, powerful limbs ending in massive lizard-like claws, yanked Mairead out of Hannah's and George's grasp. With a massive roar, it threw her into the pentagram, where she collapsed in a sobbing heap. Then it was gone.

Mairead staggered to her feet, dazed and clearly confused.

Hannah recovered herself and hurried to her friend. She reached out her hand into the pentagram, her fingers tingling where they crossed the boundary, almost as if she had plunged them into icy water. "Come on, Mairead." The girl said nothing, but took her hand. Her touch was ice cold too.

Hannah turned back to George. "Let's get out of here and take her home – wherever that may be – and we can see for ourselves whether what Ailsa said was right or not."

Mairead still shook with uncontrolled sobs as Hannah parked outside twenty-two Bishop Crescent. In the dark, it was virtually impossible to tell whether the house looked neglected or not, although Hannah got the impression that weeds had taken hold in some areas. George helped her steer the distraught woman up her path and, as they neared the front door, Hannah could see that, contrary to her first impression, the small front garden appeared well-tended.

With shaking hands, Mairead finally managed to insert her door key and let them in.

Down the passageway, a light shone under a closed door. "Mum's up still."

"It's only just after nine," George said.

"She's often in bed after the six o'clock news. She doesn't sleep well. It all depends on the MS."

Mairead took a deep, ragged breath, slipped her coat off and hung it over the bannister. Hannah and George followed her. In the cozy living room, a woman of maybe sixty, with grey hair and a blanket over her legs, smiled as Mairead walked in. Her look of surprise wasn't lost on Hannah, but not for the reason she had expected.

"Hello, dear," the woman said. "You're late tonight."

Hannah and George exchanged glances. "Tonight?" George mouthed.

"I know." Mairead replied. "It's been a bit of a confusing day. Sorry, I know I should have asked first but Hannah and George were kind enough to give me a ride home."

"That's very kind of you both," Mairead's mother said. "My daughter hardly ever brings anyone home. It's my condition, you see. Unpredictable. She always asks me first. But I'm quite well today, so it's perfectly all right. Will you have a cup of tea?"

"That's very kind, Mrs. Ferguson," Hannah said, "But we really must be going now. Very nice to have met you."

George muttered similar sentiments and two minutes later, they were sitting in Hannah's car.

"If I wasn't confused before, I certainly am now," George said. "For a start, this house is nothing like the way Ailsa described it. Secondly, how is it Mairead's mother also seems to think she saw her daughter earlier today? In fact, how come she's there at all? She's supposed to have died two years ago, according to Ailsa."

Hannah started the engine and moved off. "I think we've wandered into a Penn & Teller illusion. Maybe we're the ones who are delusional."

A flash lit up the dark interior. George had turned his phone on again. He swiped the screen a few times. "I'm getting news updates and they're all dated today. November twelfth. So, we've definitely got the right date. Mairead clearly has no memory of being anywhere out of the ordinary. No concept of passing time. But it's her mother I can't puzzle out. Even allowing for the fact that maybe Ailsa was given the wrong information by that neighbor, how can she be caught up in this as well? She's never been anywhere near Henderson Close."

"Not as far as we know anyway. I'm still trying to understand how Ailsa could have got it all so wrong. Did she go to a different address?"

"We can check with her. She's back the day after tomorrow. Unfortunately."

"She can't expect you to fall on your sword when it wasn't your fault in the first place."

"I was in charge, Hannah. To Ailsa it's an open and shut case. I was acting manager and I failed to prevent a vandal from daubing our walls with obscene words and, for all I know, blasphemous symbols."

It was pretty useless. Whatever words of comfort Hannah offered would fall on deaf ears. She also knew George was right. Ailsa was looking for a culprit and if George couldn't find the real one, he would have to do. She made one last effort.

"You reported it to the police, made a statement and they said they would look into it. You couldn't do more than that."

"They also said they hadn't seen anything like that before and it didn't match the handiwork of the usual suspects. I could tell by their tone they weren't really interested and the chances of catching whoever did it are remote at best. Especially as nothing showed up on CCTV. The trouble is, there are no cameras covering that area. They haven't been fitted yet. The nearest one is at Miss Carmichael's corner and its range doesn't reach quite far enough."

"That's hardly your fault. Ailsa should probably have got the CCTV installed earlier."

"She won't see it that way. Anyway, frankly, Hannah, I think she'd be doing me a favor if she did fire me. At least I could escape all this. I used to love this job but now I'd leave it and never look back. I've had enough of Ailsa's moods. She's so much worse these days. Sometimes I barely recognize her."

"You'd go and leave me to it? Thanks, mate."

"You know I don't mean it that way. Oh, hell."

Hannah smiled. "I know. I'm only grateful for your friendship through all this."

"Friendship?" George looked at her and Hannah knew in an instant how easy it would be for her to lose herself. George was kind. George was divorced and single. He looked out for her and he was the friend she needed right now. Anything else would only complicate things. There had been no one since Roger, and Hannah had never thought there would be. With everything else going on, she couldn't afford to become distracted.

"Friendship," she said firmly. She squeezed his hand, glad that he returned the gesture and that the smile extended from his lips to his eyes.

★   ★   ★

The following day, Hannah weaved her way through crowds of shoppers, some excited, others weary. Everywhere, fairy lights twinkled, Noddy Holder screamed "It's *Christmas*" from one shop doorway to the next, and windows glittered with holly, tinsel and chubby Santas. She arrived at work to find George waiting for her. His anxious expression told her she would not like what he was about to tell her.

"Mairead's not here again," George said. "I haven't said

anything about our encounter with her last night. Right now, I'm beginning to wonder if I imagined it – or dreamed it. Maybe I dreamed the whole thing. That would be reassuring." His wry smile mirrored her own thoughts.

"If only," Hannah said. "But I remember it too, so either we both had the same dream, or it really did happen."

"It happened. All of it."

"'Fraid so."

The entrance door to Henderson Close flew open and Morag dashed into the shop. "You guys have to come and see this. I need someone else to tell me I'm not going crazy."

"What have you seen?" George asked.

"More graffiti."

George groaned.

"No, George, not like yesterday. This is different."

They followed her down the stairs.

Morag stopped in front of the new boards they had erected the day before.

"Have a look at this." She shone her torch high up on the wall. There, in elegant, old-fashioned handwriting, three words.

"'Find my killer'," Hannah read out.

"I'm not going mad then?" Morag said. "And it wasn't there yesterday?"

"No to both," George said.

Morag switched off her torch. "I always thought the haunting stories were just so much hokum."

Hannah sighed. "Bet you've changed your mind. I know I have."

"Well, there's something odd going on here. Oh, and someone has drawn a pentagram on the floor in Farquhars Close."

George looked at Hannah. He raised his hand. Hannah followed suit. "Guilty as charged," George said.

"What did you do that for? Ailsa'll go apeshit."

"Ailsa's already going apeshit," George said. "Believe it or not, Hannah and I were trying to stop all this. The pentagram was to trap the Auld De'il."

Morag blinked rapidly a few times. "Dear God," she said.

"Has the whole world gone completely mad? You're *not* telling me the Auld De'il exists? I used to be threatened with him if I didn't behave. My mother used to get so mad with my nan. She said it would give me nightmares, and she was right."

Hannah and George nodded. "Unfortunately, we believe we've both encountered it."

"What exactly did your nan tell you about the Auld De'il?" Hannah asked.

"That if I didn't behave myself right away, he'd come for me and whisk me away to his lair underground. If I answered her back and said he'd have a fight on his hands, she'd tell me it would do no good as I wouldn't know who it was when he came. He could turn himself into anyone he chose. She used to say the devil has many faces."

"And did it make you behave?" George smiled at her.

Morag gave a wry grin. "Depends how awkward I was being. It did scare me though. I don't really think it's appropriate to threaten a six-year-old with a shapeshifting monster." She glanced at her watch. "I've got to get up to the shop. I'll leave you to it. Try not to uncover any more demons while you're down here."

After she had gone, George shone his torch on the new graffiti. "And that's the kind of skepticism which means no one will ever believe us unless we can bring them cast-iron proof. I wish I knew how to find Miss Carmichael's killer."

"So you do believe that Miss Carmichael herself has been trying to make contact and not just the shapeshifting monster posing as her?"

"I have to believe it. Why would the creature we saw be telling you to find its killer? That doesn't make sense. The voices in your head. You've heard her."

"I *think* I've heard her. And I've heard the other voice too. The raucous male voice. Whoever – whatever – that tells me I belong in the graveyard and calls me Kirsten."

"What if that is the voice of Miss Carmichael's killer? What if Miss Carmichael was killed by the Auld De'il?"

Hannah chewed her lip. "It doesn't match the stories circulating at the time, or the eye-witness accounts. Miss Carmichael was murdered by a gang of ruffians, chief among them a young man in his twenties who was never caught. That sounds like a human to me. Nothing like what we've seen. Except...."

She remembered her encounter with the strange, unpleasant man when she had slipped back to Murdoch Maclean's time. Who was he? "Supposing we did find him, what then? Is he human? Is he the Auld De'il? Both? What does she want us to do with him?"

"Exorcise him. Banish him. Something on those lines, I would imagine."

Hannah looked around. "So where is he?"

The voice sounded harsh, raucous. *"Closer than you think."*

"Did you hear that?"

George looked at her blankly. "Hear what?"

"Damn voice in my head again. It sounded so loud this time."

"What did it say?"

"It...he said he was closer than we think."

Cold, icy fingers of air rustled the hairs on the back of Hannah's neck.

She whirled around. "Stop it!"

George grabbed her hand. "What's happened?"

"Something breathed on me." Powerful hands closed around Hannah's throat. In flashes, a contorted – but human – mouth, blackened teeth, filthy skin. Eyes filled with hate. Strength borne of madness and a hatred that was almost impersonal. Her attacker wasn't trying to kill her; he was attempting to kill anyone like her.

From far away, she heard George shouting as she sank lower and lower into unconsciousness. She clawed at the invisible assailant. A dark mist descended in her mind as she struggled to breathe. Her windpipe was closing. The smell of sulfur burned her nostrils and blackness enveloped her.

CHAPTER ELEVEN

September 1881

Miss Carmichael opened the door of her home and the sweet scent of lavender greeted her. She inhaled it gratefully. After the noxious odors of the Old Town, the fresh aroma cleansed her nostrils and calmed her soul.

She stood in front of the hall mirror and removed her hat, careful not to disturb her tidy bun with her hatpin. She started to hang her coat in the wardrobe, saw the mud on the hem and tutted. That would never do. She would tell Lucy, her maid, to take it to be cleaned tomorrow. Meanwhile, she hung it on the coat stand well away from anything that could become contaminated by goodness knew what made up that mud. She lifted each foot in turn and unbuttoned her boots. Lucy would clean those later. Wash them more like. They too had become caked in the Old Town filth.

Smoothing down her skirt – miraculously free from staining – she slid her feet into her slippers and made her way into her tidy sitting room. The glass-domed mantel clock tinkled its chime, announcing the hour. Four p.m. A cup of tea would be welcome and Miss Carmichael pressed the bell.

In less than a minute, the familiar, cheerful nineteen-year-old maid-of-all-work stood before her.

"I think a pot of tea would be nice please, Lucy. And some of your delicious scones if there are any left. I'm afraid Miss Gascoigne and I made rather a dent in them yesterday afternoon."

Lucy smiled. "I tried out a new recipe. I'm glad you enjoyed them. I think there's a couple left. Would you like Earl Grey or Assam?"

"Earl Grey I think today, please."

"Very good, Miss. I noticed your coat and boots had got a bit dirty. I'll look after them for you."

"Thank you, Lucy."

The girl smiled again and left, closing the door quietly behind her. Miss Carmichael sighed and settled herself comfortably on her settee.

The rattle of the crockery woke her. "My goodness, I must have dropped off," she said as Lucy set the tray down on the occasional table next to her.

"I'm not surprised, Miss. You work too hard. Spending all that time in the Old Town. I hope they appreciate it."

"I'm sure they do, Lucy. And it's important to help those less fortunate than ourselves. I am so lucky to have my little house and a regular income from my investments when there are families in Henderson Close that scratch around for a stale hunk of bread."

Lucy looked a little skeptical. "There's a lot that could do more for themselves. Thieves and vagabonds many of them. Feckless too."

"Now, Lucy. That's unfair and, in my experience, untrue."

"You can't deny it's a dangerous place, Miss. I wouldn't go there alone. I worry about you."

"Most kind, Lucy. Thank you, but I assure you I'm not worried. What could they possibly want with an old lady like me?"

"You're hardly old, Miss. You've barely a grey hair on your head."

A bit of an exaggeration but the girl meant well. Miss Carmichael was only too aware of the middle-aged woman who stared back at her from her dressing table mirror every morning as she arranged her hair. Where had all the years gone? Flown by.

Lucy left her and Miss Carmichael sipped her tea. Tomorrow she would return to Henderson Close and take some children's clothes donated by kindly members of the parish. She and Lucy had spent a couple of productive evenings mending and repairing sleeves, cuffs, hems and loose buttons. Freshly laundered, they were now ready to provide protection in the windy, wet and freezing winter months, which would all too soon be upon them. Poor Mrs. McDonald had been at her wits' end wondering how she was going to clothe her fast-growing family. And she wasn't the only mother who would benefit from Miss Carmichael's visits.

*   *   *

The sun did its best to brighten up the filthy streets but the effort was too great. All it achieved was to shine a spotlight on the muck and hopelessness of the place. The noise of humanity selling its wares, conducting its business and fighting its foes nearly deafened Miss Carmichael as she quickened her step along the street on her way to Henderson Close. How often had she made this same journey? Countless times. Yet she could never get used to the racket or the stench.

She stood in front of number seventeen and raised her hand to rap at the door.

"Gi'e me the bag, ye auld cow."

The boy couldn't have been more than fourteen. The smell of his unwashed body assaulted her nose and she fought the urge to gag. His face and neck were covered in pimples and bites. Dear God, had this child got no home, no parents? There were plenty who hadn't around here.

He took a step closer and the smell sickened her. She fought hard to give no reaction and to stand her ground.

"Are ye deaf? I said gi'e me that bag."

Miss Carmichael tightened her hold on the Gladstone bag she was carrying. "There is nothing in here that could possibly interest you."

"I'll decide that. Now *gi'e it to me.*"

The door of number seventeen burst open and a furious Mr. McDonald pushed past Miss Carmichael, drew his fist back and landed a punch on the boy that sent him spinning into the dirt. Blood poured from the boy's split lip.

"*Awa' wi' ye!*" Mr. McDonald yelled.

The boy struggled to his feet, glared at Miss Carmichael and spat blood and phlegm. "Ye'll regret this. I'll molicate ye."

Mr. McDonald drew his fist back again. "*Get.*"

With one last defiant look, the boy staggered away.

Mr. McDonald took Miss Carmichael's arm. His wife appeared at the door and helped her in. "I'll make you some tea. We still have some left from the quarter pound you brought last time."

Miss Carmichael smiled gratefully. "Thank you. I'm sorry to be so shaken but that's the first time I've ever felt threatened here."

Mrs. McDonald's eyebrows rose. "Really? Well, I suppose that's because most folk around here know that you come to help us. But that Bain lad...." She shook her head.

"He threatened to molicate her," Mr. McDonald said. "That's no way to speak to a lady."

"Molicate?" Miss Carmichael asked. "I'm afraid I'm not familiar with that word."

"No," Mrs. McDonald said, "I shouldn't think you are. That's not a word you'd hear in the New Town. That no good Bain lad threatened to beat you up, but don't worry. He'll no' touch a hair o' your heid. My Andy will talk to his faither. Ye'll no be having any more trouble with him. Round here we know how to teach our bairns to behave."

Miss Carmichael was sure they did. If battering the child's backside black and blue counted.

Half an hour later, Miss Carmichael, now less shaken, left the McDonalds still fondling the clothing she had brought them. She had stayed a little longer than she intended and the light was fading fast. She must get a move on. It really wouldn't do to get caught in this part of the city after dark.

Her anxiety spurred her on. The street was less crowded now. In dark corners, shadows moved. Across the narrow Close, one in particular seemed to match her step for step. She shook her head. Fancy being scared of her own shadow. Even so, she walked a little faster.

And that's when she realized it wasn't her shadow at all. Someone was following her. Deliberately. Her heart beat quicker. She must remain calm. Show any fear and, if someone really was following her, they would know they had her in their power. That's what she had been taught and she knew it was a valuable lesson.

Miss Carmichael turned out of the Close and onto the High Street. Out of the corner of her eye, she saw the figure stop and slink back into the shadows of Henderson Close. But not before she had got a look at it.

A sight she would never forget.

CHAPTER TWELVE

Mairead stood uncertainly. Her head buzzed and she staggered, trying to make sense of her surroundings. She looked down to see she had been sitting on a bench in a churchyard. Staring around her, she saw no one, but the church looked familiar. Greyfriars. How had she managed to get herself here without any recollection of doing so? The last thing she could remember was being at...at work. She had gone for her keys before she and Hannah were due to go to the pub. But, if that was the case, how had she got here?

She rubbed her eyes. It was all so vague. She wrapped her shawl more closely around her. That was a clue. She must have been at work because here she was dressed as Emily Macfarlane. She reached up to her head and felt her servant's cap firmly in place and her hair tucked neatly inside it.

She looked at her wrist but dressed in character meant she did not wear her watch. It was daytime and.... It was all wrong. It couldn't be more wrong.

Mairead made her way to the exit, her heart beating faster with each step she took. She stopped and stared. Horses and carts clattered up and down Candlemaker Row. People dressed in Victorian style meandered along. The occasional glance came her way only to be swiftly averted when she caught their eye. Mairead descended the steps. At least one sight was familiar. A small statue atop its drinking fountain. Greyfriars Bobby – the faithful little Skye terrier who had guarded his master's grave for fourteen years before finally expiring himself. A small dog stopped to drink from the trough. Mairead watched it, her mind reeling in disbelief.

No water had flowed through this fountain or into the trough since it was switched off in the mid-1970s.

What was going on? The oddest ideas flashed through her mind only for her to dismiss them instantly. Maybe they had closed the area off so that scenes for a film could be shot. But, if that were the case, where were the cameras? Director? Crew? Maybe she was still asleep. A sharp pain stabbed her foot as her thin soles made contact with a stone. Awake. Definitely awake.

She must get to Henderson Close. It wasn't far. Maybe by that time she would have walked through this weird time-shift and back onto familiar territory.

She kept her head down and pressed on, along George IV Bridge, and turned right into the High Street. Still nothing was right. No motor vehicles. Only horse-drawn carriages and unfamiliar shops selling old-fashioned wares.

Ahead of her, the familiar bell tower of St. Giles' Cathedral, on her side of the street, so she should be approaching the entrance to Henderson Close any second now.

She almost missed it.

The rubbish-strewn street, dirty, ragged children playing in the filth. Mairead wandered, as if in a nightmare, casting quick glances over her shoulder, ignoring ribald comments from men with rotten teeth, avoiding the eyes of careworn women who eyed her suspiciously. Compared to them, she was well-dressed if a little conspicuous. Her clothes would have been worn by their grandmothers, or even great-grandmothers. Life was short here.

At last she saw a sign she recognized. 'Murdoch Maclean. Printer'.

In all this craziness, relief swept over her. She made straight for his shop, never pausing to consider that he was a complete stranger.

She opened the door and stepped in. The man had his back to her but as he heard her, he turned and wiped ink-stained fingers on his apron.

"Ah, Miss Car— Ye look different today, lassie."

Mairead stared at him. "Sorry?"

"Ye're the image of her but you're no' her, are ye?"

"I'm really confused. Who do you think I am?"

"It does na' matter. There's a lady who comes from the New Town. Miss Carmichael. You're no' her sister, perhaps?"

"I don't have a sister."

"Aye. So what can I do for ye?"

"Please...could you tell me what date it is?"

"The date? September 7th. Wednesday."

Mairead took a deep breath. "And what year, please?"

Murdoch Maclean laughed. "What year? Lassie where ha' ye bin? It's 1881 of course."

"It can't be 1881. Are you sure?"

The smile died around Maclean's lips. "Are ye no' well?" He tapped his head.

"No. Nothing like that. It's just…. I'm having a most peculiar day."

"Aye and ye're no' the only one. Another lassie came into my shop a few days ago. She was no' right either. Dressed like my auld granny. And you are too."

Mairead's eyes lit up. Hannah. It had to be. George had told her their friend's strange story. "Mr. Maclean, do you know where she went after she left here?"

"I hae no idea. One minute she was here. Standing where ye are now. And the next, she had gone. Why two lassies like the two of ye should be here in the Closes, I cannae imagine. Ye dinna belong here. Go home to your own kind."

Mairead's eyes filled with tears. "I don't think I can. I think I'm trapped here for some reason and I have no idea how I got here in the first place, so how can I get back?"

Murdoch Maclean made a tutting noise. "Ye cannae stay here. It's no' safe for ye. Go up to the New Town. Go to St. Andrew's and St. George's Kirk. It's on George Street. Anyone round there will tell ye'. Go up to Princes Street. Can ye find your way there?"

Mairead nodded.

"It'll be dark soon. Ye don't want to be here when it is. Who knows what might happen to ye? A young woman out alone. When ye get to the kirk, ask them for Miss Carmichael. She'll look after ye. Off with ye now and watch yersel'."

Mairead turned to leave. At the door, the stench hit her with renewed energy. She gagged. The printer had been right. The light was fading, and it was getting colder. She had no alternative but to follow his advice if she wasn't to be left sleeping rough in the worst part of town.

Mairead crossed over Waverley Bridge, unable to believe the sight below her. Steam trains belched smoke into the air, creating a fog that made her choke and set her eyes watering. She recognized Princes Street by the Scott Monument and some familiar buildings but everywhere seemed coated in a thick layer of soot.

She was losing the light fast as she hurried along the wide street, which bustled with all manner of traffic – human, horse-drawn and mechanical. After some minutes, she found herself at the junction with George Street and then she saw the church. *Please let there be someone there.*

As she approached, she saw a light through a window. Then it extinguished. Her spirits sank, but the door opened and a man she took, by his dress, to be a minister of the church emerged. He saw her instantly and his eyes widened.

"Please can you help me?" Mairead asked. "I'm trying to find Miss Carmichael."

"Trying to find her? I thought you *were* her for a moment. Certainly a few years ago she could have been your twin."

"I need her help."

The minister hesitated for a moment. "She lives nearby. Come, my child, I will take you to her."

They walked mostly in silence until the minister stopped in front of the shiny, black door of the small Georgian townhouse that was Miss Carmichael's home.

"Now, let us see if she can help you." The minister rang the doorbell.

A maid answered. Her shocked glance as she took in Mairead's appearance told her that, yet again, here was someone who was taken aback by the resemblance between her and the woman she was about to meet. The maid held the door open wider. "Please come in and I'll tell Miss Carmichael you are here."

They waited in the hall.

"My dear," the minister said, "I quite forgot to ask your name."

"Mairead. Mairead Ferguson."

The maid reappeared. "Please follow me. Miss Carmichael will see you now."

The minister led the way into a comfortable room, cluttered with furniture, photographs and plants in typical Victorian fashion.

"Ah, Miss Carmichael, I've brought a young lady who is most anxious to see you. Mairead Ferguson." The minister stepped back and the two women had their first sight of each other.

They both gasped and Miss Carmichael's teacup wobbled precariously in her saucer.

"Good gracious," the older woman said. "How extraordinary. It's like looking at myself years ago."

The minister nodded. "She could certainly pass herself off as you. Especially if she wore your spectacles and kept her own hair totally hidden."

Mairead touched her head and found a few wisps of blonde hair that had escaped her cap.

Miss Carmichael laid her cup and saucer down on the table and stood. Mairead's nerves had got the better of her and, try as she might, words wouldn't form themselves. The shock of seeing someone who looked so much like her! When Miss Carmichael took her arm, she offered no resistance. She sat where indicated.

"Lucy," Miss Carmichael said to the girl who hovered at the door, apparently mesmerized by their new visitor. "Please make us some fresh tea. Two more cups please."

"Alas, no, Miss Carmichael," said the minister. "I was on my way to visit old Mrs. Sykes. I merely took a diversion in order to bring this young lady to you, but I must away now. She's expecting me for afternoon tea."

"Of course, Reverend. Please give Mrs. Sykes my kind regards. I will see you on Sunday then."

Lucy and the minister left.

"Now, my dear. What brings you here and what can I do for you? I sense you are greatly distressed and the clothes you are wearing.... Tell me all about it."

Mairead did her best but found there was little she could say that sounded even vaguely comprehensible and it was becoming vague, as if reality was somehow slipping away. Still, at least, she could speak now. "I found myself in Greyfriars Kirkyard but I have no idea when I got there or why I was there. I knew I had to get to Henderson Close because...because...." She had nothing more to say. The memory had left her with swathes of emptiness where she knew her past life must lie. The name Emily Macfarlane meant something to her. But what? She knew her name was Mairead Ferguson. She belonged in 2018, not here, not now. But she couldn't tell Miss Carmichael that.

The clock ticked. The fire crackled. Finally Miss Carmichael cleared her throat. "Miss Ferguson, I believe Mr. Maclean advised you well today. I am so glad you chose to take heed of him and come to me."

"I didn't know what else to do."

"I believe you were sent here for a purpose. As yet, I have no idea what that purpose is, but I believe it may have something to do with my work."

"Your work?"

"With families living in Henderson Close and the surrounding area. I try to help as best I can, with food, clothing, sometimes even a little money. I have been doing it most of my life. I used to go there every Sunday afternoon with my father, following services. When he died, I carried on and increased my efforts. There is so much misery down there."

"I know," Mairead said.

"Do you, my dear? Really? How could you possibly know? You are not from there, are you?"

Mairead shook her head.

Miss Carmichael looked at her harder, seemingly puzzled. "You speak with barely an accent. Where do you live exactly?"

"At...." Where was it? Another blank. It was there...but now it had gone. She had made for Henderson Close but she didn't live there. So, where did she live? Why couldn't she remember? She was aware of Miss Carmichael staring at her. Concern growing in her eyes.

"I.... This is going to sound crazy. I can't remember." Mairead's mind raged. She wanted to tell Miss Carmichael about coming to in Greyfriars Kirkyard, of having this overwhelming urge to get to Henderson Close, and of knowing she didn't belong there at that time, but how would this God-fearing woman possibly believe her? At best she would think her demented and, in this day and age, would probably feel it her duty to have her committed to an asylum for her own protection.

Miss Carmichael removed her spectacles and polished them with a soft cloth. "You've had a nasty experience. A temporary amnesia perhaps, brought on by some trauma. I have heard it can happen."

Mairead breathed evenly. At least she wasn't sending for the local constabulary yet.

Miss Carmichael replaced her glasses on her nose. "Given your name and how much alike we are, I'm not certain but I think we may be related. My grandmother was a Ferguson. She married a man called Francis Carmichael, hence my name. I know I had a great-uncle, also a Ferguson. Maybe that's where the connection lies."

"That certainly seems possible. What was his first name?"

"I never met him unfortunately. He died before I was born. I can't quite.... Richard. Yes, that was his name. Richard Ferguson."

The name meant nothing to Mairead, but then right now, precious little did. Even with her memory intact, she would have had to trawl back a lot further into her ancestry than Miss Carmichael could have imagined. Mairead made an expansive gesture with her hands and shook her head.

"Ah well, never mind. Maybe when your memory returns and you go back home you can ask your relations."

"I haven't really got many relations. Only my mother." So, she remembered that at least.

"Oh, I see. Well, it seems that today you may have gained at least one more." Miss Carmichael smiled. "You shall stay with me. Just until you regain your memory of where you live. I do feel I should be summoning the doctor. Perhaps you were hit on the head?"

Mairead shook her head vigorously. That was the last thing she wanted. Some Victorian quack prodding and poking at her. He'd probably prescribe opium or something equally addictive. "No really, Miss Carmichael. You have been so kind and I would like to stay with you. At least for tonight. But I am quite certain I don't need a doctor. I have no pain. I can see and hear clearly. I'm sure I haven't been assaulted in any way."

"Then this is a most curious affair." Miss Carmichael slapped her hands on her legs. "Right, I shall ask Lucy to make up the guest room for you. You shall have a good rest this evening, and tomorrow you can come and help me. I am visiting a family in Henderson Close. The McDonalds. Their eldest boy, Robbie, shows a lot of promise." She sighed. "He is an intelligent child with an enquiring mind. How cruel he should be born in such an environment. A few streets further to the west and he would undoubtedly have been enjoying a first-class education with university in the offing. As it is...."

"Can nothing be done?"

Miss Carmichael smiled. "Possibly, my dear. I have some ideas but Mr. McDonald, for all their poverty, is a proud man. I have to be careful how I approach him even with what I provide so far. To announce that I intend to educate one of his sons would quite possibly prove unacceptable to him."

"But if it will help raise his child out of the slums...."

"I will pursue the matter. Robbie is nine years old and already put to labor. He works in a grocer's shop so at least he is spared dangerous tasks. He still attends school and his reading and arithmetic are advanced among his peers. I supply him with books and every week we discuss a topic from one of them. He knows a great deal about the book of Genesis, and also about the achievements of Isambard Kingdom Brunel. I think he wishes to be an engineer himself one day although his father tells him to stop daydreaming."

"He sounds like a very special little boy."

"He is." The way she said it showed almost parental pride. Mairead hoped she would succeed and that Robbie would live his dream.

A wave of tiredness overcame her and she stifled a yawn.

Miss Carmichael rang for Lucy. "Some of your lovely oxtail soup for Miss Ferguson please, Lucy, and she will be staying as my guest, so if you could make up the guest room and sort out some nightclothes and a couple of my day dresses. It seems, for the time being at least, poor Miss Ferguson has been left with only the clothes she stands up in. Fortunately it would seem we are of similar build and may even be related. Now what do you think about that?"

Lucy's astonished look was quickly replaced with a nod. "That would certainly explain the resemblance, Miss."

After Lucy had left, Miss Carmichael patted Mairead's hand. "I can see we are going to be great friends."

Mairead smiled back at her. If only she could tell her the truth. If only she could remember any of it.

⋆   ⋆   ⋆

Miss Carmichael seemed a little jittery as they approached Henderson Close late next morning. She and Mairead both carried parcels wrapped in brown paper and string. More gifts for families in the Old Town. They had already dropped off bread and pies and yet more children's clothing with a couple of families in Farquhars Close, and the McDonalds would be their last stop. As they rounded the corner, Mairead had a sudden flash of recognition. Ahead of her lay Murdoch Maclean's print shop. Miss Carmichael's step faltered and she stopped, her face white.

That corner. Mairead recognized it. *Miss Carmichael's corner.* On this very spot....

"Are you all right, Miss Carmichael?" Mairead laid her hand on the woman's trembling arm.

"Oh dear me. I...the most odd feeling...." Miss Carmichael shook her head and a tiny blush of color returned to her cheeks.

Mairead felt it too. A strange sensation as if everything around had become momentarily muffled and indistinct. Her vision grew hazy and then corrected itself. The moment passed.

Mairead steered her companion away from the spot and life returned to normal. Or as normal as anything could be for Mairead at present.

Miss Carmichael straightened her jacket and raised her hand to knock at the door. Mairead cast a glance back at the corner, from where a tall, thin man glared at them.

Something about him. Did she know him?

"You bitch."

Mairead gave a start. The voice. Male. So vicious.

Miss Carmichael was looking at her with a concerned expression. "Are you all right, my dear?"

"Sorry, I thought you spoke."

"No, dear." She gave the door a sharp rap.

Mairead looked back. He'd gone. The corner was deserted. *They call it Miss Carmichael's corner.*

Mairead shivered. The face of the young man flashed into her mind. Young man? Those eyes…the sharp angle of the jaw. Something in the way he stood. The long arms….

The door opened.

CHAPTER THIRTEEN

The tired-looking woman drew her thin shawl closer around her. "My goodness. You look so much alike," Mrs. McDonald said. "If I didn't know better, I would swear you were mother...I mean...sisters."

Miss Carmichael smiled. "They say everyone has a double somewhere. Mairead is mine."

It seemed everywhere Mairead looked, a small child was sitting, playing, sucking its fingers or trying to pull peeling paper off the damp walls. Mrs. McDonald's bulging tummy ensured there would be another mouth to feed in the coming months, or maybe only weeks. She looked pale. Her hair hung loosely where it had escaped from a couple of hair grips. Though she clearly did her best, judging by the relatively clean washing hanging in front of the meager fire, nothing could be done to stop the spread of grime from the outside world. It covered everything in a fine layer of soot. There was no sign of Mr. McDonald.

"He has some work today," his wife said, managing a smile. "Some laboring. Might last two or even three days if we're lucky."

"You make sure you get the money off him, Moira. You don't want him drinking it away."

"A man needs his pleasures, Miss."

Mairead refrained from saying that, judging by the size of his family, he already took his pleasures. Frequently. Her gaze kept being drawn to the closed door. What had she seen across the Close? Whatever it was.... The malevolence it had given off.... Was it even human?

She became aware that Miss Carmichael was addressing her. "This is Robbie."

A young boy in a frayed red jumper put out his small, thin hand and Mairead shook it. The boy looked solemn, his brown eyes serious, yet glowing with intelligence.

"I have heard a lot about you, Robbie. Miss Carmichael tells me you want to be an engineer like Brunel."

Robbie opened his mouth to reply but was cut short by his mother.

"Oh, I don't think so, Miss. That sort of work isn't for the likes of us. When Robbie's old enough, he'll go to work at the brewery. It's good, regular, honest work."

Something stirred in Mairead's memory. Something she had read a long time ago. Back in her other life. Breweries in Victorian Britain. Terrible working conditions in those places. Long hours, no concept of health and safety, and brutal bosses. Miss Carmichael was right. The New Town might only be around a mile away, but it might as well be the other side of the world where Robbie's prospects were concerned.

"We will take our leave now, Moira. My best wishes to Mr. McDonald."

"Thank you, Miss Carmichael, and bless you." Mrs. McDonald turned to Mairead. "I hope you find your way back soon."

Did she mean back to this house? Mairead couldn't help feeling she meant something else entirely. There was something in the woman's eyes. She had made contact with Mairead in a way she didn't understand. It bothered her. Like everything else in this strange new life of hers.

Back outside, in the melee of Henderson Close, Mairead's eyes were once again drawn to the corner. A few people milled about. But, of the strange male figure, no sign. She shivered.

"Are you cold, my dear?"

"No. Thank you, but I'm fine." How could she tell Miss Carmichael that, for some reason she couldn't explain, she knew that in ten years' time, this kind woman's blood would stain this very street and she would lay dying on that same spot?

★   ★   ★

A few days later, Mairead returned to Henderson Close. Reluctantly on her own this time. Miss Carmichael had been taken ill with a severe cold but had insisted Mairead must go.

"We can't let Mrs. McDonald down, nor the others. They depend on us so."

Once again, she approached the corner of the Close with some trepidation. The sound of the clattering printing press issued from the open door of Murdoch Maclean's shop. It still made her feel strange. In her mind she had such a different picture of it. Underground for some reason.

She heard a sound behind her and whirled round, almost dropping the carefully wrapped parcel she carried under her arm.

A tall, black shadow retreated into a shop doorway, much darker than its neighbors. A smell of sulfur mingled with the other smells of the street. Mairead looked around. People chattered in small groups, tobacco smoke wafted around her. No one took any notice of her. Everything became hazy and she looked down to see where she was standing. Somehow she had crossed the street and now stood on Miss Carmichael's corner. Why did she keep calling it that?

Mairead shut her eyes. The street noise grew distant and faded to an echo. New sounds emerged, growing closer. Familiar voices. Memories washed back over her. Edinburgh 2018. Henderson Close, where she worked as Emily Macfarlane.

Those voices. Who were they? Of course. George. Hannah.

Mairead opened her eyes. She was back. In her own time. The remains of Henderson Close all around her. She looked down at her dress and felt her head. Exactly the same clothes she had been wearing when the world had gone mad and she had emerged in 1881 a few days earlier. No, it couldn't be. It must still be the same day or she would have changed her clothes. Then her memory of all she had experienced on the previous days deserted her.

She had come down here for something. What was it? She couldn't remember. She must get back.

Voices. Hannah. George. They must have come looking for her.

She called out to her colleagues.

CHAPTER FOURTEEN

Hannah struggled to move, but her arms and legs were bound fast with ropes that dug into her wrists and ankles. She tried to focus and her eyes adjusted to the dimly lit surroundings. She appeared to be in a room with no windows and only a flickering candle for illumination. Whoever had left her here had at least not gagged her. She cried out and her agonized voice echoed against the bare walls.

She wriggled herself into a sitting position and leaned against a cold, sweaty wall. There was something oddly familiar about the room. She had been here before. If only the light were brighter she could be sure, but she seemed to be underground. Someone had brought her here, left her in almost total darkness. But for what purpose? And how long had she been here? Questions. Only questions. No answers.

She cried out again.

A noise. Faint at first but getting a little louder. In this strange, still atmosphere, her breathing sounded like a wind. She held her breath. There. Someone moving around beyond the room.

The candle flickered wildly. *Don't let it go out.*

A small figure in white appeared. A little girl. Behind her, concealed in shadow, must be the entrance to this place. Her exit to freedom, she hoped. The little girl stared at her, the candle illuminating her pale features. Hannah pasted a smile on her face.

"Can you help me?" she asked.

The child hesitated. Then inched forward.

"Please, could you untie me? Someone's been playing a silly game with me but they've gone and forgotten I'm still tied up here. Please could you help?"

The child continued to stare at her, then clutched something to her chest. It looked like an old raggedy doll.

Hannah tried again. "My name's Hannah. What's yours?"

The little girl opened her mouth. "Isobel," she said in a tiny voice even smaller than she was.

"Hello, Isobel. Please, would you help me? This rope is very uncomfortable."

Still the child hesitated. What was the matter with her?

Hannah wriggled some more. If she could get off the makeshift bed she sat on…. If she could get a little closer to the child, maybe she could make better contact. Maybe the child wouldn't be so scared and actually do something, instead of standing there staring at her.

Isobel lowered her doll and took another step forward. Now Hannah could make out her features. She would be a pretty child if she wasn't so grubby. Her white dress was spotted and stained and her blonde hair hadn't been washed in days if not weeks.

"Isobel, please help me. If you could just loosen the knots on my wrists I could do the rest."

A sudden noise behind the girl. She put her finger to her lips, turned her head.

And vanished.

Hannah stared at the space that until a second ago had been occupied by a child of around six or seven.

Heavy footsteps drew closer, then stopped. She saw a young man's face in the glow of the lamp he carried – his boots clattered on the stone floor.

"Ye're awake then."

"Yes. Who are you and why am I tied up down here?"

"Ye don't belong here. None of you. This is *my* place. Your place is in the kirkyard under six feet of earth with all the other bitches."

"What are you talking about? Who are you?"

The man set his lamp on the floor and stood within a couple of feet of her. "Donald Bain and ye would do well ta mind it."

"And why would I need to mind…remember…you."

He threw back his head and laughed and the sound wheezed with the croak of a hundred old men. For a horrifying instant faceless shadows writhed behind him – gone as soon as his laughter died.

Bain's face twisted into an ugly grimace. "Go back to your friends. Tell them Donald Bain is waiting for them."

"And how am I supposed to do that?" She indicated her bound hands.

He lifted up his lamp. Hannah recoiled from the twisted, contorted features that writhed in the glow. At first human, then reptilian, its red eyes burned with unnatural fire, boring into her soul. She cried out as daggers of pain stabbed her temples. Excruciating, with the power of a dozen migraines. She wanted to cradle her head. Wanted to smash it into the wall. Anything to make the pain stop. The ropes cut deeper. A wave of nausea rushed up from her stomach and she heaved. Sour-tasting bile poured in a stream from her mouth, soiling the already filthy floor. The pain redoubled. The creature became the young man again and laughed. Loud, long, raucous.

And was gone.

In the same moment, the pain vanished, leaving only the acrid taste to remind her how sick she had just been.

The pressure on her ankles and wrists eased as Hannah's bonds loosened. The pain of her brutally bloodied skin left her. When she lifted her hands, she found no trace of the rope that had tied them so tightly. No marks that she could see. She swung her freed legs onto the floor and stood. Grabbing the candle, she half staggered, half ran out of the doorway. Ahead of her, she saw the emergency lights of Henderson Close. No wonder she had recognized the room – it was the one she entered to tell the tale of Eliza McTavish. But a few moments ago, it had been foul, almost as it might have been in Eliza's day.

"What the hell happened to you, Hannah?" George steadied her as a sudden wave of light-headedness made her dizzy. "One minute you were there and the next, you'd gone."

Her experience was already fading into some half-remembered nightmare. "I don't know, George. I found myself trussed up like a turkey, in Eliza's room. A little girl came to see me. She told me her name was Isobel."

"Isobel? Really?"

"Does that mean something to you?"

"Yes. Until a couple of months before you started, we used to take the visitors to a tiny room where legend had it that a little girl was walled up alive during the plague of 1645. As they were sealing her in, she kept crying for her doll. As an act of...well, their version of charity I suppose, someone chucked in an old rag doll to keep her company. She was supposed to haunt the area right by her room."

"Why don't we go there now?"

"Structural problems. Part of the ceiling caved in and it hasn't been excavated since. That's the part that was going to be repaired at the same time as opening up Farquhars Close."

"But surely we could still tell the tale."

"Now you've seen her, we definitely should."

"There was someone else. The one who I think dragged me down there and tied me up. He said his name was Donald Bain."

"Donald Bain. That name's familiar."

"He said he would be waiting for us all. Who is he?"

"Was, rather than is. I can't remember. Something to do with Miss Carmichael, I think."

"Isobel seemed afraid of him."

"I need to check the files. I'm getting an impression of a nasty piece of work, but I can't remember in what context."

Hannah shuddered. "It must have been a trick of the light from his lamp but there were times he seemed to...change. I got a sense of pure evil from him. He said I belong in the kirkyard. 'With all the other bitches,' he said. This is his territory and he clearly hates women."

"Come on, let's get out of here."

★   ★   ★

Over a double Scotch in the pub, George tapped his forehead. "Donald Bain. I'm sure his name cropped up when they convicted Miss Carmichael's murderers. I think he was suspected of being the one that got away. The ringleader."

"That would explain the aura of evil."

"And presumably why he continues to haunt Henderson Close."

"Can you remember what happened to him?"

"Nothing. As far as I can recall. He was certainly never tried for her murder. I should imagine he melted into the criminal underworld at the time and carried on his sordid line of business, robbing, threatening. Killing perhaps."

"Now Mairead's disappeared again, I can't help wondering if he's got her for some reason. Considering she's the spitting image of Miss Carmichael, could he have become confused? Maybe he thinks she's still alive. Oh God, George, what if he intends to kill her all over again? Supposing he already has?"

"Whoa, let's not get ahead of ourselves. That's one hell of a lot of 'supposing'. Mairead could be back tomorrow."

"Do you honestly believe that?"

"I will if you will."

CHAPTER FIFTEEN

Old newspapers fluttered across the floor as a sharp breeze blew through a broken window.

Mairead opened one eye, then both, and leaped to her feet. Now what? She picked her way carefully over ruined chairs and torn carpet, stained with mildew. She recognized these things. A porcelain doll, fashioned as a Japanese girl, in a scarlet kimono, holding a parasol. Her mother's pride and joy. But the parasol was broken and the girl's pert nose chipped off.

What's happened here?

Her mind clouded over and she struggled to recall the events of the past evening. George and Hannah had brought her home. Mum was still up even though it was past nine.

Mum?

That couldn't be right.

Mairead staggered a little as she made her way to the door. It creaked open on rusty hinges. The hall was a mess of peeling paint and the front door looked as if someone had taken some well-aimed kicks at it from the inside. Mairead went through into the living room. An old smashed television lay on the floor and her mother's favorite chair – latterly the only one she felt comfortable in – lay crookedly against the wall.

The mirror lay in splinters. Someone had scrawled 'Fuck you, witch' across the wall in red paint – at least she hoped it was only paint. A weak sunlight tried to force its way through the window which had been haphazardly boarded up.

Panic set in. She had to get out of there. She ran to the front door, tripping more than once on the ruined debris of her earlier life. She tried the handle but it had seized up and refused to turn.

She raced to the back door. Same story. But in the kitchen, a window had somehow been forgotten. The leg of a broken chair would do it. She grabbed it and smashed the glass above the draining board, praying the ear-splitting crash didn't bring the neighbors running.

She crawled up onto the drainer and carefully stepped out onto the narrow ledge. Her ankle-length skirt hindered her every move and she was tempted to take it off, but she could hardly run through the streets in her panties. It was bad enough to be dressed as an eighteenth-century maid without any more indignity. A filthy tea towel wrapped around her hands provided a barrier against the jagged edges of the window frame and the skirt snagged and tore. She dropped onto the path below and looked around her at the overgrown remains of the small garden. Whatever was she doing there? Why had Hannah and George left her there like this? They had come in with her. Seen Mum....

The impossibility of it all hit her like a bulldozer. With one last glance at the derelict house, Mairead ran.

People stared. Some pointed. Others laughed. She had no money, nowhere to go and, just like 1881, only the clothes she stood up in. She belonged in Edinburgh – but where? Her memories were fast retreating. This had happened before....

Thunder rumbled overhead as the sky darkened. A flash of lightning forked across the horizon. Rain pattered, then pelted down, blinding her. Her skirt flapped against her legs, heavy with rain, nearly tripping her. The wind whipped her cap off and sent it sailing into the trees. Her hair, released from its loose bun, slapped against her face. She pushed it back out of her eyes only for another gust of wind to whip her breath away.

Mairead turned into a small side street. Mercifully, an underground parking lot stood open. She raced down the entrance. The dimly lit interior would at least provide shelter until she had a chance to decide what to do and the rain had stopped.

She panted. The effort of running against the storm had left her drained of all energy. Thankfully, the small car park was almost empty. No prying eyes to stare at her or question her presence there, especially looking as she did.

Only half a dozen quite fancy cars occupied its spaces. Behind her, she heard a clanging noise as the iron grill closing off the entrance rattled downward. It clumped to a halt and silence descended. She moved into the shadows and saw a welcome sign pointing her to the ladies' toilets. The light came on as she entered, illuminating a face she barely recognized in the mirror. Her hair was a mess but, fortunately, the elastic band she had tied it up in still clung onto the small bunch of hair that remained caught up in it. She released the band, tossed her head forward and tried to dry her hair as best she could with the hand-dryer. Then she scooped it into a tight, thick ponytail, secured firmly once more.

She used the toilet, washed her face and hands and leaned against the sink, exhausted. Outside she heard a noise. Footsteps. Coming closer. A woman's high heels clipping across the concrete. Any second now she would no longer be alone. What would the stranger make of the bedraggled, confused young woman?

The footsteps sounded louder, louder. And then kept on walking, straight past. Shortly afterward, a car engine started and moved off. The entrance grill clattered and clanged. Up, and then a minute later, down.

Mairead waited a few moments more and then opened the door. Peering out, she again found she was alone. She made her way as swiftly as she could to the pedestrian entrance, still battling the long, wet skirt. She got there only to find she would need to swipe a card to open the door.

Unless she could find another exit, she would have to wait until another driver arrived before she could leave. The rain seemed to have stopped but once again the darkness was descending and with it, the chill of early evening air. How would she survive a night here? Better than outside obviously but....

CCTV cameras perched high on the walls. Was someone watching her at this very moment? If they were and she stayed out in the open any longer, whoever was on security would realize she wasn't a customer, if they hadn't done so already. Maybe they had already seen her unsuccessfully trying to get out of the door. She would be arrested for trespassing or vagrancy. How crazy when she had a perfectly good home of her own? If only she could remember....

She could stay the night in the ladies' toilet. It was clean and she could sit down, maybe even doze off a little. She certainly felt tired enough. A gnawing pain in her stomach reminded her she hadn't eaten for a long time. She couldn't even remember when. Nothing to be done about that now. Maybe drinking plenty of water would stave off the pangs a little.

She returned to the ladies' washroom and into a cubicle, which she locked behind her. At least she'd be safe here. She hugged herself tightly as she sat, huddled, on the toilet seat.

Gradually she drifted off to some kind of sleep only to be woken by someone entering. The sound of a bucket. A voice and rapping on the cubicle door.

A female voice of east European origin. "Hello in there?"

Mairead struggled up, stiff from sitting in the same position for hours. She unlocked the door and opened it.

A short, plump woman of around sixty looked her up and down. "This is not sleeping place. This car park. You have car here?"

Mairead didn't bother to answer. The woman had already shaken her head.

"You go now, please. I have card. I let you out. You don't come back."

Mairead nodded and followed the woman. No more words were exchanged between them. Quite where she would go was another matter. Something stirred in her head.

Henderson Close. She had no idea what the time was but it had to be early morning. The venue would open in a few hours at worst. Why hadn't she thought of that yesterday? Why hadn't she gone there?

Because yesterday she couldn't remember where it was or that it even existed. Now she could have kissed the ground.

★   ★   ★

Hannah stopped in the action of opening the door of the shop. "Mairead, for God's sake. What happened to you? Why are you still dressed like that? My God, your clothes are soaking wet. Don't tell me you were out in the storm last night."

The cold night in the washroom had done little to dry Mairead's skirt and even her blouse remained damp.

Hannah wrapped her arms around her and Mairead wept on her shoulder.

"Why did you leave me there?"

"Where?"

"In that house."

"We'll talk later. Let's get you inside and out of those clothes. You'll end up with pneumonia." She ushered Mairead into the staff room. "No one will be here for ages yet. I'm always the first in."

While Mairead changed into fresh working clothes, Hannah put the kettle on and measured out instant coffee into two mugs. "Tell me what happened. How you got into that state," she said. "George and I took you home, met your mum and then we went home. Did you go out again?"

"But it couldn't have happened like that. You didn't." How could they have got it so wrong?

"Sorry? How do you mean we didn't?"

"You couldn't have left me at home. With Mum."

"Why ever not?"

"Because she died two years ago."

The spoon clattered into the sink. Hannah wheeled around.

Mairead continued. "I woke up there yesterday afternoon. The place was all boarded up – from the *outside*. I had to break out. It took me ages and then I ran, but I couldn't remember where I needed to go."

Hannah sat down. "I don't understand. Ailsa said that Bishop Crescent was the address she had for you and when she turned up there, the place was derelict and a neighbor said you had moved out after your mother died. But when we took you home, your mother was living there and it was clear you were too. It was dark but the house certainly wasn't derelict. It was warm and comfortable. Your mum welcomed us."

Mairead shook her head. "I don't know what's going on. I only know what I've told you. There are so many gaps in my memory now. So much I can't explain."

"Like where you really do live now?"

Mairead nodded.

Hannah took a deep sip of her coffee. "It's all linked up. It has to be. What happened to me. What happened to you, and George too. I need to tell you about Donald Bain."

When she had done so, Mairead exhaled. "All this craziness seems to have started when they opened up Farquhars Close. Surely that means the legends were true. They must be. Something was walled up there and now it's loose."

"OK, I'm going to suggest something really crazy," Hannah said. "Suppose Donald Bain and the Auld De'il are one and the same. Suppose it was Donald Bain who was walled up."

"And now he's free."

"Yes, God help us."

CHAPTER SIXTEEN

Hannah shut her apartment door behind her. Peace, quiet and normality at last. She put her bag on the hall table and slipped her coat off. In the living room, she made straight for a bottle of Burgundy, uncorked it and poured herself a large glass. She kicked off her shoes, sank into the comfort of her sofa, leaned back and closed her eyes, enjoying the smooth, rich wine and a chance to rest her aching feet.

Half a glass later, she stirred herself. Time to get a relaxing bath, change into a comfy caftan and fix herself a sandwich. She couldn't face a cooked meal tonight.

It felt good to slip into the warmth of the fragrant suds. Her fears and confusion seemed to melt into insignificance as she inhaled the soothing aroma. She leaned against the edge as the water gently lapped her body. From behind closed eyes, she sensed the room growing darker. That shouldn't be.

Her eyes snapped open. She wasn't imagining it. The room was growing darker, as if someone was depressing a dimmer switch. Only she hadn't got one. It couldn't be the bulb. They just snapped off when they went or were switched off. Besides, there was no one else in her apartment....

Hannah stood and stepped out of her bath. She wrapped her toweling robe around her and padded out into the hall. All the lights had dimmed, so that she was in a half-light. In the bedroom, shadows covered half the room. Unnatural shadows that writhed and twisted.

No. It couldn't have followed. It mustn't.

Whatever it was belonged in Henderson Close. Not here.

Out of the corner of her eye, Hannah caught a movement. Too swift to be human, it shot across her peripheral vision. She stepped out into the hall. No sign of anyone. Or anything. She crept along and into the living room.

The smell hit her at the doorway. Lavender. An old lady's

smell. The sort of scent Miss Carmichael might have worn.

Miss Carmichael.

"Is anyone there?" The scent wafted stronger than ever. Darkness crept across the room, spreading like a cloak. "Miss Carmichael, are you there?"

The darkness settled. Hannah tried the light switch. Nothing. She flicked it twice, three times. Still nothing. "We're trying to help you, Miss Carmichael. We're trying to find your killer. I think I know who it is but we need your help. He isn't like...." What? Not like a normal ghost?

The lights came up all at once. Hannah was left shaking her head in disbelief.

Finally daring to move, she returned to the bedroom and dressed quickly. She ditched the caftan in favor of more practical jeans and jumper.

Back in the living room, she rescued her glass of wine, topped it up and glanced out of the window at the rain-swept street beneath. The streetlamps lit up patches of the shiny surface and under one, a figure moved into the light.

Hannah gasped. The woman stared up at her, her wire-framed glasses glinting. She raised her hand and beckoned to Hannah.

Without hesitation, without a thought, Hannah dashed out into the hall, thrust her feet into her winter boots, arms into her warm coat, grabbed her keys and left.

She tore down the stairs and out through the front door, in time to see the figure slowly moving along the deserted street.

Hannah raced to catch up with her, but however slowly the woman moved, she could not reach her. She followed the silent figure down the High Street, stopping at the entrance to Henderson Close. The woman turned and looked at her, her face expressionless.

She vanished.

Hannah stood, unsure what she was meant to do next. Maybe the woman would return. Miss Carmichael. The temperature continued to drop until it had to be hovering around freezing. Hannah's feet and hands were growing numb. Still nothing happened. She must go home or freeze to death.

In her apartment, the warmth of the central heating greeted her at the door. But in the bedroom, the chill turned her breath to vapor.

A small figure in a dirty white shift faced the window.

The hair on Hannah's neck bristled. "Who are you? What are you doing here?"

The girl said nothing. She continued to face out of the room.

"I said, who are you? What do you want here?"

As if in slow motion, the girl slowly turned.

Hannah cried out. The child had no face.

She kept on turning, her movements graceful as a ballerina on a music box, until she faced the window again.

Hannah stood, trembling. Her eyes must be deceiving her. But she knew they weren't. The little girl spread her arms wide. In one hand, she clutched an old rag doll. Isobel's rag doll. She dropped it, and soared through the closed window.

Hannah crouched down, half expecting the doll to disappear. It didn't. She picked it up, noting how grubby it looked. How worn and patched. At some stage this doll had received some serious damage. It had to be the same one and the girl had to be Isobel. How and why were different matters entirely.

Hannah laid the doll on her bedside chair. What could she do with it? Throwing it away could not be an option. The girl might come back for it. Probably would if she could. But the thought of living with it, seeing it every time she opened her eyes? No. Hannah steeled herself to pick the doll up again. She carried it out into the hall and opened a large fitted cupboard where she stored all manner of things not needed every day. She cleared a space next to the Christmas tree and laid the doll down. She closed the door firmly and went back into the bedroom. No sign of the little girl, but she knew she wouldn't sleep that night.

★　★　★

At work the next day, she was greatly relieved to see Mairead.

"Where did you spend last night? I looked for you when we closed but you'd already gone. I wondered if you wanted to stay with me for a few days."

"Thanks, Hannah. I stayed with Morag. It's crazy not being able to remember where I live."

"Have you done a search on yourself online?"

Mairead nodded. "I can't find any trace of me. It's as if I don't exist."

"But what about your bank account?"

"Like my employee record here, it shows twenty-two Bishop Crescent. I do my banking online. I can remember that much. It's crazy. It's as if someone or something has filtered out great chunks of my memory and left random ones behind."

Hannah thought for a moment. "Do you have a credit card?"

"Again, I don't remember, so I rummaged through my bag, went through my purse again and again. Nothing. I don't have a credit card to my name apparently."

"That's weird. But no weirder than anything else that's been happening."

Mairead sighed. "It looks like I'll have to start my life all over again. At least I can get money now."

"So you have a bank debit card?"

Mairead nodded. "And, oddly, I can remember my password. I have to go shopping at lunchtime. Jumpers, jeans, underwear.... You name it, I need it."

"If I can help with anything, let me know."

"I will. Thanks, Hannah."

★   ★   ★

"You look tired, Hannah." George handed her a coffee. "Still not sleeping?"

Hannah shook her head. "I keep thinking I'm hearing things, and when I do get to sleep, all I can dream about is that child, Isobel, and that bloody doll of hers."

"Do you think she left you the doll on purpose? As a gesture perhaps? She hasn't threatened you in any way, has she?"

"No, but I keep expecting her to come back for it. Or *someone* to come back for it. And I can't understand why she had no face. When I saw her down in Eliza's room, she had normal features."

"Maybe it's symbolic."

"Perhaps."

Morag dashed into the staff room. "Ailsa's back, and she doesn't look happy."

An understatement. Ailsa was incandescent. "I go away for a few days' holiday and come back to this shambles. George, what has been going on here? I've had the Phantoms Paranormal Society onto me, complaining that you cut short their séance. I've had customer complaints galore about obscene graffiti and a woman has threatened to sue us for physical harm she suffered on one of the tours. She claims something bit her, *and* she has the photographs to prove it. Explanation please, George. Now."

Hannah wanted to slash right through the awkward atmosphere. She sensed all but one person in that room sympathized with George's plight, and equally, they were only too glad they weren't wearing his shoes at this moment.

She heard a voice and realized it was hers. "It's not George's fault," she said. Ailsa turned her cold gaze toward her.

"Oh really? Then if not his, who *is* responsible? You? In my absence, I put George in charge. He's the Deputy Manager."

Hannah looked for support from the others. They avoided her eyes. All except Mairead.

"All I meant was that nothing George could have done would have stopped what's been going on. The graffiti appeared overnight. No one was left down there, so we haven't a clue how it was done."

"You're going to tell me we have real ghosts down there, aren't you?"

"Yes," said Mairead. "We have."

"Not you as well. I would be very careful if I were you, Mairead. You're in enough trouble as it is. Disappearing like that and giving a false address."

"It wasn't a false address...." Mairead's voice tailed off.

Ailsa ignored her. "George? I'm waiting."

George ran his hand through his hair. "I stopped the séance because something was happening to Hannah. Whatever we'd tapped into had latched on to her. It wanted her. She had a bizarre experience and understandably didn't want to continue. I thought it best to stop altogether before things got completely out of hand."

Ailsa's lips remained in a tight line. "Hannah? Is this what happened?"

"Yes. It was pretty full-on. No way could I have carried on. George made the right decision. I'm sure of it."

"It's a pity the Phantoms don't agree. Up until then, they said it had been the best experience ever. You deciding to cut it short ruined it for them. Full refund of course – but then you promised them that anyway, George. Not satisfied with that, they have then proceeded to damn us all over social media. Apparently we're little short of fraudulent. The company has already been onto me demanding a full explanation."

"I'll resign," George said. "You don't need to take the flak for any of this. I made the decision and all of this happened on my watch."

Ailsa nodded. "Magnanimous of you. I'll consider it. Now get back to work, all of you and make sure the visitors have the experience of their lives. In a good way."

Hannah left with the others, George by her side. "I don't see why you should have to resign, George. It's so unfair."

"That's life. It's either that or wait for Ailsa to sack me. I don't honestly see what else she can do in the circumstances."

"I'm sorry, I have a group waiting and I'm only just going to make it on time. Let's meet up after work, go for a curry or something."

George managed a weak smile. "Thanks, Hannah. I'd like that."

Hannah nodded and left him. She pasted on a smile and became Mary Stratton. A small group of fifteen happy faces greeted her and five minutes later they were all negotiating the uneven ground of Henderson Close.

A short distance past the printing shop, one of the female American visitors piped up. "My goodness this place is creepy. Real spooky."

Others in the group snickered. A man, probably in his late forties, joined in. "You can almost hear the ghosts rattling their chains."

More snickers.

The woman cried out and stopped in her tracks, then started to laugh.

"Are you all right, madam?" Hannah asked, taking care to remain in character.

All eyes were on the woman. "Oh yes. I am now. But you

really had me going there for a second. I wasn't expecting the child. Great touch."

Hannah's blood turned icy. "Child? What child?"

"The little girl. She popped her head up and looked out the window, over there." She pointed at a darkened window of one of the locked dwellings. "Didn't anyone else see her?"

The rest of the group looked at each other in a general chorus of shaking heads. Hannah must keep control. Already the woman was showing signs of jitteriness.

"Oh, *that* little girl." She improvised wildly. "Now that will be young Nell McCarroll. She'll be looking out to see if her daddy's coming home from work."

"Is that a waxwork then?" the woman asked. "So clever."

Hannah nodded, mentally crossing her fingers. Satisfied with her explanation, the group moved on.

They reached the end of the Close, where the recently painted-over boards indicated the start of Farquhars Close. Hannah began her story. "There is a legend of a character people called the Auld De'il who was responsible for a series of murders a couple of years after the infamous Jack the Ripper struck in London. It is said he sold his soul to the devil himself and one day the residents caught him, trapped him and walled him up here." Hannah pointed to the boards. "The murders stopped immediately."

A man in his twenties, holding the hand of a terrified looking girl with long blonde hair, spoke. "The murders stopped abruptly in Whitechapel too, didn't they? Could he have come up here and begun again?"

His girlfriend looked even more frightened now. She stared up at him, her eyes wide.

Hannah nodded. "Indeed that is one theory. Serial killers don't tend to stop until something, or someone, stops them. She turned to the board. "Maybe the Auld De'il and Jack the Ripper are one and the same. I'm afraid we shall never know. Whoever he was, he took his secret to the grave."

A few nervous laughs greeted this.

A massive bang shook the boards. Followed by another and another.

The group shifted uneasily. A few gasped. The American woman gave another cry. Hannah prayed. What the hell was going on? She must stay calm. She must make them think this was normal. All part of the show. Or....

"Don't worry, ladies and gentlemen. It isn't the Auld De'il. It's the workmen, carrying out excavations. We are planning to open up Farquhars Close next year. Let's leave them to it. I have one more thing to show you before you return to your own time."

She forced herself to move steadily when every pore of her being screamed at her to run. The visitors had recovered and were now chatting excitedly among themselves, moving slowly. Oh, so slowly. Behind them the banging had become an incessant loud thumping. At any minute, it sounded as if the boards would give way and something would crash through and into the Close. Hannah dreaded what that something might be.

As they approached Miss Carmichael's corner, Hannah toyed with the idea of simply carrying on back up the Close and ending the tour, but she had already promised them one last stop. She would make it a quick one. Taking a deep breath, she plunged in. "Now don't come too close, ladies and gentlemen, but look down and you will see the stain that can never be removed."

The middle-aged man crouched down and touched it. "That's a good one. Fresh blood!" He grinned and held out his finger, stained red. "No, not really," he said with a laugh. He sniffed his finger and a surprised look passed over his face.

Hannah spoke quickly before he could say any more. "Miss Carmichael was a philanthropic lady of the late nineteenth century who worked tirelessly for the benefit of poor families living in Henderson Close and the surrounding area. She raised money, collected clothes, food and anything else she could lay her hands on. Local people were horrified that one of their own could have murdered her. They set up vigilante groups as none of them trusted the local police force. Her assailants were caught, except for one and, to this day, no one knows who that was or what became of him, although there are plenty of theories. Maybe it was the Auld De'il himself."

If only the thumping from behind the boards would stop. Hannah couldn't take any more. Forcing herself to keep her voice steady, she said, "Now, we don't want to bump into the next tour so let's go back up into the gift shop and I'll be happy to answer any further questions you may have." The group obediently followed her. At the foot of the stairs, the American lady remembered. "Oh, aren't we supposed to have our pictures taken?"

This was greeted by nods and murmurs from visitors clearly wanting to get their money's worth.

"Of course," Hannah said, fixing her smile once more. In ones and twos, the visitors stood at the bottom of the stairs and smiled up at the camera. Flash after flash lit up the street. The banging stopped.

"Eugh, what's that smell?" A young woman pinched her nostrils and screwed up her face. Others began to copy her.

Then the smell hit Hannah. A horrible sulfurous odor that swept up the Close. As the last couple posed for their picture, their smiles turned into expressions of disgust.

"Sorry about that, ladies and gentlemen. Let's make our way upstairs now." Hannah stayed at the foot of the stairs, ready to follow her last guest up.

She put her foot on the step and cast a quick look behind her.

The towering shadow leaped, wrapped itself around her, cloaking her in a stinking blackness that cut out the light, sound and presence of Henderson Close. Hannah fought. She beat against the amorphous mass, her fists meeting nothing solid. Her ears filled with a rushing noise of a wind that seemed to come from within the mass. She tried to cry out but whatever held her muffled her voice. She was drowning in an impossible sea.

Then it left her.

But something remained.

CHAPTER SEVENTEEN

1881

Miss Carmichael heard the boys jeering and taunting as she rounded the corner on Henderson Close. It wasn't the first time. These young hooligans loved nothing more than to turn on someone usually younger, smaller and weaker than they were. This time, there were four of them, circled around a small girl who clung on to an ancient, but obviously much-loved rag doll.

The tallest of the boys made a grab for the doll and managed to snatch it out of the little girl's hands. Tears streaked down her grubby face.

"That's enough, boys," Miss Carmichael said, "Give her the doll back. You don't want it."

The boy holding the doll rounded on her. "What's it to do with ye, interfering old cow?"

"Don't speak to me like that and give the little girl her doll back."

"Who's going to make me? You?" He laughed and the other boys joined in. Miss Carmichael wished she had brought her umbrella. Right now, there was nothing she would like to do more than set about these cruel ruffians, even if to do so would drag her down to their level. Someone needed to teach these lads some manners.

Anger gave her courage and she kept her voice calm. "Give the doll back to the little girl," she said. Whether it was the authority in her voice or whether he was simply tired of the game, the older boy lowered the doll. He stared her straight in the eyes and ripped off its arms, before throwing it down onto the filthy street.

With a raucous laugh, he set off, his fellow bullies running after him. Miss Carmichael quickly retrieved the doll before any further damage could be done to it. The street was busy with people going about their business. Not one person had come to her aid, or the aid of a distressed little girl, who still stood, her eyes streaming with tears.

Miss Carmichael turned the forlorn and filthy toy over in her hands. "I'm afraid she's in a sad way. What do you call her?"

The little girl turned her reddened eyes up to her. "She doesna' have a name. Just Dolly."

"Well, Dolly is a name. And a very pretty name too. What's your name?"

"Isobel."

"That's a very pretty name too. Now, Isobel. I have an idea. Why don't I borrow Dolly, take her home with me and see if I can repair her? Would you like that? I could give her a bit of a wash too. Then she would be all clean and pretty."

At that moment she wished she could take Isobel home with her too. At this rate the doll would be cleaner than its owner.

Isobel hesitated, then nodded, a hint of a smile warming her face. The child would be really quite attractive if she was scrubbed up and happier.

"Then that's decided. I'll walk you home and then I'll know where to bring Dolly when she's mended and washed." A sudden thought struck her. "You do have a home, don't you, Isobel? With your mummy and daddy?"

Isobel paused, then nodded.

"Take my hand and show me where you live. I'll make sure you get home safely."

Once again, hesitation. Miss Carmichael had the distinct impression there was something Isobel wasn't telling her, but now she slid her hand into Miss Carmichael's and the two made their way along the Close, weaving in and out of the other pedestrians, taking care not to step into the stinking gutter. At the junction with Farquhars Close, Isobel withdrew her hand. Miss Carmichael looked down.

"I must awa' now," Isobel said.

They were outside a recently collapsed tenement. The place was uninhabitable. Ceilings had caved in, all the windows were gone. Surely she couldn't live here? "Let me take you home, Isobel. If I don't know where you live, how will I return Dolly to you?"

The little girl skipped off, turned and waved. Three men, the worse for drink, veered in front of her, blocking her from Miss Carmichael's sight. She moved to one side to let them pass and when they had done so, there was no sign of Isobel.

Miss Carmichael caught up to where she had last seen her, by the side of the ruined building. "Isobel?" She called her name repeatedly but to no response.

Most extraordinary. Peering through into the building, she could see nothing but fallen timbers, ruined plaster and broken furniture.

An elderly man stopped next to her. "I wouldn't go in there, Miss. It isn't safe."

"No, I can see that," she said. "Does anyone still live there?"

The man raised his eyebrows. "People will make a home almost anywhere if they have no roof over their heads, but no one goes in there. Not since it fell."

She looked back at the building. "It does look extremely dangerous."

"Oh, it's not only that. Some folk would live with that. No, it's the ghosts, you see."

"Ghosts?"

The man nodded. "Some strange things happened in that place. Murders and such. The dead come back, they say. At night. Sometimes in the day. Doesn't do to linger around here."

Miss Carmichael wondered if he was having a little fun at her expense but he looked serious enough. "Have you seen any... ghosts here?"

"I've seen things I can't explain. Shadows. Things that couldn't be there. People...." He shook his head. "It doesn't do to talk too much about such things. If you take my advice, you'll get back to the New Town. Not so many ghosts there."

"Thank you for your advice," Miss Carmichael said.

His glance took in the doll she was carrying. He seemed startled to see it. He pointed at it. "Where did you get that?"

"A little girl gave it to me."

The man crossed himself. "God bless you, Miss. I must leave you now. Please, go back home. Throw that thing away."

"Oh, I couldn't possibly...." The man had gone, moving faster than she would have thought someone of his obvious age could manage.

★   ★   ★

"What an odd thing to say," Lucy said, handling the doll with obvious distaste.

"I thought so too. Do you think it can be saved?"

"It'll need a good wash first and then I should be able to sew the arms back on. It's very old, isn't it? Must have been in that child's family for generations."

"I should imagine so. Probably the only toy the poor girl has. I'm still worried about how I can get it back to her. There are so many dwellings packed together. She could live in any one of them."

"It's only small. You could take it with you each time you go down there. You saw her there once. You're almost bound to see her again."

"That's another odd thing though. I've got to know most people and the children by sight if not by name around there and I've never seen this child before in my life."

"Maybe her family just moved to the Closes."

"Possibly." Miss Carmichael sighed. "You're probably right though. Now I've seen her once I'll most likely run into her every time I go there."

"I'll get started on this then," Lucy said and left her to mull over the day's events and the little girl with the sad eyes.

There was something else bothering Miss Carmichael about Isobel. Yes, that was it, the child looked strangely out of time. Her dress, if you could even call it that – more like a shift or a nightdress – was fairly shapeless, but definitely old-fashioned, and the child's face...not a *modern* face.

Who are you, Isobel?

★   ★   ★

"Robbie has something he wants to say to ye, Miss Carmichael."
Mrs. McDonald pushed the boy forward. Miss Carmichael smiled
down at him as she stood in the McDonalds' one room.

The boy put out his hand as Miss Carmichael was certain he had
been instructed.

"Now what do ye say, laddie?"

"Thank ye, Miss Carmichael," the boy said shyly.

"He loves the books you brought, Miss. His faither says he
should put them down and get on with some proper work but
every spare minute, he has his nose in a book."

"You are most welcome, Robbie. I shall bring along some more
next week."

The boy smiled. Now was the time. Mr. McDonald had again
secured a couple of days' laboring. For a short time, at least, things
weren't so desperate for the family.

"Moira, I've been thinking. Robbie is a bright lad. He deserves
a good education. I know he attends school now, but not all the
time and probably not to the standard of which he is capable. As
you know, I have no relatives, but I do have the resources to ensure
Robbie has the education that he richly deserves. He can also come
and live with me so that he may be close to his school and...." Miss
Carmichael faltered. Her carefully, oft-rehearsed speech had deserted
her. One more sentence and she would have ruined everything. She
didn't want to imply the obvious truth. That Robbie could hardly
be educated at a good, private school by day, only to return home in
his smart uniform to a slum in the Old Town.

"It's all right, Miss Carmichael," Moira McDonald said. "I
know what you mean and I thank ye from the bottom o' my heart
for thinking so much of my laddie. But my Andy won't hear of it.
He's a proud man, Miss."

"I know he is, Moira. And like so many of his gender, a stubborn
one. But he's also a good man who wants the best for his children.
I'm sure you can persuade him that he could have so much more
if you would simply take me up on my offer. Promise me you'll
consider it."

Robbie's eyes looked as if they grew any larger, they would pop right out of his head.

"And how about you, Robbie? Would you like to go to a good school where they have more books than you could ever read in a lifetime?"

The boy hesitated for a moment, looked at his mother, then back at Miss Carmichael. A broad grin lit up his face. He nodded vigorously.

Miss Carmichael took his chin between her thumb and forefinger.

"See what you can do, Moira. I'll be back next week and you can give me your answer then."

"I will…and thank you, Miss. Thank ye for everything you do for us. Please be careful in the street. Andy tried to have a word with the Bain lad's faither but he's in prison for thieving. The lad's roaming wild again. I swear he has the de'il himself in him."

"I'll be careful, Moira. Thank you for warning me."

Another encounter with the Bain boy was not a prospect she relished. Ever since the girl, Mairead, had gone wherever she had gone to and Miss Carmichael had returned to visiting the Old Town on her own, she had dreaded encountering him – with or without his motley assortment of friends.

Now, with the daylight hours shortening as autumn progressed, dusk was already falling, casting the usual gloom over the Old Town.

Deep in the shadows, a figure moved slowly into the light as Miss Carmichael approached.

"Ah, it's the old cow again, I see. What have ye got for me today?"

Miss Carmichael pulled her coat tighter around her and pressed on. The boy barred her way. Miss Carmichael felt panic rising. She must show no fear. Boys like him thrived on it.

"Out of my way, please," she said, proud that her voice remained firm.

"Make me." He grinned.

Miss Carmichael sidestepped this way and that, but each time, the Bain boy stopped her.

"Young man, kindly remove yourself."

"No. Not till ye gi'e me yer purse."

"She'll no' be daeing that." Mr. McDonald's voice boomed out across the street. "But I'll be seeing ta ye in ways ye cannae imagine if yer dinnae leave her be."

"Y'auld Jessie. Ye dinnae scare me."

"Nae? We'll see aboot that."

Miss Carmichael ducked out of the way as Andy McDonald's fist met with Donald Bain's eye. The boy backed off, muttering obscenities. His eyes blazed and for a second, Miss Carmichael truly believed she had witnessed a devil in the boy. He scarpered as fast as his feet could carry him.

"Are ye awreet, miss?" Mr. McDonald said. "He'll get himsel' in prison like his faither and good riddance that'll be."

"Thank you once again for coming to my aid, Mr. McDonald. I'm not quite sure how that would have ended had you not arrived when you did."

"Shall I walk ye back to yer hoose, Miss?"

"I'm sure I shall be all right now, but if you could accompany me to the High Street, I should be most grateful. There are usually enough people there to deter ruffians like Donald Bain."

Mr. McDonald looked uncertain about this, but Miss Carmichael was adamant. He said his farewells as the High Street became Lawnmarket.

Anxious to get home before full night descended, Miss Carmichael kept up a steady pace, hindered by a stiff wind that whistled around her head and threatened to dislodge her hat.

Back in the comfort of her own home, she ordered tea. Lucy brought it, set it down and handed Miss Carmichael the child's doll.

"I washed it and mended as best I could, Miss, but it was in such a state."

Miss Carmichael turned the doll over in her hands. Lucy's neat stitches were barely in evidence. The doll was rather more patchwork than it had been, but she knew the little girl would love it. If only she could find her again.

★ ★ ★

The little girl found her. It was as if she had been waiting for her, on the corner of Henderson Close.

"There you are, Isobel." Miss Carmichael handed over the repaired doll to the little girl with wide eyes.

She grabbed it and cuddled it so tightly, Miss Carmichael feared the stitches would burst, but Lucy's needlework held firm and the child's grubby face broke into an angelic grin.

"Now you must promise to take good care of it. Probably best if you don't take it out on the street with you. Here, take my hand and I'll walk you home."

The little girl seemed reluctant to tear one hand away from clutching the doll but she did so and clutched Miss Carmichael's hand. A few yards away, she caught sight of the Bain boy, on his own, smoking. He glared at her but didn't move. *Don't come any closer. Please.*

Distracted, Miss Carmichael barely registered the little girl removing her hand from hers. She looked down and behind her. No sign. It was as if the girl had vanished. Again.

Donald Bain slunk away, grinning.

Pull yourself together, Miss Carmichael told herself. She made her way back up Henderson Close, intent on visiting a few shops on Princes Street. A new every-day hat had proved a necessity when Lucy announced that, sadly, her old winter one had fallen victim to moths.

"I don't understand it. I put it in mothballs but the little bug – blighters chomped through it anyway."

"Never mind, Lucy. I think I deserve a new hat. That one is years old. The moths are welcome to it."

She smiled at the memory, then gasped as Bain charged out in front of her.

This part of the street was unusually deserted. The boy barred her way but there was something different about him. Surely he hadn't been so tall a few minutes ago? Nor as broad-shouldered.

The boy stared at her, malevolence in his eyes. His lips parted to reveal his rotten teeth. He was Donald Bain but he wasn't the Donald Bain who had taunted her, threatened her and tried to steal her purse. No, this was another creature entirely. This was the creature she had seen that day, skulking in the shadows, and he had taken on Donald Bain's form.

Silently, she recited the twenty-third Psalm.

"Yea, though I walk through the valley of the shadow of death, I will fear no evil: for thou art with me; thy rod and thy staff they comfort me...."

He spoke and the voice wasn't his. His lips moved, but the words weren't his. The sky darkened. "You do not belong here, woman. Get back to your own place. Leave us alone."

The harsh, rasping voice grated on her nerves with its inhuman pitch. She fingered the small gold cross she always wore. The creature saw her.

"That will do you no good. I am master here. Not your God... not your...Christ." He spat the word out and was gone. As if he had never been there.

The sky lightened. Miss Carmichael stood, too stunned to move, for a few seconds. Had she really seen him? Maybe she had suffered a momentary delusion. One person went by and eyed her curiously before moving on. A couple she recognized walked past on the other side of the street. The man doffed his cap to her.

Miss Carmichael nodded at them, shook herself and resumed her walk. But she wouldn't buy a hat today.

Back home, Lucy opened the door. For the life of her, Miss Carmichael had been unable to get her key to stay in the lock, her hands trembled so much.

"Miss, whatever's happened?"

Lucy helped her over the threshold and off with her coat and hat. "You look as if you've seen a ghost."

"At least I could blame that on my over-active imagination." Miss Carmichael struggled to regain her composure, angry that tears pricked her eyelids. She hoped Lucy hadn't seen them.

"You go into the warm now and I'll bring you some nice, strong tea." Lucy opened the living room door and Miss Carmichael settled herself in her chair. She took a deep breath, wishing it calmed her more than it did. Her tea arrived promptly and Lucy poured her a cup.

"Lucy, please would you ask Reverend Smalley to call on me at his earliest convenience? I feel I am in need of some spiritual guidance."

"Of course, Miss. I'll pop around there straightaway, as long as you'll be all right while I'm out."

"Yes, thank you, Lucy. I shall drink my tea and I'll be fine."

Miss Carmichael knew Lucy was longing to know what had discomposed her so badly but until she had spoken to the Reverend, she didn't trust herself to tell anyone what she found so hard to comprehend herself.

★   ★   ★

Reverend Smalley put down his teacup. "From your account, I would say you have indeed had an encounter with pure evil, Miss Carmichael. I must confess that in all my years in the ministry I have never witnessed anything as extreme as your experience yesterday. I was called once to a young woman who was flailing her arms and screaming obscenities but the poor girl turned out to be afflicted with epilepsy and I believe another mental disorder. Certainly not possessed by a demon. I am not at all surprised you felt so shocked and unnerved."

"But what is to be done about it, Reverend? The boy lives on the streets down there. There's no telling what he might do. He seems particularly averse to females of any age and I fear for us all."

Reverend Smalley shook his head. "I think I must consult with the bishop on this. It really is so far out of my own experience, I feel I too need some spiritual guidance."

★   ★   ★

Miss Carmichael closed her front door and polished her spectacles, deep in troubled thoughts. With evil of such a nature as the Reverend believed unleashed on the streets of Edinburgh, was anyone safe?

★   ★   ★

"It is good of ye to think about our lad, Miss Carmichael." Andy McDonald leaned back in the rickety chair which protested at the shifting of his weight. "But the likes of us dinnae belang in the New Town."

Miss Carmichael sighed. She knew he would be hard work and he was certainly proving her right. Why couldn't the man see that her suggestion was the only way their boy could escape the dreadful existence he was forced to live?

"Mr. McDonald, Robbie is young, only nine years old, and at his age well able to cope with such change as a move to the New Town would afford. His chance to have a good education and a real future is in your hands. He has already said he would like to come and stay with me, go to a good school and achieve what he is capable of. Please don't stand in his way."

Andy McDonald's face showed a mix of emotions from fear to confusion and everything in between.

Robbie, crouched in a corner of the room, switched his gaze from his father to his would-be benefactor and back again. Mrs. McDonald sat sewing an already much mended child's undergarment. She said nothing, but looked anxious.

Miss Carmichael waited, offering up silent prayers that the proud man would make the right decision.

Andy McDonald cleared his throat. "I dinnae want ye to think we're no' grateful."

"Then let him come with me. You can see him whenever you want. I can bring him here or...."

Mr. McDonald shook his head. "We'll no' be visiting the New Town. I'll no' have folk staring and pointing, turning up their fine noses at us."

"I'm sure they...." She had been going to say 'wouldn't' but he was probably right. Some people could be so cruel.

"Pa, please let me stay wi' Miss Carmichael." Miss Carmichael hadn't expected the boy to speak up. He rarely did in her hearing. From his father's reaction, he was just as astonished.

"Robbie lad? Are ye' sure?"

The boy nodded vigorously.

Husband and wife exchanged glances. There was a pleading in Moira's eyes that tugged at Miss Carmichael's heart. A tear glistened in the corner of the mother's eye.

Mr. McDonald nodded. "Ye'll no' forget us, laddie."

Robbie ran into his father's outstretched arms. Miss Carmichael dabbed at her eyes with her handkerchief, touched by the sight of the parents letting a beloved child go.

A few minutes later, Robbie and his few meager possessions left Henderson Close, clutching Miss Carmichael's hand.

★　★　★

"Reverend, you have some news for me?"

Lucy closed the door and Miss Carmichael waited for the minister to sit down. She poured him a cup of tea. Robbie was in his new room, playing with some tin soldiers she had bought for him and which he seemed loath to leave alone for more than five minutes.

"I saw the bishop this morning and told him of your experience. He agrees with me that you had an encounter with an evil presence a few days ago."

"And what was his advice? What should I do?"

"The answer is in prayer, Miss Carmichael."

"I prayed at the time but the…whatever it was…told me prayer was no good. It wouldn't work. That he was master there."

"The Devil lies. It is one of his most powerful weapons. He makes us believe that which is blasphemous. You are a good Christian woman, Miss Carmichael. You know to reject the Devil and all his works. You did so at your confirmation. Your parents did so on your behalf at your baptism."

Miss Carmichael felt a knot tighten in her stomach. Of course she had her own firmly held beliefs in the power of prayer but in the light of what she had experienced, she now needed practical help to back it up. "But should I carry something with me? Holy water? A crucifix?"

Reverend Smalley's normally pallid complexion turned puce. "Miss Carmichael. Let's have none of that Papist nonsense here. You don't need any of those trappings. Your faith and prayer. That is what will protect you." He stood up. "Thank you for tea, Miss Carmichael. I trust you will be bringing the young lad to Sunday service?"

"I will indeed, Reverend." She rang for Lucy, who opened the door almost at once. Had she been listening? What if she had? She wouldn't have learned anything more than Miss Carmichael had herself.

As the minister left, Miss Carmichael uttered a deep sigh that emanated from the very core of her being. She had been a firm Christian all her life, attended church on all but a handful of Sundays when illness of one sort or another had kept her confined to home. Now, on the one occasion she had needed to call on one of its officials for practical help, it had been found wanting.

Her relationship with the church would never be quite the same again.

CHAPTER EIGHTEEN

"I've never seen anything like that," George said. "Look at these."

The last tour drifted over to the photo section, eagerly anticipating their pictures.

Hannah put her hand to her head.

"Are you OK? You don't look well."

"I've suddenly got a ferocious headache. I'll take some paracetamol in a minute. What's the problem?"

"See for yourself."

George turned his computer screen to face her, careful to ensure that none of the visitors could see it.

Hannah stared. Every single photo was swathed in a fog so thick, it was impossible to tell who was being pictured. "We'll have to explain that there's been a fault and invite them to go down and have them taken again."

"And if the same thing happens?"

"Your guess is as good as mine."

A middle-aged man approached them. "Are they ready yet? Only I have a train to catch."

"I'm so sorry," Hannah began. "There's been a technical problem and I'm afraid we will have to take your pictures again."

The man's face reddened. "That's ridiculous. I can't hang around here all morning. My train leaves in less than an hour."

"I can only apologize," George said. "If you would like to come with me, I'll take you down right away."

The man looked as if he was about to explode but George was already heading in the direction of the door. With a glare at Hannah, the man followed him.

"Ladies and gentlemen," Hannah said, wishing her head would stop pounding, "please follow my colleague and we will take your pictures again. I am so sorry for the inconvenience."

Amid some muttering, the group wandered off toward the entrance.

Hannah handed them over to Morag and went to take her tablets.

In the staff room, something bothered her. She could remember being down in the Close with that group but she couldn't remember returning with them. And suddenly it seemed vital that she did remember. If only she knew why. It was as if her own mind was playing tricks on her, keeping something from her. Thoughts. A memory. A far distant memory. Not of herself, but of someone else, closely connected with her. However she struggled to make sense of these unfamiliar feelings, she failed.

★   ★   ★

Her sense of unease stayed with her all through the rest of the day and lingered after she got home. Restlessness and insecurity took hold and she couldn't concentrate. Finally, disgusted with herself, she went to bed, falling asleep almost instantly but waking suddenly, knowing she wasn't alone.

The little girl stood facing out of her bedroom window, her hair blowing gently in the breeze. Once again, a smell of lavender wafted under Hannah's nose and she sat up in bed, strangely unafraid of the apparition in front of her.

"It's Isobel, isn't it? Why are you here?"

"I've lost ma dolly." The tiny voice, barely audible.

Hannah swallowed, picturing the rag doll in the closet. "I'll get it for you."

She padded out into the hall and opened the closet door. She reached up and pulled the doll down. Its black button eyes glinted up at her.

In the bedroom, the girl stood stock still by the window. Hannah approached her, heart thumping. She held out the doll. "Here you are."

The child did not move at first. Hannah edged a little closer. A chill enveloped her, growing stronger the closer she came. An age seemed to pass before the girl showed any signs of movement. Her hair fluttered in a breeze that failed to reach Hannah.

"Isobel? Can you help me? Do you know who killed Miss Carmichael? Can you help me bring him to justice? She cannot rest, Isobel. Not until he pays for his crime."

The girl turned.

Hannah gasped as, once again, instead of a face, a swirling mass of dark clouds swept across an oval space. The swirling became a silent storm. Hannah backed away.

Isobel spun faster and faster until she became a writhing, twisting tornado trapped within some sort of force-field. As Hannah retreated further the spinning slowed until Isobel once more stood in front of her, facing out of the window. She held her doll. She turned once more. "Thank you," she said, and the voice made the clouds of her face vibrate.

She vanished.

Hannah rubbed her eyes, uncertain of what she had seen or even if she had seen it. Deep within her, a nameless sensation surged and subsided, like someone taking the deepest of breaths. She ran to the bathroom and vomited, sinking to her knees as she emptied the contents of her stomach and more besides into the toilet.

Shattered, she leaned against the cool tiles, her head banging with renewed fervor.

She lost track of time and didn't know how long she had sat there before she managed to struggle to her feet and stagger into the kitchen. Her headache had subsided a little and two more paracetamol would hopefully send it on its way. She poured a glass of water, took the pills and drained the glass, then another as an unquenchable thirst took hold.

She flopped down onto the sofa, another glass of water in her hand. Maybe she had eaten something that had disagreed with her, or was coming down with some sort of tummy bug. Flu even. She didn't feel feverish but maybe that would come later. At least the next day was her day off. She would rest up and see if anything developed. It would be good to have a duvet day. She couldn't remember the last time she'd done that. And she would call Jenna. It was her turn to call and it would be good to catch up on all her news.

A little before four in the morning, Hannah went back to bed. This time, she was alone in her room. At times it seemed she had imagined everything, but then the image of the girl's face – or lack of it – flashed into her mind. The way she had transformed. No way had she imagined that. Then there was the doll. So real and yet it too had vanished with the girl.

Hannah slept fitfully and finally got up around lunchtime. Her empty stomach demanded to be fed and she made some toast and honey. Best to take it steady after being so sick.

The weather was fine, if grey and cold. She needed to get out. She would wrap up warmly and go for a walk in the New Town.

The streets thronged with people of all nationalities as always. Hannah hadn't a particular destination in mind, just a desire to wander around the Georgian streets for a while, admiring the architecture. She made her way along Princes Street until she came to South Charlotte Street. Reaching Charlotte Square, she wandered up to the Albert Memorial. Every major town and city in Britain seemed to have its own Albert Memorial. This one showed him astride a horse and looking every inch a personage of great standing. Queen Victoria must have loved it.

Hannah carried on with her walk, passing elegant town houses and hotels. One house in particular attracted her attention. She stopped and looked up at it. There was nothing different about it. The same, typical Georgian architecture, a glossy black front door with highly polished brass knocker. But something drew her to it. An inscription on a plaque informed her that the building housed a firm of solicitors.

She mounted the steps and raised her arm. What was she thinking of? Knocking on their door? What possible reason would she give for being there?

She descended to the street again and hurried off. Back on Princes Street she found a café and ordered a mocha. The chocolatey warmth calmed her and brought her back to whatever passed for sanity these days. But that house. She couldn't get it off her mind.

★ ★ ★

Mairead closed Ailsa's office door and drew a deep breath. It could have been worse. At least Ailsa had only issued her a written warning. She had also relented where George was concerned, refusing to accept his resignation. So Mairead's job was safe, for now. OK, the warning would stay on her record for a year, but she could live with that. What she couldn't live with was all the uncertainty, the gaps in her memory. Ailsa had suggested she seek psychiatric help, but the thought of unburdening herself to a total stranger, on demand, wasn't a prospect she was prepared to entertain.

Then there was the small matter of where she lived. Presumably she was paying rent or a mortgage but her bank account showed no sign of either. She had obtained statements for the past three years. All they showed was that she had never paid council rent on Bishop close. Why the council hadn't let the house again was a mystery. Maybe she should go back and call on that nosy neighbor who had spoken to Ailsa, but she couldn't face seeing that place again. Not after last time. Meanwhile, she had taken a room at a cheap and cheerful bed and breakfast. It would suffice for now and was all she could afford. If only she could wake up one day and find her memory restored, with all the gaps filled in, but as each new day arrived, it remained stubbornly like an impossible jigsaw.

Mairead made her way into the gift shop to collect her latest tour group. They were all there, ready and waiting, eagerly anticipating the stories and spookiness to follow. She could only hope the spirits would be quiet and let her get on with her job.

"Ladies and gentlemen, my name is Emily...."

Every group of visitors had its own identity, even though they were mostly strangers to each other. They shared a common purpose and interest, maybe that was it.

Mairead told her stories, made her usual stops, and as the tour progressed and nothing untoward took place, some of her confidence trickled back again. Outside Murdoch Maclean's shop, she told them about the printer and how he had been the last to leave the Close in 1906.

"Of course, he wasn't living here then. But he still conducted his business from these very premises. By that time, the Close had been sealed up at one end, so there was one way in and one way out. The council buildings above had been constructed, resulting in the demolition of the upper stories of the houses here."

"It must have been awfully dark," said one young woman with braided hair and scarlet-framed glasses.

"There were gas lamps but, yes, it would have been dark down here."

"Not much passing trade then," an older man piped up.

"Indeed not, sir," Mairead said. "It would have been hard to make a living but by the end of his time here, Murdoch Maclean was a very old man. He always maintained they would have to carry him out in a pine box. In the event, he left on foot, hauling a cart with his possessions on it. After he had gone, the council immediately sealed up the Close and built on it. That's why you enter it from inside the gift shop."

"What's down there?" The young woman pointed to the end of the street where the boards blocked off Farquhars Close.

A shiver traveled the length of Mairead's spine. "That's our next destination. Well, near it anyway."

A woman gave a little cry. "Oh my God, *no*. It *stared* at me." The woman gripped the arm of her female companion. "Did you see it, Dawn?"

A middle-aged woman in pink shook her head. "See what?"

"Is everything all right, ladies?" Mairead asked, knowing it wasn't.

The woman pointed a shaking finger at a locked building. "There. In the window. A face...only it wasn't a face.... I can't describe it."

The rest of the group crowded round, jockeying for position, trying to see what the woman had just witnessed.

"There's nothing there, Wendy," Dawn said. "Must have been a trick of the light."

"No, I'm telling you, I *saw* it. Hideous. A face shape but no actual face. No lips, nose, eyes. Just...like dark clouds."

"People do report seeing strange phenomena down here," Mairead said, keeping a firm grasp on the pressure cooker of emotions mounting inside her. "But mostly it is as the other lady said. The light's pretty dim and it plays tricks on the brain. I shouldn't worry about it." *I'll do quite enough worrying for all of us.* "Now, gather round while I tell you the tragic story of poor Miss Carmichael...."

"No, I'm sorry," the woman called Wendy said. "There was definitely something there."

A few impatient murmurings. Mairead must contain this. "Would you like to go back to the shop? I can take you if you wish as long as the rest of you don't mind waiting here for a few minutes."

"No, it's all right," Wendy said. "I'll carry on. I don't want to hold anyone up. I just know what I saw, that's all."

"Well, I wish I'd seen it," an older man said. "That's what I came for and I haven't seen one ghost yet."

Laughter erupted from some of the visitors and Mairead breathed a silent sigh of relief. The tension lifted and she got on with her story.

That's when the banging started.

"It's coming from behind those boards," an Australian woman said.

"I think perhaps we should move on now," Mairead said.

"But what is it?" the woman asked.

"Probably workmen," Mairead said.

"Or heavy-duty rats," the older man said, lifting the tension once again.

"Precisely," Mairead said. "Now let's get you all back to your own time." She forced herself to keep her voice steady while she told them of poor Miss Carmichael's fate and then the party trooped back, had their photographs taken at the foot of the stairs and, much to Mairead's relief, returned safely up to the gift shop.

Hannah stood by the photo section. "Let's hope these work," she said.

"I heard what happened to those pictures a couple of days ago, but they've been all right since, haven't they?"

Hannah nodded. "Anything kick off while you were down there?"

"One woman swore she saw a figure near Miss Carmichael's corner. She said it had no face."

"No face?"

"Yes. No eyes, lips, its facial features like swirling dark clouds. I told her it was a trick of the light but she wouldn't have it. Hannah, what's wrong? You've gone white."

"I've seen that. Not here. In my bedroom. A little girl with a doll. But when she turns around, she has no face, only these clouds. The last time...." No, she really didn't want to remember the last time. "She seems so real until then. Too solid for a ghost. At least, too solid compared with how I always imagined a ghost might be. I'm almost sure she's the same girl who came to me when I was tied up in Eliza's room. If it is her, her name's Isobel."

"That's not all though. This loud thumping started from behind the boards. It went on and on. I got them out of there then. Fortunately we were at the end of the tour anyway and this brilliant guy suggested it was heavy-duty rats."

Hannah breathed. "I wish he was right."

Mairead looked over at the group, mingling around, picking up books, postcards and a host of tourist mementoes. "They seem happy enough."

"Thank God for that. The photos have come out all right."

Mairead peered over her shoulder as Hannah tapped through them one by one.

"Hang on a second," Mairead said. "I saw something. Go back... back again...there." In the bottom left hand corner of a photograph, the figure of a small child crouched. Her long, straggly blonde hair concealed her face and she wore what looked like a grubby white shift.

"That's her," Hannah whispered. "The girl who comes into my room. Isobel."

"I can't see her doll."

"Let's look at the other photos." The next four were perfectly normal. Then....

Hannah exclaimed. "That's the doll. She came back for it and it's there. In the photograph. She's holding it."

"Keep your voice down." Mairead indicated a couple of curious faces. "Smile."

A more forced smile Mairead couldn't imagine but it seemed to satisfy the curious, who resumed their search for gifts.

"The only thing we can do is play dumb and hope they don't notice. At least not until they've left. Most people are more concerned with how they look than any of the scenery."

"True," Hannah said, as the first couple approached them with their order.

As the last of that group left, Ailsa came up to them. "Everything all right, Mairead?"

Mairead nodded. No way would she tell her about the knocking downstairs, but.... "I think you should see these pictures. They're of the latest group of visitors."

Ailsa leaned over Mairead's shoulder as she clicked through the photographs on the laptop. "Interesting. Are we sure there were no children down there?"

"Positive."

"Probably wisest to take these down off the public screen. That group have all left now and if anyone makes a late request, we'll have it on computer."

"You never know," Hannah said. "If we keep them up. It might attract more business. Perhaps we should go for some free publicity. Get the papers onto it. Social media."

Ailsa blinked at her. "And did either of you think to get the visitors' permission to use their images? I thought not."

"We could always pixilate their faces," Mairead said.

"Nice try, Mairead. No. Take them down."

Hannah and Mairead stared after her as she moved on.

"You know," Mairead said. "Sometimes I really don't understand Ailsa. She goes on about increasing business and then when an opportunity like this presents itself, she's left the building."

"Crazy," Hannah said, returning to the photos of the little girl. "It's only a matter of time though."

"What is?"

"Until something serious happens. To our guests, I mean. Hell, enough has been happening to us. The banging you heard? I heard it too. The other day. I tried to put it out of my mind, but it was excessive. Really loud. And then...something weird.... I can't explain it."

"Was that the tour when you came up a few minutes after the last of your visitors? George said you looked terrible and had a splitting headache."

"Yes, I think so. I had a mental blank about the end of that tour. I'd no idea I was late back."

"Not excessively. Only a couple of minutes or so. Maybe you were tidying something up, or picking up litter or something."

"If I was, I don't recall it."

"I don't think we can afford to do nothing for much longer."

"No, you're right, but I haven't a clue what to do to make it stop. I wish that psychic medium – Cerys – hadn't binned us. I've tried to contact someone else I knew years ago, but she hasn't been back in touch either."

"There's only one thing for it. We're going to have to go it alone. Do it ourselves. Go down to the Close after work and try and contact Miss Carmichael."

Hannah's eyes widened. "You're not serious? Another séance? After what happened last time?"

"I wasn't there last time. But if we don't do something, these occurrences are only going to get worse. You and I both know that, and so does George."

Hannah went quiet. She bit her lip. Mairead waited, served a customer who had just come in and went back to her. "So, what do you think?"

"I wish you weren't right, but we know something has been unleashed down there and it's spreading. You've been targeted, so has George and so have I. Before long, it could get much worse and then, who knows who'll be next in the firing line? We're obviously not going to get any help from Ailsa so we're going to have to try and put it right ourselves."

"I have no idea why we three have been targeted, but we have, so it's down to us."

"God help us."

CHAPTER NINETEEN

October 1891

Donald Bain wiped the kitchen knife on his filthy trousers and cast quick glances up and down Farquhars Close. Three o'clock on an icy morning did not lend itself to a throng of people. The street was deserted, except for him. And the body that lay slumped on the ground at his feet. He hadn't intended to kill him. If the daft bastard had simply handed over his wallet, none of this would have happened. He brought it on himself. He could see Donald had a knife. Purely for protection, of course, and to 'encourage' his mark to follow his orders. But there was always one who thought he could get the better of him. He did it to himself really. Charging at him like that. Impaling himself on Bain's ma's only kitchen knife. Suicide.

The blood had pooled from the deep gash in the man's chest. Donald Bain bent down and rifled through the well-dressed stranger's pockets. He smiled as he found what he was looking for and retrieved a fat wallet from the man's coat. What was such a fine gentleman doing down here anyway? Probably looking to give Nancy or one of the other girls a bit of trade.

Donald flipped open the wallet and removed the wad of notes. He stuffed them in his pocket and dropped the notecase on the ground. He must get away before anyone saw him. Now he was sure all the man's pockets were empty, he stood, looked around one last time and then raced up the street toward Henderson Close. A couple of minutes and in the distance behind him he heard shouting, a police whistle. Good job he could run so fast. They must have found the body, but he was well out of sight by now. Lucky for him the night was still pitch dark and he knew the streets so well. A sudden noise nearby startled him and he melted into the shadows of a doorway. A figure moved toward him. It seemed to glide over the rough ground, making no sound. As it neared him, it stopped.

Donald held his breath. The…whatever it was…swayed and writhed. Like nothing he had ever seen before. Not human or animal. It coiled like some strange serpent, but Donald could see straight through it. The dark, dank street rippled behind the smoke-like substance. Donald shrank as far back as the door behind him would allow. The figure knew he was there and it wanted him for some purpose he would rather not think about. If he had believed in anything but his own wits, he would have prayed, but he knew no one was listening. No one had ever listened to Donald Bain – except when he pointed a knife at them.

As he stared, the apparition began to take on form. Long, thin legs like poles protruded from a wasted, skeletal body. An emaciated face with a long, pointed nose and mismatched eyes grimaced at him, opening a tight-lipped mouth to reveal teeth even more rotten than Donald's own. Claw-like hands reached for him in an ugly embrace and an old memory stirred. Donald choked as the breath was squeezed out of him. The creature lowered its head and a strong stench of sulfur leaked from its half-open mouth.

"You belong here."

The voice was harsh, not quite human, more like an icy breath.

Donald's head swam, lack of oxygen and the odor sapping his consciousness. The creature tightened its grip on him and he sank to the ground in a dead faint.

★   ★   ★

"Ye cannae sleep here."

Donald opened his eyes and looked up into the bearded face of a policeman. He struggled to his feet, soaked through from a steady, freezing rain that had created puddles and sloshing mud. The street bustled with people going about their business. How long had he been out?

"Get along wi'ye." The policeman fingered his truncheon.

Donald nodded quickly and did his best to run but his feet

and legs were numb from cold and lying in the same position for hours.

He felt in his pocket, relieved to find the wad of cash still there. His knife pressed against his bare leg; the cold metal stung his flesh. Memories of the creature from the previous night drifted back into his mind. Maybe he had dreamt it. But he felt different this morning. Today he could do anything he wanted. He had money in his pocket. He could enjoy himself. Eat and drink well. Maybe pay Nancy a call himself – after he'd cleaned himself up a bit. Give the whore a treat and give himself some fun.

He smiled, then frowned. These thoughts should give him pleasure. Such rare treats. As he turned into Farquhars Close, he realized there was only one thing he wanted to do today.

The murder had invigorated him. He wanted more.

CHAPTER TWENTY

The woman's fear. So strong he smelled it. Donald looked down at her as she lay on the bed, trapped under his weight. A little nick here…a little nick there…. How she screamed.

"Shut it, you whore, or I'll give ye something to scream about." He smashed his fist into her face and she passed out cold.

"That's better." Blood poured from her ruined nose. "Dirty bitch."

He stripped her flimsy blouse. The much-washed material ripped like paper. It revealed breasts discolored with the bruises of her previous dozen clients. "Filthy cunt," he said, gritting his teeth. He balled up saliva in his mouth and spat at her. His ma's kitchen knife gleamed on the bed beside him. He picked it up and stroked it against her right nipple. It instantly budded and that angered him. "Ye're like alla them. Cheap dirty cow." He raised his arm and brought the knife down, stabbing her through her right breast. Blood streamed from the wound, soaking into the stained and malodorous sheets. The pain must have cut through her unconsciousness because she managed to cry out once, the sound dying on her lips as she expired.

A barrier rose in his mind and he stabbed, laughing with each thrust. Again and again he raised his arm and brought it down until a bloody, mashed, butchered corpse was all that remained of Nancy McGonagall.

He wiped his hand across his mouth and stood, turning his back on his handiwork. His shirt was soaked in her blood. He must find a change of clothes. Dump these, away from here. Drunk with bloodlust, he opened her rotten door and staggered out into the black and silent night.

Luck was on his side. The luck of the devil. Two doors away, someone had carelessly left their washing on a line. He reached up and grabbed a pair of worn trousers and a shirt. Damp, but they would suffice. Better than what he was wearing. He quickly stripped and re-dressed, shivering as the clammy material made contact with his skin. As an afterthought, he snatched a sheet and balled up the bloodstained clothes in it.

Back home in the foul hovel he occasionally shared with what passed for his family, he shoved the sheet and its contents under the bed where two of his brothers were sleeping top and tail. Tomorrow he would find a rubbish heap and bury it.

Tired but exhilarated, he hauled a thin blanket off his mother, who snored in the corner of the room, an empty gin bottle by her side. He stared down at her, filled with an almost irresistible urge to stab her with her own kitchen knife.

Only the problem of what to do with her lousy, stinking body stopped him.

★   ★   ★

The next morning, he smelled the crisp dawn air through the miasma of rot and decay. No sun today. Clouds. He felt alive as he had never felt before, as if killing Nancy had refreshed his blood, opened his mind and possessed his soul.

He almost skipped down Henderson Close, stopping abruptly as a tall, impossibly thin man stepped out in front of him.

"Ye should look where ye're going," Donald said.

The man opened his mouth, revealing rotten teeth. There was something familiar about him.

For once, Donald knew fear. "What do you—"

The cloak cut off his words. Nearly choked him. He coughed. Spluttered. Memories of the previous day's encounter flooded back. The man forced Donald's mouth open, pushing filthy fingers inside. Donald gagged. Images swirled in front of his eyes. He saw himself, knife raised, a woman, helpless and screaming beneath him. He brought the knife down. Once. Twice. Three times. Again and again, slashing, slicing. The man released his hold and Donald laughed. Harder than he ever had before, his pitch rising to maniacal proportions.

He was alone in the street. He wiped the back of his hand across his mouth. A faint stink of sulfur, like a massive egg-fueled fart, made him wrinkle his nose. He felt the knife in his jacket and he knew what he must do.

He would find them at the corner of Farquhars Close where it intersected with Henderson Close. Even at this early hour, they would be about, waiting for any man drunk enough or hungry enough to give them some business. It didn't take him long. One found him within minutes.

"Want a little company?" she asked. She was like all the rest of these whores. Unkempt, blousy, in her thirties. Well into her thirties. He said nothing, but went with her.

"I'm Rose," she said. As if he cared. "What's your name?"

"Victor," he replied. Knowing he would indeed win.

"That's a nice name."

He wished she would shut her filthy mouth. Her breath stank of stale tobacco and gin. He'd do this one from behind, then he wouldn't have to smell it. Or look at her.

She produced a key from her floppy cleavage, running her tongue over her lips. Supposed to make him ready for her? Stupid bitch! He'd show her.

She unlocked the door and he pushed her in, eager to get on with it.

"Oh, you're keen, ain'tcha?" That accent. Not Scots. English. A goddamned fuckin' Sassenach. She'd get double for that.

The room was surprisingly clean, if irredeemably dingy. The bed was neatly made up although when she pulled the eiderdown off, he could see he wasn't the first to grace its sheets today. Or maybe even this month. Fury swelled within him, fueled by his encounter with the strange man. If man he was. Demon maybe. He'd passed something on to Donald that only heightened his own bloodlust.

He shoved her down on her back on the bed.

"Hey. Money first. Pleasure after."

He grunted, fumbled in his pocket and found a few notes, which he scattered on the rickety table next to her bed. He would pick them up again later.

She glanced over and seemed satisfied with his payment.

"Now, my lover, what's your pleasure?"

He drew his fist back and slammed it into her face. She screamed. Blood spurted from her nose and smashed lip.

"Don't ever call me that. I am not your lover. I am your destroyer." He marveled at his new voice. Deeper, more raucous than before.

She struggled to raise her hands to shield her face but he straddled her, landing blow after blow until her face became a pulpy mess and she lost consciousness.

Roughly he threw her over onto her front, lifted her skirt and thrust his hardened cock into her, ramming her mercilessly until he climaxed. He withdrew instantly, taking pleasure in seeing the flow of blood staining her legs and the sheets beneath.

She groaned.

"Still alive, are ye? Enjoying it?"

More groans.

"Ye bitches are all cunts and whores. My mother's just like ye. She'd send me out of the room while she fucked her latest for pennies. Then sent me down the ale house for gin. She'd drink hersel' stupid while us bairns starved. Any wonder I hate the whole fuckin', mawkin lot of ye?"

The woman struggled to speak. "Please...."

"Oh, please, is it? Ye want more o' the same? I never refuse a *lady*."

He grabbed his knife out of his jacket. The first stab was up high between her legs. She tried to scream but he shoved her face hard into the blood-drenched pillow and ignored her feeble struggles, which grew weaker by the second. Then she was still.

He jumped down off the bed, taking care to avoid the blood pouring out of her insides. He threw her over onto her back, pausing for one second. She was dead all right. Her eyes were wide open, glazed. The last thing she'd seen had been the pillow but the last person she had seen had been him. He couldn't take the risk. The police took photographs of dead people's eyes to see if they had captured the deceased's last sight.

He gouged out one, then the other, before slicing them until nothing but a mess of blood, muscle and fluid remained. He tossed them on the floor.

His hands. He must wash them carefully before he left, but he wasn't done yet. He sliced off her breasts, then struggled with disemboweling her. The knife would need sharpening before his next escapade. In the end, a mass of intestines and organs he didn't even know the names of lay in an untidy heap all around her. The smell of blood and shit, mingled with the damp and fustiness of the old room invaded his nose and satisfied his spirit. Enough for today. She was done. Well done.

He left her and found a ewer of cold water. He took precious minutes washing his hands and the knife. The woman had made a fair amount of noise at first but no one had come. The neighbors were probably used to it. Cries of fake ecstasy to try and entice more money out of her punters. They would just think she had been particularly enthusiastic.

He checked his appearance in the cracked mirror, noted a few specks of blood that had splashed onto his face, and wiped them off. Satisfied he gave no visible evidence of the massacre he had committed, he left the room and emerged onto Henderson Close in a hailstorm.

He whistled as he sauntered up the street, hands in his pockets. Another few hours and he would be back. Meanwhile he must get that knife sharpened.

He passed a shop doorway, briefly glancing at a well-dressed man whose eyes seemed to follow him. Maybe he was one of those…. Donald wheeled round to face him. "Do ye want something?"

The man smiled. He couldn't be much older than him – probably younger. But what he was doing in this part of the city was anyone's guess. Smart suit, snowy white shirt, starched collar. He didn't belong here.

"I would appreciate a few minutes of your time if you can spare it." Hardly a trace of an accent.

"Why?"

"I can assure you it will prove beneficial to you. To both of us." The man laughed. "Ah, no, you misunderstand. I am not after your body. I have a…business proposition for you. Purely business. My business."

Donald Bain studied his face, searching for any clue as to the nature of his business or if he was about to walk into a trap of some kind. He didn't trust this sort. But if there was money in it. And he did have his knife….

He nodded. "You can have five minutes. Over there." He pointed to the nearest ale house. Let this man try any funny business with Big Jock Docherty looking on.

The man smiled. "I can assure you, you won't regret it."

CHAPTER TWENTY-ONE

November 2018

Hannah, Mairead and George made their way down the steps to Henderson Close.

"God knows what Ailsa would say if she knew what we were doing here tonight," Hannah said, shivering as one of the Close's unexplained drafts hit her.

"It's a good job she's in London then, isn't it?" George said. "I notice *we* didn't get an invite to the company's fancy Christmas party."

"Would you have gone if you had?" Mairead asked.

"Probably not. Can't stand those posh dos. Give me haggis and a pint any day."

Hannah laughed. It broke her increasing tension. "Is it me or is it exceptionally cold down here tonight?"

"I feel it too," Mairead said.

Hannah squeezed her hand. "Anyway, we're here now. Miss Carmichael's corner and there are the boards. Nothing seems to have changed in the past few hours."

George bent down and touched the stain. "The blood's dried."

"I'd love to know whether that's a good or a bad sign," Hannah said. A sigh echoed around them. "Please tell me I'm not the only one who heard that."

"I heard someone breathing hard or sighing," Mairead said.

"So did I." George opened the partition door. "Come on, let's see what we can do."

The ruined Close was lit only by a few security lights, and shadows were everywhere. "Don't stare at anything too long," George said. "You'll start to imagine all sorts of gremlins and we've enough to contend with here as it is."

Hannah nodded. Wise advice. Already she could picture a

hunched figure leaping out of a shadowy doorway a few yards away. *Shadows. Only shadows....*

"So what do we do now?" Mairead asked.

George shrugged. "Maybe join hands next to the pentagram and call out to Miss Carmichael."

"And what if we contact something else? Like last time," Hannah said.

"I don't know," George said, "and that's the God's honest truth. We know the three of us have been targeted. Maybe as we're all here, that could give us an advantage."

"Or give whatever *it* is an advantage," Hannah said. A twist of fear was working its way up from the pit of her stomach. "I feel something's watching us. I don't feel I can trust anything I hear or anything I see."

"Me too," Mairead said. "I don't like it. And the whole atmosphere seems...charged. Like a thunderstorm's about to happen."

A crash sent them reeling. A few feet away, a shadow moved. It curled and writhed.

"Join hands," George said and grabbed Hannah's right wrist. "We've got to stick together."

The three of them gripped each other's hands. The misty apparition hovered a few inches off the ground. Hannah saw the dimly lit Close through it. A few feet away, a door lay on the ground, recently parted from its frame.

George's voice echoed. "Please, if there is a spirit out there who can help us, do so now. Miss Carmichael, if you're there, please help us. Chase this evil spirit back into the pentagram."

The apparition ceased writhing. Hannah felt the hairs on the back of her neck rise. "Mairead, is there anything behind me? I can feel something."

"I don't think so. But it's so dark behind you, I can't be sure."

"It wasn't so dark a moment ago," George said, his voice a whisper.

The darkness behind Hannah drifted around them, until they were encased in blackness, unable to see each other. Only the pressure of their hands on hers told Hannah the others were still there.

"What's...happening?" Mairead's voice shook.

"Keep hold of my hand," Hannah said. Seconds ticked by.

A sudden wrench sent a shard of pain through Hannah's wrist. She had broken contact with Mairead. "Hold my hand, Mairead."

Fingers closed around hers and Hannah breathed. "God, I thought I'd lost you then."

"Kirsten."

The voice sounded soft, male, seductive.

"Kirsten."

"I've heard that name before. Who's Kirsten?" Hannah asked, her mouth dry.

"Who?" George asked, gripping her hand tighter.

"I've heard that voice before too," Mairead said. "I know I have. I can't remember. My damn memory...but that voice, calling out for Kirsten."

The mist suddenly vanished and Hannah gasped. She was holding on to George's hand and he had Mairead's but between the two women, a space had opened up.

"You were holding my hand," Hannah said.

"I know. I was," Mairead said. "Something wrenched my hand out of yours but I found it again almost immediately and never let go again."

"I think the answer's obvious, don't you?" George said. "Someone, or something, joined us."

"The apparition's gone," Mairead said.

Hannah dropped George's hand. "It's as if the thing is playing with us. It knows we haven't got a clue how to beat it."

"The atmosphere's changed again. It's not so oppressive now." Mairead looked around.

"I vote we go to the pub, sink a couple and try and come up with some sort of plan."

"George is right," Hannah said. "We'll get nowhere like this, and I do have one idea."

"That's one more than I've got right now," George said.

Mairead nodded and the three of them made their way back.

★   ★   ★

Ten minutes later, with drinks in front of them, George spoke. "Right, Hannah, what's this idea of yours?"

"Miss Carmichael's plaque in the graveyard."

"What about it?"

"Remember at the séance, I was told to go alone to Greyfriars that night. I didn't and when I did go, I went with you." She took a deep breath. "I think I should go alone. Maybe I'll get further."

"I don't think that's at all a good idea," George said. "Remember what happened when we were both there. If you were on your own...."

"But that's my point. Because I didn't follow instructions, that...whatever it was...was angry."

"It told you that you belonged there. In the graveyard. Presumably six feet under it, to be precise."

"Oh my God, Hannah. Really?"

"It was while you were...away, Mairead. Don't think I'm making this suggestion lightly. Frankly, I'm all out of ideas, so if either of you have a better one, I'd be more than happy to hear it."

George traced condensation down his beer glass with his finger. "I wish I did, but...." He shook his head.

Mairead sipped her white wine.

Hannah struggled to quash down the surreal feeling of not really being there. She swallowed hard. "That's decided then. I go alone."

"Not entirely alone," George said. "We can wait by the kirk. We'll be able to see you from there. The moon's almost full and it's a clear night. If anything happens we can get to you in seconds."

A tinge of relief eased a little of Hannah's apprehension. "Tonight it is then. Let's do it." She drained her cider and stood.

★　★　★

Their breath misted in the cold night air. The street illuminations and the twinkling of Christmas lights coming from houses backing onto the kirkyard seemed strangely out of place so close to the gravestones and monuments of Greyfriars. Hannah tightened her woolen scarf more closely around her neck and mouth in an effort to keep out the biting cold.

"OK," George said. "This is where we leave you. For now."

Hannah nodded. She pulled her scarf away from her mouth. "Wish me luck," she said.

Mairead and George nodded. Mairead squeezed her hand.

Hannah couldn't remember ever feeling quite as alone as she did on that short, but seemingly endless walk to the far wall. She fought for every step, her senses screaming at her to go back to her friends. But she knew she couldn't. She had to face this. Within her, something stirred. An inexplicable excitement she could not comprehend.

She stared up at the plaque, shadowy in the moonlight.

"Well, Miss Carmichael, I'm here and I'm alone. Please tell me what you want from me and how we can trap that devil back in the pentagram."

She waited. Her toes began to numb up inside their thick woolen socks and cozy boots. She walked in a tight circle, trying to get some feeling back into them. Her fingers too were losing sensation deep in her winter gloves.

"Someone told me I belonged here. In this graveyard. But why, Miss Carmichael? Why would I belong here? I'm not even from Edinburgh."

A sudden blast of cold air whipped past her ears, stinging them with the sharp chill. But in the trees not a leaf stirred. It was the stillest of nights.

Hannah shivered. "Please, Miss Carmichael, I don't know how much longer I can stand this cold."

"*You belong here.*" The voice was male, as before but, as Hannah peered through a sudden mist, she could just make out a faint outline. A figure of a woman. The same woman she had seen before.

"Miss Carmichael. Please help me. Help us."

The figure became clearer. Still ghostly, but now with definition. She wore narrow metal-rimmed glasses and a stern expression.

She mouthed the words but Hannah heard them in her mind. *"Find my killer."*

"But your killer must be dead by now. Unless he is the Auld De'il."

The woman opened her mouth again and Hannah heard the words in her brain once more.

"Find my killer."

"Donald Bain. Miss Carmichael, was your killer Donald Bain?"

"He was not alone. The devil was beside him. And he has returned." Slowly Miss Carmichael's hand rose. She pointed at Hannah. A sharp, stabbing pain scythed through her chest. She cried out.

The sound of running feet. Coming closer. Hannah was still doubled up, the pain subsiding a little, but it had winded her.

"Hannah, what happened?" George put his arms around her and Hannah took her first full breath.

"Miss Carmichael. She was here."

"Did she say anything to you?"

Hannah nodded. "She told me to find her killer. Then she pointed at me and that's when…I had asked her if her killer was Donald Bain."

"What did she say?" Mairead asked.

Hannah told them what Miss Carmichael had said. "We're not much further forward."

"Maybe we are." George pointed up at Miss Carmichael's plaque. A deep crack had appeared, barely visible in the pale light.

"That wasn't there when I last saw it," Hannah said.

"But why would Miss Carmichael damage her own memorial tablet?" Mairead asked.

"How's this for a suggestion?" George said. "Supposing the plaque was paid for by her killer?"

In a weird way, Hannah could see what George was getting at and it made some kind of sense. "I was standing right there. In front of the plaque but with my back toward it when she raised her hand. What if she wasn't aiming at me? What if she meant to damage the plaque all along and I simply happened to be in the way?"

"So she shot right through you," George said. "That must have been some charge."

"Believe me. It was. Like a massive electric shock."

Mairead let out a shriek. "Oh my God! Get it off me!"

"*Mairead.*" George and Hannah each grabbed an arm as Mairead rose inches off the ground only to be dashed down again. She fell against George. A scurrying sound, like someone running away, but Hannah could see nothing.

"What the hell just happened?" George's breath clouded in the freezing air.

Mairead shook her head. She was shivering, either with cold or fear or a mixture of the two. "Something grabbed me. From behind. I couldn't see anyone. I felt this...this.... I don't know what it was, lift me off my feet and then it dropped me when you grabbed hold of me."

"Miss Carmichael?" Hannah asked.

"No. She wouldn't do that."

Mairead's certainty took Hannah by surprise. "How do you know?"

"Because...I met her."

George and Hannah exchanged glances. "You *met* her?" George asked. "When, for heaven's sake?"

Mairead put her hand to her head. "Something's just clicked in my brain. I can't.... It happened when you say I disappeared the first time. When I lost those weeks. I...it's all cloudy and vague but I'm sure I stayed at her house. In the New Town. I remember she took me to Henderson Close. She helped families there. One was a poor family who lived in one room. McDonald. That was their name. There were a lot of children.... It's all so disjointed. My memory...there was a boy...Robbie. Nine years old I think. Miss Carmichael took him under her wing. She was going to send him to an expensive private school.... I'm sorry. That's all I can remember."

"That's pretty good going," Hannah said. "Your memory's coming back all right."

Mairead gave a half-smile. "I wish I could fill in all the gaps. I still have no idea where I've been living for the past two years or more. Part of me still thinks it was Bishop Crescent, even though I know that's impossible."

"Can you remember exactly where you met Miss Carmichael?" Hannah asked. "Maybe if we went there we could…I don't know, maybe establish a stronger contact with her."

"I might. I'm not sure. But not tonight. I'm freezing and I'm suddenly so tired I can barely stand."

"I agree," Hannah said. "Are you up for early tomorrow morning? Before work? Say eight thirty?"

"Sounds good to me," George said, and Mairead nodded.

"How about we meet at the Albert Memorial in Charlotte Square?" Mairead suggested.

"I was around there recently," Hannah said. "That's fine with me."

"Let's get out of here," George said. "I've had enough of this place for one night."

★   ★   ★

Half an hour at her laptop and Hannah finally found what she was looking for. An obscure website with detailed information on the many and various uses of the pentagram. The devil's trap – a variation of the Grand Pentacle – seemed to hold the key to getting rid of the Auld De'il once and for all. Hannah read the description with mounting hope. "Once a demon has entered the outer circle of the devil's trap, it is imprisoned there for all time."

Pray God it will work.

Hannah printed out the article, including a drawing of the special pentagram. She examined the strange symbols, which resembled nothing she had ever seen before. Who cared? As long as it did the job. She folded the paper up. It would stay with her until she had a chance to use it.

★   ★   ★

The rain pelted down between seven and eight the next morning before settling down into an unpleasantly cold drizzle that seemed to penetrate every pore of Hannah's skin. Tightly bundled up in a waterproof coat over a chunky wool jumper, accompanied by thick socks, jeans and knee-high boots, she crammed her imitation Barbour hat on her head, taking care to tuck her hair firmly in. No point in battling the wind for control of an umbrella today. She thrust her gloved hands into her pockets and left her apartment, clumping down the stairs and out into the weather.

Pre-Christmas shopping tourists were already out in force and Hannah negotiated shopping trolleys, ambling pedestrians, and cyclists who seemed to think they could ride wherever they chose.

Mairead and George arrived at the same time, having met up on George Street.

"Ready?" George asked.

Hannah and Mairead nodded.

"Have you any idea where we're going?" Hannah asked Mairead.

"I'm not sure. I'm going to follow my instinct, wherever that takes us. There's something in the back of my mind. It may not even be a memory. Perhaps a dream I had so, sorry in advance if this is a wild goose chase."

"Right now, any lead is worth following," George said.

"Definitely," Hannah agreed.

Mairead had already begun to walk, across the green and onto South Charlotte Street. She turned off down Rose Street and Hannah recognized the route from her previous walk around there.

"I feel I want to go down here," Mairead said, turning left off the bustling pedestrianized street.

Hannah was growing increasingly curious as to where Mairead was leading them. A feeling of déjà vu began to swarm over her.

Mairead stopped in front of a smart Georgian building. "Here," she said. "Don't ask me why but I'm as sure as I can be that Miss Carmichael lived here."

Hannah stared up at the familiar black glossy door. Fleming, McLintoch and Campbell, Solicitors, on a gleaming brass plaque. "I've been here before too," she said. "I had a wander around the New Town and ended up right here. It was weird. I had the strange compulsion to knock on the door. I didn't in the end, but I came close."

"What drew you to it?" George asked. He sounded surprised but Hannah didn't think it was down to her revelation.

"I haven't the faintest idea," Hannah said. "I had such a compulsion to go inside but I've no idea why. As far as I know I had never been down this street before, let alone visited this place."

"It used to be flats," George said, staring at the upper stories. "I know it well."

"Really?" Hannah asked.

George nodded. "I used to live here. Right up there." He pointed. "On the top floor. I grew up there."

A shiver traveled at the speed of light up Hannah's spine. "So, in some way that none of us understand, we're all connected to this building."

George took hold of the brass door handle. "Come on. Let's go inside."

"What?" Hannah grabbed his hand. "Whatever reason do we have for going in?"

"Do you know what?" George said. "I usually find honesty works best. I'll tell them I used to live here and that I'd like to have a look around. Oh, and you want to make a Will." He indicated Mairead.

"I do?"

"Yes."

"I can't afford their prices. They're going to be sky high."

"You're not really going to make a Will. We'll make you an appointment when we've had a look around and then you can cancel it later."

"I always said you were mad, George Mackay." Mairead smacked him on the arm and George turned the handle.

★　★　★

"You lived here? When was that?"

Hannah had the distinct impression the middle-aged receptionist was testing George, making sure he was telling the truth.

"We moved here when I was ten, in 1979, stayed five years and then left. I think it was converted to offices soon after."

The woman nodded and a slight smile grazed the corners of her lips. "That fits. The practice opened here in 1986, soon after the conversion. I'm afraid there won't be too much you remember. No bedrooms or original furniture. You rented, I presume?" She led them up the stairs.

"Yes. The landlord was a bit grim. I can't for the life of me remember his name."

"I never knew it. He died, I believe, and the house was sold to commercial property developers."

"The stairs look familiar though," George said, patting the bannister.

The woman reached the first landing. "Yes, I believe they're original." She pointed up at the next flight of stairs. "So you were up at the top then?"

"That's right."

"There's nothing to see. Just closed doors, I'm afraid."

"Nevertheless…would you mind? This means so much to me."

He could charm a crocodile, Hannah thought, and it was clear that this receptionist was not oblivious to his cheeky smile. Considering George was around her age, he could turn on the boyish charm when he wanted to.

"As long as we don't make too much noise I'm sure the partners won't mind. Miss Fox and Mr. Napier are both out so there's only Mr. Campbell up there at present. He's with a client. He'll be the one you see, Miss Ferguson."

"Thank you," Mairead said simply, averting her eyes from the woman's gaze.

Climbing the stairs next to her, George whispered in Hannah's ear, "Do you feel anything?"

Hannah shook her head.

At the top of the stairs, George looked around. He spoke quietly. "I can picture it how it used to be. A door at the top of the stairs, short hall, then rooms off. Two bedrooms, kitchen, bathroom and living room. The offices must be quite large. There's only three of them."

"Well, the solicitors do have quite a collection of legal books," the receptionist said. "And they take up a lot of space."

She led them back down to the first floor. Mairead staggered. Hannah steadied her.

"I feel something here," Mairead whispered. Her face was white and her eyes wide. "I've been here before. I know it. I stayed in a room on this floor."

"Miss Ferguson, you don't look at all well," the receptionist said. "Let's get you back downstairs and I'll make you a cup of strong tea."

They steered her down the stairs and into an empty waiting room. At the sight of it, Mairead gasped again. A strange tingling and the feeling of déjà vu once again hit Hannah.

"I'll go and make that tea now," the receptionist said.

When she had gone, George and Hannah crowded around Mairead, whose face was even more blanched.

"I can't explain what I feel," she said. "All I know is that I stayed here at some time and that this," she looked around, "was Miss Carmichael's living room."

"I've only encountered her ghost," Hannah said. "How's it possible that I'm sure I've been here before?"

George blinked. "What?"

"I know I've been here before. I can feel it and...." How could she explain that she could see the room, not as it was now but as it might have appeared in Miss Carmichael's day? "Mairead, do you remember this room?"

Mairead nodded slowly. "Miss Carmichael had it stuffed full of furniture and knick-knacks."

Hannah nodded. She could 'see' the occasional tables with their lace doilies, photographs in silver frames. "There was a mantel clock over there." Hannah pointed to a redundant fireplace.

"Yes," Mairead said. "It used to chime the quarter hours. A real tinkly chime. Quite pretty."

"And she had an aspidistra," Hannah said. "On the windowsill."

"Yes, she did and a glass display cabinet full of china."

George was watching the two, eyes wide. "You two knew each other back then?"

"I don't know," Hannah said. "We seem to share the same memories of this room, but I don't remember anywhere else in the house. The first and second floors meant nothing to me at all."

"I don't remember the top floor but, as I said, I had a room on the first. It's so strange. So real."

"Am I dreaming this?" George asked. "Because it certainly feels like it."

"Not unless we all are," Hannah said.

"This is the weirdest feeling—" Mairead didn't get a chance to finish her sentence because the receptionist returned with a tray loaded with mugs of tea.

"I thought you could probably all do with a cup," she said, smiling as she laid the tray on a table in the center of the room. "How are you feeling now, Miss Ferguson? You've got a little color back in your cheeks."

"I'm fine now, thanks."

"Enjoy your tea and I'll make that appointment for you. Is next week possible?"

"Er…yes. I'm sure that will be fine."

The receptionist once again left them alone.

George handed out mugs of tea and sipped his own. "This is no coincidence. I lived here when I was growing up and you two seem to have some shared memory of sharing a home with Miss Carmichael."

"Mairead does. I don't. I just remember the room the way it was back then, and I know I have been here. More than that…." Hannah shrugged.

"We haven't got long. She'll be back soon. What are we going to do?"

"Mairead could always make that Will," Hannah said. "We could all chip in to pay for it. That way we have the perfect excuse for coming back."

"What do you reckon, Mairead? Are you up for it?"

"Not that I have anything to leave or anyone to leave it to, but they say everyone should have a Will or the state gets it. In cases like mine anyway."

"I made one when my marriage broke up," Hannah said. "Just to make sure Roger didn't inherit anything."

"OK. I'll do it." Mairead set down her empty mug.

The receptionist returned carrying an appointment card. "Next Tuesday at nine with Mr. Campbell." She handed the card to Mairead.

"Thanks."

"Right, well, if you're quite recovered, I'll show you out."

Hannah, for one, was glad to leave. A few minutes earlier, she had been struck with an almost overwhelming sense of being in another woman's body. It had been unpleasant. That other woman, from another time who shared none of her memories and whose spiteful character left an unpleasant taste in Hannah's mouth. Now, as they emerged into the grey, drizzling morning, the feeling lifted. But it had been there.

And she never wanted to feel it again.

★　★　★

Back home that night, Hannah booted up her computer and checked her mail. Nothing much. Mostly junk, but one item grabbed her attention. A minute later she was signing in to Facebook. Rosanna had finally accepted her friendship request and sent her a message.

"Hannah, how wonderful to meet you again after all these years. Trust you are well. I shall look forward to catching up with all your news."

Hannah responded immediately. *"Hello, Rosanna. Great to hear from you. I'm living in Edinburgh now. Are you still in Spain? There's something I would like your advice on. Do you have Skype? I could call you."*

Hannah sent her message and waited. If only luck was with her for a change. Maybe Rosanna was still online. Seconds ticked by and then....

"Yes!" Hannah punched the air. Rosanna had sent her Skype details.

★　★　★

"Hannah. Hello."

The familiar face looked little changed from the excitable woman Hannah had known all those years earlier. Maybe the soft light had smoothed out any wrinkles. Maybe it was Spanish good living.

"Rosanna. Thank you so much for connecting with me. I hope you're keeping well, and your family?"

The smile Rosanna had worn when the call first connected

was fading. She looked troubled. "Yes, we are all well. Thank you. But you...I sense...something is wrong. You wanted to ask me something."

She looked uncomfortable, as if she was...yes, she was squirming. As if she couldn't wait to get away.

"OK, we'll catch up later." She took a deep breath. "Some strange stuff has been happening here."

"Yes. I can tell."

"You can? How?"

"I feel it. I can see it. It is all around you. Remember when Jacquetta and your daughter were friends? I told you I sensed an aura around you. Something dangerous. I know you didn't believe me then but I was right and I am right now."

"You mean the same thing you told me about then? It's still with me?"

"It is much stronger now. You have been in contact with a force so powerful, it has drawn out the presence from within you."

"But how is that possible?"

Rosanna shook her head. "I never pretend I have all the answers, but I do know you were drawn to the place you are now. It is a place of great danger for you." She clapped her hand in front of her mouth. Her eyes shot wide open.

"Rosanna, tell me. How do I get rid of this? It's not just hurting me, it's targeted my friends as well. Maybe more people will be hurt by it."

"It's growing stronger. Maybe it is already too strong."

"What can I do? How can we protect ourselves?"

Rosanna lowered her hand, but her eyes stayed wide, scared. "It's all around you, Hannah. I have no idea how to help you. I have never seen anything so strong. So...evil."

"But you must know something that will help."

"I'm sorry, Hannah. Truly I am. I will pray for you."

She cut the call.

"Rosanna!"

Hannah stared at the screen. She tried to call back but there was no answer. When she returned to Facebook, she found Rosanna had unfriended her.

CHAPTER TWENTY-TWO

Once again, the heavy atmosphere of Henderson Close cloaked Hannah in an unpleasant embrace that had become all too familiar and made her nerve endings itch. The day passed uneventfully enough, for which she felt relieved, but she knew it was only a brief respite. All the joy she had ever felt for this job had evaporated. Now each working day was a hill to climb. If she could, she would simply leave. Maybe go away from Edinburgh. But it would do no good. Rosanna had made that clear. Whatever was after her here had been after her probably all her life. Everything had been leading up to this encounter. She wondered if it was the same for her friends.

She said as much to Mairead and George as the three sat in the café opposite their place of work.

"I don't know," George said. "Who does? It's a shame Rosanna was too scared to help any further."

"You should have seen her face." Hannah shuddered. "I think she knew she would be way out of her depth. She genuinely didn't seem to know how we could help ourselves. We're going to have to go on our own instincts and hope it gets us through."

"We're still the only ones to notice anything really wrong," Mairead said. "Morag laughed when I asked her if her groups had experienced anything out of the ordinary. She still thinks everything is pretty much as it was. The usual chills, over-imaginative visitors, but nothing to what we've been through."

Hannah had received the same reaction from Ailsa, combined with a look that seemed to question her sanity. "Things only seem to happen to members of *our* groups. A Canadian woman yesterday screamed when she saw a tall thin man in the shadows. I've had people tell me they've been pushed. One man said a gruff voice swore at him, another said he heard a young girl sobbing. It was a relief to have a peaceful day today for a change."

"There have always been visitors who have heard, seen and felt things," Hannah said. "But it's the way it's escalated that worries me, and Rosanna telling me it was now so strong it might be impossible to defeat."

"Something happened when those workmen knocked down the wall into Farquhars Close. We know that for a fact," George said.

"That accelerated something for sure," Mairead said. "But think about it. Before that happened. What are the chances of the three of us – each with our own connection to Miss Carmichael's house – coming together in the same workplace at this time?"

"That's what Rosanna was getting at. It's been engineered that way, but not only for me. For all three of us," Hannah said.

"Either that or our being here has acted as some sort of catalyst."

"I get that," George said. "So, what I suspected has to be true. We have a collective strength, if only we knew how to use it."

"If we could go back in time again," Hannah said, thinking aloud. "If we could control it. Maybe go back together. Find Miss Carmichael."

"And stop her being killed?" George said.

"No, I don't think we can do that," Hannah said. "Surely that would kick off some kind of chain reaction. I don't think we can change history, but if we could be more aware of it. Know exactly what happened and who was responsible…. Maybe, just maybe, we could trap the evil back in its own time."

"Murdoch Maclean," Mairead said.

George and Hannah looked at her.

"Don't you see? His shop is some kind of…I don't know… portal. Both Hannah and I found ourselves back in Miss Carmichael's time when we went near the shop."

"Yes," Hannah said, "but it's so random. I've done countless tours and had no reaction there whatsoever."

"Hannah, it was in Murdoch's shop you found the newspapers disturbed and saw the photograph of Miss Carmichael," George said. "Mairead could be on to something. And if we're right about the collective strength of the three of us.... There's never been an occasion when all of us have been there at the same time, has there?"

Hannah thought back. She shook her head. "It's got to be worth a try. Miss Carmichael isn't going to rest until we find her killer, and we have to find a way of cleansing Henderson Close of that demon or whatever it is that's escaped."

"And the little girl with no face," Mairead said. "Isobel. What's her link to all this?"

Hannah shook her head. "Maybe we'll find that out too."

★　★　★

The last of the visitors had left. It was Ailsa's day off and George locked up the shop.

"OK, let's do this," he said.

Still dressed in their character clothes, the three guides trooped down to Henderson Close. Hannah shivered.

"You feel it too?" Mairead asked, hugging herself, while George blew on his hands.

Hannah spoke and her breath misted in front of her. "The temperature must have gone down ten degrees or more since my last tour."

"Come on, ladies. Let's get this over with."

George led the way along the familiar rough surface until they reached Murdoch Maclean's shop.

"Can you feel that?" Mairead asked. "It's like something's waiting."

The unnatural silence hung heavy. Hannah glanced quickly around. A shadow moved.

"Let's go inside," George said and Hannah followed him, Mairead bringing up the rear.

"Should we hold hands, or something?" Hannah said. "With any luck that'll make sure if we go anywhere, we go together."

She linked hands with the others.

"OK," George said. "I guess we just wait and see if anything happens."

"There's something outside the shop," Mairead said.

"Where?" George stared into the gloom.

"I can't see it. Not properly. But there's definitely something there."

"I feel it too. And it's not friendly." Hannah's senses were taut. Something tugged at her mind, trying to get in. She fought against it. It pushed harder. Her head throbbed. Both Mairead and George had their eyes closed tightly. George's face had contorted into a grimace. Mairead looked in extreme pain.

"What...are you...both feeling?" Hannah asked, barely able to get the words out for the pain that stabbed at her.

Mairead struggled to speak, her eyes still shut. "A force. Something thrusting its way in. It's...so hard...to...stop it."

"Same here," George said through clenched teeth, as a new wave of excruciating pain left Hannah breathless. She shut her eyes and, instantly, the atmosphere changed. She felt Mairead and George's hands tighten their grip on hers. A smell of rotting vegetation and manure swamped her nostrils. Then the noise began. Faint at first, then building. Voices, clattering hooves, neighing horses.

"What? Three of ye and none of ye look like ye belang here."

Hannah recognized the gruff male voice. She opened her eyes as Mairead and George did the same. Murdoch Maclean wiped ink-stained hands on his apron.

"I think ye'd better tell me what your business is here."

George looked from Hannah to Mairead. The look of sheer bewilderment on his face spoke volumes.

"Mr. Maclean," Hannah began. "I realize we must seem very odd to you, but I assure you we mean no harm to you or anyone here. If possible, we could do with your help. We need to find Donald Bain."

If Murdoch Maclean's eyes could have grown any larger they would have surely popped out of his head. "Donal' Bain? Now what would ye be wanting wi' that young skellum?"

George recovered himself. "Do you know him, Mr. Maclean?"

The printer made a sucking noise with his remaining teeth. "Yes, I know him. All the folk around here know him. He's the de'il himsel' when he has a mind."

"That's why we need to find him," Mairead said. "He's committed a terrible crime."

"Just the one?" Murdoch Maclean let out a laugh. "The lad hasna' a guid bone in his body. He came out wrong and he's been wrong ever since."

"What do you mean? Came out wrong?" George asked.

"Came out erse end firs'."

"Ah. Breech."

"Aye. His faither said when he opened his eyes, he saw the de'il himself staring out at him."

"That must have been frightening."

Again the printer let out a mirthless laugh. "Mackenzie Bain doesna' know the difference between a lie and the truth. I nivver believe a word that comes out of his mouth."

Hannah tried again. "Do you know where we can find his son? It's really important."

Murdoch Maclean looked at them disbelievingly. "Ye go out in the Close looking like that and ye won't have to find him. He'll find ye. And he'll have the clothes off ye. Even if they do look like ye've stepped off the stage of the Music Hall."

"There's a reason we're dressed this way but it isn't important," Hannah said. "Finding Donald Bain is. We don't know how much time we have here."

The printer looked from one to the other, shrugged and cleared his throat. "Ye'll more than likely find him in Farquhars Close. Up to na good as usual."

"Thank you, Mr. Maclean."

They left. Hannah was only too aware of the printer's eyes watching them go.

As they emerged into the pale sunlight, the shadow that had watched them drifted away.

"You saw that, right?" Hannah asked, nodding in the direction she had last seen the apparition.

George nodded. "If you mean the thing that looked like a scarecrow, yes."

"To me it looked more like a tall, skinny man," Mairead said.

Hannah shook her head. "I saw a shadow. Dark and indistinct.

I couldn't have told you what it was, whether it was human or animal or neither."

George exhaled loudly. "So now we're all seeing different things."

Hannah looked up and down the busy street. "Maybe it's because whatever it is moves so fast. Our brains are interpreting the signals in different ways."

"Sounds plausible," George said. "Come on, let's find this Donald Bain."

"Who's looking for me?"

Hannah jumped. Where had he appeared from? Judging by the expressions on her friends' faces, they hadn't heard him approach either. Instinctively she moved to one side, away from him.

"Are you Donald Bain?" George asked.

"Aye. What of it?" The young man puffed on a thin cigarette. His cold, grey eyes looked the two women up and down.

"He is. I recognize him." Hannah said. "Although he looks a little different than when I last saw him. Are you familiar with a Miss Carmichael?"

"Why would I be?"

The gravelly voice belied his years. He sounded like an old man, a lifelong heavy smoker. He even wheezed like one. Hannah could feel hatred and anger pouring out of him. As far as this man was concerned, the world and everyone in it was his enemy.

George spoke. "She visits around here, helping the people who live here."

"That stuck-up auld cow. I've na time for her type. She's dead anyway."

"*What?*" Hannah grabbed Mairead's hand. "What's the date?"

"What?"

"The date. What is today's date?"

"April 3rd."

"And the year?"

He laughed. "You're quair folk. It's 1892."

"We're too late," Mairead said. She shook Hannah's hand off and took a step toward the boy. "You murdering bastard."

George held her back. "Mairead."

"Aye, ye do right ta warn her off," Bain said. "I'll no ha' any slag threatening me."

Hannah clenched her fists. "I heard they caught her killers," she said.

Mairead and George stared at her. Then George slowly and almost imperceptibly inclined his head, while he kept a firm restraining hand on Mairead.

Hannah cleared her throat. "They hanged them didn't they?"

Bain eyed her suspiciously. "Aye."

"But one escaped. The one who actually killed her. They haven't found him, have they?"

"There's nae one ta find."

Hannah took a deep breath. "Some say it was you."

Bain's eyes flashed. His lip curled. "Some folk need ta mind their own."

Mairead's voice shook. "Miss Carmichael was a good friend to the people around here."

"She was an interfering auld cow."

"You killed her."

Donald Bain balled his hand into a fist and drew his arm back. George pushed Mairead behind him and took the full force of the blow to his cheek. He fell back. Mairead tripped and steadied herself. She seemed disoriented but Hannah couldn't worry about that now. She grabbed Bain's arm, catching him off-guard.

"Let go of me, cow!" he yelled.

George gave him no chance to wriggle free. Recovering himself, he grabbed the other arm. "It's time you faced justice for what you did."

"Justice was more than what you gave Miss Carmichael," Hannah said.

Bain struggled but Hannah's anger gave her added strength, and George was probably twice his size.

Conversations paused, people turned to stare and a few smiled at the sight of Henderson Close's least favorite resident being frog-marched up the street. At the junction with Farquhars Close, a group of men stood in a huddle. Armed with improvised weapons, they looked in surprise at Bain, who was mouthing obscenities.

"Here's your murderer," George said, keeping a firm grip on the man's right arm.

One of the men brandished a plank of wood studded with nails. "Ye saved us a job. We guard this street from the likes of him."

"He's the killer who was never caught. He killed Miss Carmichael."

The man stared, then slowly shook his head. His friends muttered among themselves, also shaking their heads.

"But he has to be," Hannah said. "He and the Auld De'il are one and the same."

One of the men laughed. "Eh lassie, that's a good one."

"I nivver touched her," Bain said.

"If I didnae know different, I'd say the same as these folks." The leader fingered his weapon. "Ye're certainly capable of it and we ken that it was ye who robbed the Lamonts and took all their food and what little money they had. Ye're a wrong 'un and na mistake but ye're no Auld De'il. Gi'e him ta us and we'll tak' care o'him."

George tightened his grip. "How do you know it wasn't him?"

"Because the day she died, he was locked up. Drunk and disorderly."

Hannah and George exchanged looks.

★   ★   ★

Mairead was aware her friends had dragged Bain off. She managed to follow them for a few steps, then faltered. She stared at the little girl in front of her. Isobel – she was clutching a doll. It had to be her. All around them, it seemed as if time had stopped. Nothing moved, only the child and her.

The little girl raised her hand and pointed at Mairead's head. A memory shot back, clear as if it had only happened moments before. A hospital. White walls. People moving around. Sick people. Not sick in body. Sick in their minds. She was in her body, looking down at her arm. A name bracelet. 'Mairead Ferguson'. Someone was speaking to her.

"You can go home, Mairead. You've done so well."

"I don't have a home."

"We've found one for you. It's a hostel. You'll be safe there. As long as you take your medication and attend your appointments."

The vision faded. The little girl had gone.

★   ★   ★

Hannah's stomach lurched. Nausea rose up her gut. George must be feeling it too. And Mairead? She was standing some distance away, almost doubled over. Hannah knew she had followed them but something hadn't been quite right with her. She had moved like an automaton. Hannah had been too preoccupied with Bain then. Now she went over to her.

"Mairead? Are you all right?"

Mairead retched.

"George?"

"I'm coming, Hannah."

Hannah reached for George and Mairead's hands as the street faded. Pressure mounted until Hannah had to close her eyes. The street sounds and smells evaporated.

A second later and they were back in their own time, in Henderson Close, outside Murdoch Maclean's shop.

Mairead coughed. "Now what do we do?"

"God knows," George said.

"We have to go back to Farquhars Close," Hannah said. "Stand near the pentagram and call out again." She moved off. The others followed.

"I don't see what good it will do," Mairead said. "But I haven't any other suggestions. I was so sure Donald Bain was the killer. Even Miss Carmichael believed it, only she said he didn't act alone."

"We all believed it," Hannah said. "As the man said, it could have been him by nature but even he couldn't be in two places at once."

"Are you sure about that?" George asked. "Right now, I'm prepared to believe almost anything where that runt is concerned." He opened the door and steered them through into Farquhars Close.

Once again, Hannah was struck by the awful stench of sulfur. Mairead covered her nose and George scowled.

"It's here. Whatever it is," he said.

The ground trembled, then settled. A ball of dark mist rolled toward them, spreading tentacles of its stinking self in all directions. The three friends reached for each other's hands. But as Hannah's fingers touched Mairead's, she recoiled from the shock.

"Oh my God." Her fingers throbbed but she tried again. Mairead reached for her but fell to one side.

"Something pushed me," she cried. "It's got me! I can't...." George and Hannah tried to reach her, but came up against an invisible wall that beat them back each time.

"Mairead. Hang on!" George surged forward again only to be thrust backward and off his feet.

Hannah helped him up and they locked hands, charging at the force-field.

Mairead was being dragged away. She clawed at the ground, trying to find a handhold. Failing. She screamed. "I can't break free!"

A rushing noise like a mighty storm filled the Close.

Mairead lurched forward again. "*No!*"

The ground trembled again and a void opened up in the ground in front of them.

"It's dragging me to the edge!" Mairead screamed.

Without warning, the force-field let Hannah and George through. They grabbed Mairead and she held on fast, but her grip weakened as the invisible force doubled its strength. A massive tug and Mairead was wrenched from their arms. Her screams descended with her into the blackness below. As they watched in horror, the ground sealed itself.

George put his arms around Hannah and she wept on his shoulder.

"We've lost her," she said.

The darkness deepened around them.

"What's that noise?" George asked.

Voices. Whispering. Murmuring indistinctly.

"It's all around us." Hannah clung tightly to George. They couldn't be separated now. "Look." Where the void had been, letters were forming on the ground.

As the words took shape, Hannah read them out. "'Find…my… killer.'" Miss Carmichael, if this is you, we've tried. We thought it was Donald Bain but we know it can't have been. Now we've lost our friend. Please help us and we'll carry on trying to find your killer. I promise."

"What the hell is going on here?" Ailsa strode into Farquhars Close and she was beyond angry.

George let Hannah go. "We're looking for Mairead. She came down here and now she's missing."

"Not again! That's it. I've had it with that one. If she's not back at work tomorrow, I'm sacking her. Who were you talking to just now? I heard you mention Miss Carmichael. It sounded like you were calling out to someone."

Hannah improvised. "It was nothing. While we looked for Mairead, I was thinking of a new scene I could act out when we finally get Farquhars Close up and running. It seemed appropriate as we were down here. Daft really, I suppose."

Hannah's eyes drifted over to where the writing had appeared. The ground had returned to its usual stony appearance. No trace of any words now.

Ailsa looked at her a little too curiously for Hannah's liking. She forced herself to maintain eye contact.

Finally Ailsa took a deep breath. "Clearly she's not here and I've just come along Henderson Close. She's not there either. I suggest we all make our way back to the shop, lock up and go home, which is what you two should have done an hour or more ago."

★   ★   ★

In the pub twenty minutes later, Hannah sipped her cider. "What was Ailsa doing there anyway? It's her day off. She had no reason to come in."

"I was thinking the same thing. There was something else about her that was odd too."

"I didn't notice anything. What did I miss?"

"Her ring. The signet ring she always wears on the third finger of her right hand."

"What about it?"

"She was wearing it on the little finger of her left hand. Now everyone knows, the fingers of the dominant hand will generally be slightly larger than those of the other hand. Ailsa is right-handed, so how could that same ring have fitted snugly on the smallest finger on her left?"

Hannah shrugged. "Maybe she had it altered?"

"Maybe, but.... Where did the mole on her left cheek come from?"

"Mole?" Hannah thought back to their encounter with their boss. She mentally traced her face. George was right. On her left cheekbone. A small mole. "You're right. It didn't register with me at the time. I was too busy trying to come up with a plausible excuse. Are you saying what I think you're saying?"

"That it wasn't Ailsa in Farquhars Close."

"George. We've got to go back. Now."

CHAPTER TWENTY-THREE

1891

"Ye're looking fine, Robbie," his mother said. "Miss Carmichael has done well by ye."

"Thank you, Ma."

"Don't be calling me Ma now. Ye've learned to speak better than that."

"Yes…Mother."

"Such a fine-looking young man. Ye'll be having all the young ladies after ye. And ye're going to be a lawyer one day?"

"Yes, Ma…Mother. I'm studying at the university."

His mother looked over at the silent figure of Robbie's father, sitting in the one good chair, puffing on a clay pipe. "What de ye think of our son now, Andy?"

Mr. McDonald withdrew the pipe from his mouth and nodded, unsmiling.

"I brought you some bread and some mutton. Lucy baked some of her cinnamon buns for you as well. She knows how much you like them."

Mr. McDonald stood. "Ye'll no' be bringing anything else frae her," he said.

Robbie looked from his father to his mother. She avoided his gaze. A pang of fear struck him.

"Father?"

"Ye'll pass on our thanks to Miss Carmichael and ye'll tell her we'll manage fine from now on. Say goodbye to yer ma now. Ye'll no' be seeing her again."

"What?"

"Yer faither's right, Robbie. Ye're not one of us now. Ye need to find your way in your new life with the fine folk ye're meeting now."

"But...you're my family."

His father turned away. "No, not anymore, lad."

"It's better this way," his mother said, reaching up and smoothing his collar. "Ye're one of them now."

Robbie shook his head, angry to find tears welling up in his eyes. "That's where you're wrong, Ma. I'm not one of them. I'll never be one of them. When they look at me all they see is a lad from the Old Town who was picked out of the gutter by some do-gooder and dressed up in fancy clothes and given an even fancier education, but whatever the gloss, I'm still the lad from the Closes. They'll never accept me."

His father thumped the table. "They will if ye leave the Old Town behind. Forget Henderson Close. Forget where ye came from. Forget us, laddie. Forget we ever existed. Ye'll be the better for it."

"No!" Robbie's tears flowed unheeded. He might as well tear his heart out right there and then. Lay it out on the table for all to see. It would do him no good anymore. His own family rejecting him.

"Come on now, lad," his father said. "Ye're a man now. Men don't cry. It's time to put yer childhood behind ye. Your whole life stretches before ye. Full of opportunity. Make the most of it. Now, come on, it's time to go."

He put his hand on Robbie's shoulder and his son made to hug him. He sidestepped him. "We'll no' be having any of that. Time to go."

His mother hugged him tight. "Goodbye, Robbie. I'll always love ye."

"Now, Moira, let the lad go. Ye promised."

His mother wrenched herself free of Robbie's grasp. "Ye have a wonderful life now."

"Ma, I—"

"Goodbye, Robbie." His father stuck out his hand. There was nothing more to do. Robbie shook it and his father opened the door. Robbie half staggered over the threshold. He turned in time to face the door as it slammed shut.

★　★　★

He had practiced the words until he could rehearse no more. He wished she wouldn't look at him like that. He never really knew whether she was mocking him or simply having a little harmless fun. Kirsten Lawless. Robbie from the Old Town would never have met the barrister's daughter, but Robert McDonald from Charlotte Square…now that was something else entirely.

Since the awful last visit to his parents, Robbie had resolved to do as his father wanted. Make these well-to-do folk in the New Town realize that he was one of them. He was entitled to walk among them and he was also entitled to ask the girl he loved to become his wife. He had known Kirsten for six months and, while she had never actually encouraged him, she had not resisted his advances either. Innocent though they may have been.

He swallowed hard. She put her teacup down delicately on her saucer.

"Kirsten. I have something to ask you."

The brown eyes flashed. "Yes, Robert?"

"Kirsten, you know I am in love with you. I am studying hard and when I qualify, I shall be in a position to offer you a good standard of living and a loving, faithful husband." It was coming out all wrong.

"My goodness, Robert," she said, her gloved hand ineffectively stifling a laugh. "You sound like a faithful hound. Shall I buy you a collar and lead?"

Robbie leaped up from his seat and knelt down in front of her, grabbing her hands. "Please, Kirsten, I'm being serious. I want us to be serious. I can't offer to marry you yet, of course."

"Of course." The mocking tone was unmistakable. Why did she have to make it so hard?

"Kirsten, I really want us to be more than friends."

"More than friends?"

"I don't mean anything improper…. Kirsten. I would like us to have an understanding that when I am in a position to make a formal offer, you would consider marrying me." Finally, he had said it. Albeit ineptly.

Kirsten withdrew her hands. "Oh get up, Robert. You're making a spectacle of yourself."

Robbie returned to his seat, feeling his ears grow hot and his palms sweat.

"What am I to do with you, you impossible young man?"

"I don't know what you mean."

"Can't you tell? Can't you see? I have been amusing myself with you. It has been a most enjoyable escape from the tedium of my life during these past months. But as for anything more than that...surely you can see it would be impossible. My father would never countenance it for a start."

"Your father has been most considerate. He has even offered me a place in his practice when I qualify."

"That's Papa all over. I shouldn't think he spelled out what that post would be, did he? Most likely tea boy or post boy."

Robbie cast his mind back to the conversation he had had with Sir Humphrey. Had an actual position been mentioned? A job title? He couldn't recall one. That terrible pang of fear he had last felt in Henderson Close now once again stabbed him.

He heard Kirsten's next words through a mist.

"Miss Carmichael probably should have left you where you were. You'd probably have been happier. You know that old saying about silk purses and sow's ears? I'm afraid you'll never be accepted as a true gentleman, and I can only marry a true gentleman. Such a shame, but the fun will have to be over now. You've ruined it by getting serious." She stood and smoothed her dress. "Goodbye, Robert, please don't contact me again."

He didn't try and stop her, what would have been the point? He heard the front door close and sank down on the chair. Damn Miss Carmichael and her do-gooding ways. Damn Kirsten! Damn them both to hell!

CHAPTER TWENTY-FOUR

Hannah and George crept down the stairs and along Henderson Close. In the distance, they could hear voices, chanting, whispering.

"It's like earlier," Hannah mouthed at George through the gloom of the emergency lights. He nodded.

They came to the boards separating the two Closes, stopped and listened. One voice rose above the others.

"Oh great Lucifer, Lord of the Underworld, Bringer of Darkness, come to us now your humble servants."

Beneath their feet, the ground rumbled. The chanting heightened, became more intense. The voice grew almost hysterical.

"Satan our Lord and Master is with us. Behold, he comes...."

The sulfurous stench poured through the boards. Hannah choked. The chanting stopped. She held her breath. She could tell George was doing the same.

The door opened.

For an instant, Ailsa stood before them. Ailsa but not Ailsa. For the first time, Hannah saw what George had seen. The mole on her face. The signet ring on the wrong finger. Fingers that seemed longer than Ailsa's. The woman seemed to stare right into her soul. Despite herself, Hannah flinched, then shook her fear off. She would not be intimidated by this creature, whoever – or whatever – she was.

The woman seemed to sense the change in Hannah. She grinned, her mouth wider than Ailsa's, with sharper teeth than Ailsa's. In seconds, her skin turned black, scaly. Her arms culminated in clawed hands with long talons that could rip flesh. Her eyes flashed red and her newly bald head glistened. When she spoke, her voice sounded familiar – but not as it should have been. Not from this creature. Not from Ailsa either.

"You have interfered for the last time."

Hannah stared. "Mairead?"

George sounded as shocked as he looked. "*No!*"

The creature stood her ground, not moving, a strange, cockeyed smile on her face. Behind her, the chanting voices started again. They grew louder and louder, until the crescendo was too much for Hannah's ears. She clamped her hands to them, desperately trying to shut out the noise. George did the same. They reeled in pain while the creature before them laughed. Scales fell away from her skin, leaving suppurating sores in their wake. Sparse blonde hair sprouted from her head, her eyes lost their red glow.

Still the cacophony continued. Hannah screwed up her face, blocking out the terrible parody of Mairead standing in front of them, still laughing.

The Mairead/Ailsa creature spoke again and the accent was much stronger. "You meddle where you dinnae belang. This place is not yours. It belangs to the maister."

The chanting stopped.

Hannah tentatively dropped her hands. "Mairead, what's happened to you?"

"I am hame. Hame at last. Where I belang."

"My God," George breathed.

The creature's eyes flashed. "Ye dinnae want to mention that name here. This is the maister's place."

"We saw you vanish into the ground," Hannah said. "Now you're here like this. What did they do to you?"

"I belang here. I have always belanged here. This is my hame."

"The Devil has many faces," George said. "We know you're not Mairead. Release her in the name of God."

The creature reared up and laughed. "You invoke the name of God? Your God will do you no good. Have you not learned this? *I* rule here. I and I alone."

A quivering motion began in Hannah's stomach. Unpleasant. It made her feel nauseous. She swallowed hard.

"I know who you are." The words were out before Hannah realized she had uttered them. In her mind, she saw it. A different world. Miss Carmichael's world. A world of stark contrasts. Rich and poor living cheek by jowl. Like a film, snapshots of a comfortable living room in an elegant house, only to be replaced with scenes of a filthy, stinking hovel. One room, peeling paint, five children, a man and a pregnant woman. One of the children – a boy with haunted eyes – stared at her. The only one who could see her. He couldn't be more than nine. He smiled at her. The smile morphed into a sneer. The scene wavered and the boy grew.

The shabby room faded as the boy became a young man. Well dressed. The haunted eyes now hard and cold. The scene shifted once more and the young man grew taller. He advanced toward Hannah and raised his hands. A part of her detached itself and went to him. She was dressed in late Victorian style. He looked at her imploringly.

"Kirsten. Don't leave me."

She laughed at him. A mocking, terrible laugh that chilled Hannah's blood. Laughed until that was all Hannah could hear. The noise rang in her ears, echoed down the Close.

"No! That can't be me."

How can that be me?

The man put his head in his hands. He wept, deep gut-wrenching sobs that tore themselves from his shaking body.

Then he stopped. He lifted his head from his hands and his eyes were red. Not from weeping, but the red of the fires of hell.

He reached out to the devil creature. Became one with it, their bodies melding together in a swirling demon dance. His expression changed from sadness to anger, to hate. Hannah could sense his thirst for revenge.

The scales grew back and embraced them both as one. Blackened and simmering with evil.

George gripped Hannah's hand.

"You can see it too?" she asked.

"Yes."

The demonic dance ended. The blackest of shadows enveloped the half-human, half-demon creature that the two had become. Unholy cries echoed off the walls, faded and disappeared.

George and Hannah were alone.

Hannah stared, not daring to move, not daring to believe what she had witnessed.

"We're next," George said. "And I haven't a clue how to stop it."

"Me neither."

"Let's get out of here."

"No, we can't. The creature isn't trapped. It's roaming free and it's...." Hannah could barely grasp what she was about to say. "It's feeding. Consuming souls and bodies."

"That's what it looked like. Ailsa, Mairead...who was the other guy?"

"I believe it was Robbie McDonald. You remember? Mairead told us about him. But I've just seen him in a different way."

"He was a young boy when she met him."

"And that's how I saw him...at first. Then he grew. There's something about him.... He wasn't what I thought he would be. We have to try and trap that thing in here. I need your help." She held her breath, certain George was going to refuse. His frown told her he was battling with his decision. The frown lifted. He took a step closer and she breathed again.

"I must be as crazy as you but I know it's the only way we have any chance of stopping this thing."

Hannah smiled and George followed her into the Close.

The pentagram was clearly marked.

George joined her inside it. "What do we do now?"

"We act as bait. Draw the creature out and into the pentagram. We get out and it's trapped inside because the force within will bind it."

"Are you sure about that?"

"Not really. But according to something I read, that's how it works. Or that's how it *will* work once I've completed the preparation." Hannah reached in her pocket and drew out a neatly folded piece of paper containing the arcane symbols she had printed out.

She retrieved the small pot of paint they had left behind and began to copy the symbols into the five points of the pentagram.

George watched her. "I hope this is worth it."

Hannah looked up. "It has to be, George. It's our only chance."

"Now what? We know what happened last time we summoned Miss Carmichael."

"Last time we weren't in the pentagram and we didn't have the extra protection I hope I've just given us." Hannah mentally crossed her fingers. It *had* to work. "OK, here goes."

She smoothed out the piece of paper and read the words. "'Oh Great Diviner of the Universe, send your spirits of protection to us that we may be safe in this your sacred design. Summon the evil in this place and trap it within, that it may never more devour the souls of the innocents.'"

Beneath their feet, the ground shifted. Hannah grabbed George's arm and continued. "'Great Spirit, hear our words, we beseech thee.'" She jabbed her finger at the paper and George repeated.

"We beseech thee."

Outside the pentagram, a furious wind whipped up the dust and small stones until it sounded like a hailstorm, but within its protective confines, Hannah and George remained untouched.

An angry roar. A tumultuous crash. Hannah clung tighter to George and he to her. From out of the shadows, the creature they had seen earlier appeared. It walked on scaly human legs bent backward. Its face continually shifted from Ailsa's to Mairead's to Donald Bain's, then to Robbie McDonald's and back to a reptilian demon with flashing red eyes.

Mairead's face looked tortured, anguished. Hannah hoped and prayed the thing would release her once it was trapped. It lashed out with its clawed hands – its feet mere millimeters away from the edge of the outer circle.

"Come on, what are you waiting for?" Hannah said.

"*Hannah!*" The horror in George's voice took her aback. Couldn't he see they had to goad the thing into the circle? The outer edge of it at any rate. No closer than that before they made their escape.

Hannah waved her arms at it, taunting it. "Come on, closer, if you dare. You want to eat my soul? Come and get it. I *dare* you."

"*Hannah*. For pity's sake!"

"George, if you're not prepared to help me, shut the fuck up."

The look of hurt in his eyes was too much but Hannah didn't have time for bruised feelings.

The creature lashed out once more. Mairead's face, locked in a paroxysm of fear and pain, flashed before her.

Another figure appeared. It stood next to the demon. The little girl in a white shift. With no face. Her doll drooped from her right hand.

Hannah was taken aback. She momentarily lost concentration. What was this child doing here, now of all times? "Isobel? You're not safe out there. Come to me. Take my hand." She put out her hand. Outside the pentagram.

George screamed at her. "Hannah, what the hell are you doing? She's not real. The girl. That thing'll have you."

Too late, Hannah realized. A trick. The child vanished. The creature grabbed Hannah's hand in a vise-like grip. It pulled her. George grabbed her from behind and held on tight but he was fast losing ground.

Hannah tugged desperately at her hand, but the harder she pulled, the tighter its grip became. The creature's face morphed into Mairead's. Her shocked, human look gave Hannah hope.

"Mairead, for God's sake, help me."

Mairead's voice issued from the creature's mouth. "I don't know how…I can't get out."

"Try, please! You're my only hope."

Mairead screamed. Her face contorted. Blood streamed from her forehead into her eyes. They grew black. Her head writhed and the creature lost its grip. Hannah snatched her hand back.

Mairead's face disintegrated. Horrified, Hannah clutched her wounded hand, red and swollen from the attack.

"We've lost her," George said. "It's killed her."

"It's all my fault. If I hadn't been so stupid."

"It's coming!"

The creature resumed its reptilian face. Then Ailsa's, contorted. Donald Bain's frigid hard stare. Only Robbie seemed calm. His cold eyes stared out of the demon's head before it switched back to the reptile.

George must have understood what Hannah had been trying to do because he took up the call. "Come on, bastard. We're ready for you. Come *on*." He took a step forward.

The creature also took a step forward. One more and it would be trapped.

It took a step. Backward.

Hannah's heart sank. Anger swelled inside her. "You fucking *coward*."

The demon circled around them. Hannah and George stood back to back, never letting it out of their sight. It roared. It spat. Ailsa's face reappeared. She opened her mouth to speak and her voice rang out. *Hers*. Not the contorted voice of the creature. "You cannot win. The Devil is in control here and I am his servant."

So now they knew, Ailsa wasn't a victim of the creature. She had never been what she seemed to be and here lay the proof.

George spat at her. "You evil bitch."

Ailsa laughed. Mirthless, harsh, grating laughter that chilled Hannah's blood.

The face morphed again. This time Robbie stared out at them.

"Robbie McDonald?" Hannah asked. "Why has it got *you*?"

Robbie said nothing. He stared at them, his face expressionless before fading and once again becoming the reptilian devil.

The creature took another step. Forward this time. Its toe almost touched the outer edge of the circle.

Hannah held her breath. *Now. Please.*

It took another step. A white mist descended all around it, so dense Hannah couldn't see George.

"Jump. George! Jump out of the pentagram. Don't touch the outer circle."

"I can't see anything."

"Nor can I. Take the biggest jump you can manage."

The creature's roars hurt her ears. Hannah took a deep breath and leaped. Instantly she was through the mist and out the other side. George appeared a second later. Behind them a rumbling started.

"Oh God, now what?" George turned to see the source of the

noise. Hannah was too preoccupied with the mist. The roars of the creature died down. The mist cleared.

"Hannah." George's voice sounded a warning tone.

"It's gone. It worked. George it worked!"

"Not so fast, Hannah. We have a problem."

"What?" She turned and looked in disbelief. A wall. Where the boards and the broken door had been. "What the hell...?"

George pressed the bricks. "Solid. We're bricked up in here. There's no other way out. We're trapped in here just as much as that...thing." He pointed to the pentagram.

"At least we're safe from it. It's trapped inside there."

"Oh, we're safe all right. Until we die of thirst and starvation."

"There has to be a way out. I won't accept this. After all we've been through."

"Come on then, let's search. Feel along this wall. See if there are any cracks or holes."

They moved along in the dim glow from the emergency lights.

Nothing. The brickwork was as solid as it had been since before the workmen knocked it down. They trudged over ancient broken crockery, rubble, plaster. Hannah was grateful that the place was relatively dry. Mold covered some walls but at least they weren't ankle deep in water. Nor had she seen any rats, but that again could mean there was no way out. Or in.

"One thing's for sure," George said as they scrambled into the next derelict house. "No one's going to come looking for us. Oh, they'll wonder how the wall got put back up but as for tearing it down again? I doubt it."

Something had been bugging Hannah and now she realized what it was. "The emergency lights. They're connected to the electricity supply."

"Yes, of course. But when the power fails, they switch to battery. Goodness knows how long they'll last."

"Yes, but couldn't we at least trace the wiring? Maybe...."

"Sorry, Hannah. There's no switch in here. They never got around to putting one in. It's one of the ones on the wall at the bottom of the stairs. You're on a hiding to nothing, I'm afraid."

"Indulge me. We're getting nowhere here. There's not even

a breeze. No sign of any exit and we're almost at the end of the excavated bit of the Close."

"If we had torches we could see the ceiling better. Maybe there's a manhole cover or something."

"And how would we get up there even if there was? It's a death trap down here."

George kicked a pile of rubble and it collapsed. "OK. But we have to do something. We've nothing to lose."

Hannah caught a movement out of the corner of her eye. "George." She pointed over to the doorway. Isobel stood, clutching her doll. She had a face. Sad, tear-streaked, but it was *her* face.

She half turned, then looked back.

George gasped. "My God, it's you."

"You know her? I didn't know you'd seen her."

"We met once. A long time ago. A lifetime ago it seems now, when I was a child. Dougie they called me then. I switched to my middle name in my teens. She came into our garden. The garden of that house...." He smacked the wall. "*Damn!* The landlord. How could I have forgotten? His name was McDonald. Robert McDonald. A relative? Coincidence?"

"Is anything a coincidence here?" Hannah said. "She wants us to go with her."

George and Hannah followed the little girl as she glided over the rough terrain. Hannah stumbled a few times, cursing stubbed toes. Then the little girl stopped outside a house. She looked up at it and then at Hannah.

"Was this your house?" Hannah asked. The little girl nodded, a tear tracking its way down her pretty face.

Isobel made to open a nonexistent door and beckoned them to follow her inside.

The room was wrecked, like all the others. Broken chairs, a worm-eaten table, moldy walls and plaster-covered floor. An ancient range with an old kettle. Besides that, a dust-covered rocking chair with a tattered cushion provided the only semi-intact furniture. In a shadowed corner, someone turned.

Hannah breathed. "Robbie McDonald."

He was smartly dressed in keeping with his time. Tailored dark grey suit, stiff white collar. On his head a bowler hat. Every inch a city gentleman. When he spoke, his voice held the merest trace of an accent.

"You don't belong here."

That voice. Hannah recognized it instantly. It had said the same thing to her more than once.

"So, where do I belong, Robbie?"

"You know where you belong. In the kirkyard. With Kirsten."

"Who *is* Kirsten?" George asked.

"She betrayed me. They all betrayed me. *She* knows." He pointed at Hannah. "It *was* you. You returned to taunt me again. You – they – said I didn't belong."

Now it all became clear. The strange feelings she had experienced. The sense of déjà vu at the house in the New Town. She *had* been there before. In a previous life. But that would mean.... She pushed the thought away. "And this was your house?" Hannah asked.

He shook his head. His gaze unnerved Hannah. It was as if he was invading her soul.

"I cannot go back there. They've all gone."

"Everyone went a long time ago, Robbie," George said. "Even you."

To her amazement Robbie threw back his head and laughed. That harsh and raucous noise he had made when he was imprisoned in the demon.

"How did you escape?" Hannah asked. "From the devil's trap?"

"What makes you think I did?"

Hannah exchanged glances with George.

"Robbie," Hannah began. "Do you know where you are?"

"I am in Isobel's house in Henderson Close. She's the only one who still accepts me. She is an old spirit. Earthbound. She has walked these streets for centuries and became my friend when I still lived here."

"If you're here," Hannah said, "you can't be in the devil's trap. You escaped from the demon."

Robbie said nothing.

George took a step closer to him. Robbie seemed to grow a couple of inches taller. Hannah noticed for the first time how thin he was. Tall and thin. Not unlike a scarecrow from a distance, in the shadows, and his eyes appeared oddly distorted as if he had been stretched somehow out of shape. He curled his lip.

"Why do you stay here?" Hannah asked. "If you have the freedom to move."

"The bitch is here."

"The bitch? You can't mean Miss Carmichael? She gave you every opportunity you could have wished for. An education. A comfortable home—"

"She took away my identity. I was never good enough for the smart people in the New Town and too educated for the Old Town. My own parents told me not to come back. They said I wasn't one of them anymore."

Hannah stared at him, aware that George was doing the same. "My God," she said. "It was you. You killed Miss Carmichael."

"Donald Bain killed her."

George spoke. "He couldn't have. He was in prison."

"Not after I stood bail for him. I paid him handsomely."

Hannah leaned against the wall, steadying herself. "How could you do that, Robbie? After all she did for you."

The ghost reared up, grew taller, thinner. Its lips parted over teeth which had outgrown their gums. "She stole my life, so I took hers."

"She *gave* you opportunities. Education, a future out of the slums."

"You know nothing about it. And now you are trapped here. As I am."

"You? Trapped?" Hannah's anger drowned her fear. "Whatever happened to you in later life was your own doing. Did you never feel remorse? Wasn't it you who paid for Miss Carmichael's plaque?"

"I know of no such thing. Why would I pay for a plaque? I wanted her forgotten, and now that woman...the one who looks exactly like her."

"Mairead."

"I believed the bitch to be dead and long ago buried but then she returned. Returned to taunt me."

"You killed Mairead too. *You*...." Hannah couldn't finish her sentence. The devil, Donald Bain and Robbie McDonald, joined as one, with whoever Ailsa really was.

A movement caught Hannah's attention.

"Ye must awa' now, Robbie." Isobel's tiny voice held surprising strength. "Your time is done."

"*No!*" Robbie's features contorted, stretched. His teeth became pointed, blackened, his hair singed. The air filled with his tortured screams while Hannah and George watched, horrified. Unable to move. Others joined him. Demons like gargoyles and a serpent-like creature who swallowed them all.

Then disappeared.

Isobel tugged Hannah's hand, her touch feather-light. "It's done now. He is trapped with the Auld De'il."

Hannah looked down at her, relieved to see her face. "We have to find a way out. Please help us."

The little girl backed away, shaking her head. Her eyes widened. She clutched her doll more tightly to her and set off running.

"*No!* Come back!" Hannah and George set off after her, but she had disappeared.

"Now what the hell do we do?" Hannah peered through the gloom.

"We turn this place upside down," George said. "What else can we do? Maybe there's still some other way out."

They searched. The dampness of the walls made Hannah shiver.

"Hannah." George's call made her turn her head.

Framed in the doorway, barely there but instantly recognizable. Miss Carmichael. Despite her own predicament, Hannah found the sadness in her eyes almost unbearable. She had given Robbie everything and to find out he was the instigator of her murder....

"Please, Miss Carmichael," Hannah said. "Help us. We're trapped here."

Miss Carmichael raised her arm and pointed behind Hannah. A shower of ancient plaster fell from the wall, cascading onto the floor in a snowfall. Bricks wobbled, released their mortar, then toppled. A hole formed. Through it, the emergency lights of Henderson Close cast their dim glow.

"Thank you. Thank you so much," Hannah said, but Miss Carmichael's ghost was already fading into nothing. Hannah watched her disappear. "Rest in peace now, Miss Carmichael."

"Come on," George said.

Hannah scrambled through the hole, oblivious to the broken bricks that grazed her face and tangled her hair.

She helped George through and they stood on the other side of the wall, watching it close up until there was no trace of the hole that had saved their lives.

"I can hear voices," George said. "They're coming this way. It's Morag." He squeezed Hannah's hand. "I'd begun to think I'd never hear another human voice."

Relief surged through Hannah as they waited for their colleague and her visitors to join them.

"Hello, Mistress Ross," Hannah said.

She waited for Morag's greeting. Nothing.

Morag brought her group to a halt, ready to begin her tale. "Ladies and gentlemen, here we are at Isobel's house. Isobel was a little girl in 1645 when the plague struck Edinburgh. I told you earlier about Eliza McTavish? Well, young Isobel was also walled up and just before they sealed her tomb, they threw in a little rag doll to keep her company. So, you see, they were all heart in those days."

One of the party shivered. "Is it me or is it extra cold just here?"

"Aye," Morag replied. "It can get a wee bit chillier here. It's only recently been excavated and restored. About a year ago."

Hannah and George looked at each other. "A year ago?" Hannah whispered. "She hasn't seen us. She's standing four feet away and she hasn't seen us."

The woman who had complained of the cold spun round and stared Hannah straight in the face.

"Are you all right there?" Morag asked.

"Yes," she replied uncertainly. "I think so."

"Why can't they see us?" Hannah asked. "Or hear us?"

George shook his head.

"Now, ladies and gentlemen," Morag said. "If I could ask you step back a little, I want to show you something you all seem to have missed. One of you is even standing on it. Yes, the lady who felt suddenly cold."

She looked down and jumped back. "Oh, my goodness. I had no idea I was standing on *that*."

"If you look closely, you'll see a five-pointed star in a circle. Anyone know what that's called?"

"A pentagram," the woman replied.

Hannah and George looked down. They were standing in the middle of it.

"But how...?" Hannah's earlier elation had evaporated, replaced by a growing nameless fear.

Morag was in full flow now. "When we excavated here a year ago, we found it. This is where Henderson Close meets Farquhars Close...."

Giggles sounded from some of the younger members of the group. Morag smiled. "Yes, we all have a little fun with that one from time to time. The poor man who owned the name grew to be a notable man of business and property here in Edinburgh. No doubt the challenge of having people snigger behind his back spurred him on. So, if you'd like to follow me, I'll take you further into Farquhars Close and tell you about the legend of the Auld De'il."

Hannah made to follow them but her legs wouldn't move. "George?"

"No, I can't move either."

Hannah sighed. It all became clear now. "We were all brought here, weren't we?" she said. "I was right. There are no coincidences here. Some force we don't understand brought us all together at this point in time. At exactly the moment when the Auld De'il was about to be released. All so that it could feed from hatred so strong it survived death."

"It seems that way. Released, the beast feeds and grows. We can only hope no one sets it free again."

A rustle sounded to the side of them. Isobel was back.

"Please, will you help us?" Hannah asked.

"Ye must stay. Keep watch."

Tears pricked Hannah's eyes. "For how long? Are we to stay trapped here forever?"

George spoke. "We're dead, Hannah. We have nowhere to go but here. Don't you see? We are the ones that will keep the Auld De'il trapped."

"Is that true, Isobel?" Hannah knew the answer before the girl nodded. Images flashed through her mind. Jenna, growing older, running a large, successful school. Happily married to Sean. The grandchildren she would never see, growing strong and healthy. Gradually the images faded and, instead of emptiness, they left pride. Her daughter would live a long and fulfilling life.

George took her hand and drew her to him in their ethereal world of spirit. "We are where we are supposed to be," he said.

★   ★   ★

In the kirkyard, the young woman stared at the damaged plaque. "Goodbye, Miss Carmichael," she said.

A small hand slipped into hers. Mairead Ferguson looked down at the little girl who cuddled her battered rag doll. Finally, her mind cleared and she had her answers. All the ones that mattered anyhow. So many illusions and false memories when all she needed to know was right there with her now.

"I'm ready," she said.

Without a word, Isobel smiled and led her deeper into the graveyard.

ACKNOWLEDGMENTS

My thanks, as always to Julia Kavan, for steering me in the right direction and pointing out any instances of sheer folly. Thanks to Shehanne Moore who, as a native Dundonian, gave me valuable advice on aspects of regional dialect. Any errors in that regard are entirely mine. Major thanks to horror editor par excellence, Don D'Auria. It's great to be working with you again, Don! And big thanks to the wonderfully supportive horror writing community, with a special nod to Stuart R. West who introduced me to the quirkiness of Kansas.

Henderson Close and Farquhars Close are products of my imagination but, if you're interested in visiting one of the actual Edinburgh Closes, take a trip to The Real Mary King's Close – a wonderfully preserved time capsule, on the Royal Mile. It's dark there, and spooky. Thoroughly recommended, as are Jan-Andrew Henderson's excellent and highly entertaining books: *Edinburgh: City of the Dead*, *The Town Below the Ground: Edinburgh's Legendary Underground City* and *The Ghost That Haunted Itself: The Story of the Mackenzie Poltergeist*.

Greyfriars Kirk is another must-see and, if you can, go on one of the night time graveyard tours. You might even encounter the Mackenzie Poltergeist himself. Oh, and while you're there, have a look for a plaque on the wall. It simply reads, 'Miss Cathcart' – and no one knows anything more about it.

FLAME TREE PRESS
FICTION WITHOUT FRONTIERS
Award-Winning Authors & Original Voices

Flame Tree Press is the trade fiction imprint of Flame Tree
Publishing, focusing on excellent writing in horror and the
supernatural, crime and mystery, science fiction and fantasy.
Our aim is to explore beyond the boundaries of the everyday,
with tales from both award-winning authors and original voices.

•

Other titles available include:

Junction by Daniel M. Bensen
Thirteen Days by Sunset Beach by Ramsey Campbell
Think Yourself Lucky by Ramsey Campbell
The House by the Cemetery by John Everson
The Toy Thief by D.W. Gillespie
The Siren and the Specter by Jonathan Janz
The Sorrows by Jonathan Janz
Savage Species by Jonathan Janz
Kosmos by Adrian Laing
The Sky Woman by J.D. Moyer
Creature by Hunter Shea
The Bad Neighbor by David Tallerman
Ten Thousand Thunders by Brian Trent
Night Shift by Robin Triggs
The Mouth of the Dark by Tim Waggoner

•

Join our mailing list for free short stories, new release details,
news about our authors and special promotions:

flametreepress.com